The Painful Journey of Love

The Painful Journey of Love

Thuso Kewana

THE REGENCY
PUBLISHERS

Copyright © 2022 Thuso Kewana.

All rights reserved. No part of this publication may be reproduced, distributed, or transmitted in any form or by any electronic or mechanical means, including information storage and retrieval systems, without a prior written permission from the publisher, except by reviewers, who may quote brief passages in a review, and certain other noncommercial uses permitted by the copyright law.

ISBN: 978-1-958517-57-4 (PB)
ISBN: 978-1-958517-56-7 (E-book)

Some characters and events in this book are fictitious and products of the author's imagination. Any similarity to real persons, living or dead, is coincidental and not intended by the author.

Book Ordering Information

The Regency Publishers, International
7 Bell Yard London WO2A2JR

info@theregencypublishers.com
www.theregencypublishers.international
+44 20 8133 0466

Printed in the United States of America

Acknowledgments

I would like to acknowledge the following people for their contribution to making this book.

Firstly, I would like to thank God Almighty through the power of the Holy Spirit for giving me the strength and guidance to complete this book.

I also want to extend my deepest sense of gratitude to my lovely wife Matshele for her persuasive encouragement to pen down my thoughts that resulted in the birth of this book. To my children, Nceba, my son, who has passed on to be with the Lord, Pitsi and Babalwa, my daughters, thank you for your unwavering support right up to completion.

Thanks to Donovan Smith for the wonderful work of art he has done to the cover of this book.

To Cathy Dippnall thank you for the sterling work you have done in editing this book.

Movies about African American lifestyle were a source of inspiration for me. Though this book is a fiction, some of the events are based on a true reflection of the South African urban black lifestyle, which is in most cases like that of African Americans.

Prologue

It was a Saturday morning in spring; the sun shone through trees, flowers were in full bloom, and green grass. It was all quiet at the cemetery, and only the chirping of birds could be heard amid tranquility. Suddenly a black hearse followed by a limousine, a convoy of ten black Mercedes Benz cars and a group of people on foot broke the silence as they slowly moved into the graveyard while negotiating the winding road in the cemetery toward an empty tomb that was well decorated with red and white flowers.

Every man inside the cars wore a black suit and a white shirt. Women wore black dresses and modest black hats, befitting the somber occasion.

Those in cars all alighted except for one occupant in the limo behind the hearse. Men were behind the coffin carrier and followed by women and children.

The limo door swung open, and the driver was stood waiting for the occupant to alight. The driver bent down and said something to the person inside the limo.

A woman came out of the limo wearing a black dress and a black hat covering her face with a thick black veil. She walked slowly toward the grave with the driver next to her.

Chapter 1

Earlier

It was a nice warm late spring morning as Thandi was jogging along Greenpoint beach. She was deep in thought as she was, and the sweat was running down her face. The two-piece jogging tights she was wearing fitted her slender body very well. Thandi ultimately stopped next to a Citi Golf.

While she was stretching, she would look at her wristwatch. She took out her towel to wipe her sweat from her face and drank water. After this, she got into her car and drove off.

Her cell phone started to ring. She answered it through the handsfree set.

"Hi, dad. How are you doing?"

"I'm well, my child. How are you doing?"

"I'm fine, daddy, thanks for asking. What can I do for you, daddy?"

"Why does it sound as if you are driving? Where are you going so early?"

"Yes, I am. I am from jogging along the beach. I am now driving back home."

"Oh, I can see. Did you leave your grandmother at home? How is she doing?" he asked.

"I guess she is doing fine, daddy. I left her still sleeping this morning when I went out. I am rushing to get to her now for her medication. How is mummy doing and my twin brothers?"

"Everybody is doing just fine. Ok, I called to tell you that your response from the university has arrived, and you are accepted for the master's program."

"Oh, that's great, daddy. Don't you think so?"

"Yes, it is. I am just worried about your grandmother's health when you are not there."

"It's just for one year, daddy, then I will be with her. Ok, daddy, I am home now. Let me rush in, will talk to you later. Bye now. Pass my greeting to mom and the twins."

"Will do so, bye baby, love you."

"Love you too, daddy."

Thandi dropped the phone, locked her car and rushed to the house.

Chapter 2

A tall young man stood in front of the mirror and took a final look at himself as he was about to leave his flat for the night shift. He brushed his mustache with both his pointing fingers and smiled to himself. It was 18h15, and he had just finished watching a match between Kaiser Chiefs and Orlando Pirates, which ended up in a goalless draw. Sipho then took his rag sack backpack with his sandwich and homemade drink. He locked his flat and off to work he went. It normally took him 30 minutes to walk to work. On his way, he met Themba, one of his work colleagues and they started talking about the match.

Sipho was the supervisor for all the machine operators at work. He had gone as far as grade 12 at school and could not go any further because his single mother could not afford to send him for tertiary education though he had good grades. His father died when he was 10 years old. He then did a three-year internship course with one steel company as a technician and passed it. One of the things that he carried all the time in his backpack was a small bible that his mother gave him, and he read it at work during lunch breaks.

It was 07h 00 when the siren rang for the change of shift and Sipho had finished doing a handover to the day shift supervisor. He went to the locker room, opened his locker and took out his backpack and headed straight to the clock machine to clock out for the day. This morning Sipho joined a group of his colleagues walking home. They were still talking about the previous day's soccer match. Themba broke their conversation by announcing that he had to go via the local clinic to collect the house keys from his wife.

"What is your wife doing at the clinic?" asked Sipho.

"She works there," replied Themba

"Oh, is she the one who does the cleaning?" continued Sipho.

"Sipho, don't you know that my wife is a professional nurse, the last time you went there, she was the one who attended to you."

"How do you know that?" asked Sipho

"She told me that there was a guy from work who was at the clinic for finger stitching."

"Oh! I didn't know that she was your wife, she is so beautiful! How the hell did you approach her, or is it one of your sisters that proposed to her on your behalf? It's nice to have sisters who can do the job for you. As for me, I would not even know where to start, I am afraid of educated women, guys, especially if they earn more than you do, it's like they can drive you crazy and then dump you in the middle of nowhere. How does a tribal-like you, Themba cope with such a beautiful and educated woman like that?"

"Sipho, my wife earns more than I do, but at home as the head of that house, I call the shots."

"He is lying, educated women like controlling guys who are not educated. Do you remember Vuyo? He was married to a lawyer, and she was calling the shots. What happened to him? That woman dumped him for a rich guy after six years of their marriage," commented Seth.

"Seth, that's not true; not all women are like that. Look at Joe; he is still married to Thembi, a lecturer at the college with a degree in education from university and Joe dropped out of school before completing grade 10, and now he is a successful businessman," said John.

"John is right. They have three kids together," commented Thabo.

"Okay, guys. It's just that I am afraid of educated girls, period. Themba give my greetings to your wife and tell her my finger is fine and say thanks to her on my behalf," said Sipho.

"Will do so," said Themba as he was breaking off from the group toward the clinic direction.

"Sipho, for how long are you intending to stay without a woman in your life?" asked Seth. "You are the only one here who does not have a girlfriend."

"Sipho is damn scared of women. I don't think he even knows how to propose to a girl," commented John with a smile.

They all laughed except Sipho.

"He is not the marrying type. It is a waste for such a handsome guy like him to deprive our sister a man like him," said Thabo with a burst of huge laughter.

"I wonder what you intend to do with all the money that you are working hard for when you do not even have a girl to take out?" continued Seth.

"I am saving it to start a small business; I don't want to work for somebody for the rest of my life. I would like to start my own business and be my own boss one day," said Sipho.

"If you think that is how Joe started, you are making a big mistake, it's not that simple you need an education, a rich wife or you must win the lotto, my friend. Joe got money from his wife to start that business," said Seth.

"Joe saved money, but whatever he saved was not enough for him to start any business. With his education and the little wages, there was no way the banks would have given him money to buy that franchise. Joe's wife bought the business for him." added John.

"Whatever you say, guys, Joe is the one who is managing the business and it is doing very well. All that I am telling you guys is that one day is one day I will have a business of my own," said Sipho giggling.

As they were approaching Sipho's block of flats, two girls were outside the flats next to a bus stop waiting for the bus. One of them, Linda, stays in the same block as Sipho. She's a fifth-year medical student at Wits Medical School and staying on the second floor with her parents. The other one is Joyce, Linda's colleague from the other side of the street and doing the same year as Linda and they were study partners.

"Wow! Sipho, look at Linda! Isn't she cute?" said Thabo. "Who is Linda?" asked Sipho.

"The girl with a yellow jersey Sipho, she stays in the same block as you. Don't tell me that you don't know her," said Thabo with a frown.

"I don't go around looking at girls in my neighborhood, more especially the high-class university girls like them," said Sipho

It was like the girls were listening to their conversation because they broke into laughter at that time.

"Can you hear that they are laughing at us right now," responded Sipho.

"Come on, Sipho, those girls did not even hear our conversation. I give up on you. I don't know how we are going to get you to start dating when you are so afraid of girls," said Seth as he crossed the road and waved goodbye to the other guys who were also leaving Sipho in front of his flat as they continued to their respective destinations. As Sipho was going up the stairs toward the main entrance of the flats, he took a last glance toward the two girls at the bus stop; unfortunately for him they did not even notice he was there; they were heavily engaged in their own conversation.

He opened the door of his flat, took out his lunch box and put it on top of the table, and switched on the radio. He then took off his clothes, put them on top of the only chair in the room, and went for a shower. After drying himself, he went straight to bed and slept.

Chapter 3

Linda and Joyce boarded the bus to university. In the bus they met other students and exchanged friendly greetings and small talk.

"This coming Friday, my parents are driving to Durban for an outing. Can you come over so that we can study at my place? I have the whole house to myself this weekend," said Linda.

"I don't have a problem with that, actually I need an excuse to get out of the house, I will talk to my parents first, but I don't foresee any problems. The other thing is I have already promised my boyfriend I will go and watch a movie with him on Saturday evening. You will have to allow me to leave you alone for two and a half hours. I promise I won't be gone for too long since he already knows I will not be able to go anywhere after the movie because I have to study for the test on Monday," responded Joyce.

"By the way how is he doing? I haven't seen him for a while now," asked Linda. "Is he still working for the same law firm?"

"Yes, he does, and he is doing well, he just bought himself the latest BMW," responded Joyce. "He is so crazy about that car."

"Wow, aren't you the luckiest girl? Which series of BMW did he buy? What color?"

"I don't know which series it is you know I am not into cars; I just know that it is red in color."

"Did he take you for a spin? Oh, I am so jealous of you my friend, please invite me one day when you go for a drive, I love BMWs."

"He is coming to see me tomorrow; I will ask him to take us for a drive, I'm sure he won't mind."

"What happened to Mike? Are you guys no longer an item?"

"I dumped him, he lost his job, and the bank repossessed his car last month."

"But girl, Mike was a nice guy and he treated you like a queen. He gave you a lot of presents, in fact he spoiled you rotten when he was still working, and you can't just dump him like that at such a critical time."

"Oh, no Joyce, you can't be serious, I am a woman remember, I have needs, what am I going to do with a man who cannot meet my needs? To make things worse he has gone back to stay with his mom. Do you want me to play nurse to mummy's boy?"

"But Linda, the material things are not needs, my friend. You can survive without them. That man needs your support even more right now and you know that."

" Oh, no, Joyce, not me, I'm sorry, I have my eyes set on something bigger and better right now, have you seen our new Histology lecturer? Oh! What a hunk! Oh! Yummy!"

"Yes, Linda I agree, he is very handsome, but he is also Judy's husband, remember the pediatrician who is practicing next to the mall, that's the wife."

"What? You can't be serious, Judy? That ugly woman who's driving a white ML. She lectured us last year in pediatrics, didn't she? I would never have thought that she was his wife, what could he possibly have seen in that woman. I wonder?" said Linda shaking her head.

"Oh! Stop it, Linda! Don't you know that life is not always about money and beauty? It is about love. You must learn to love a person beyond what he has or how he looks like. The guy loves Judy as she is, finish."

"Ok, now I know what they mean when they say love is blind," said Linda with a chuckle.

"By the way, when are you going to start dating again?" asked Joyce.

"I don't know my friend; you must talk to your boyfriend to hook me up with one of the lawyers at his workplace. Tell him I am looking for a well-established guy who's got lots of money, not these boys who are fresh from school. I am a doctor in the making remember, soon I will be driving my own big machine."

"He is coming tomorrow you can tell him all those things yourself," said Joyce with a giggle.

"Girl, please stop tittering I am serious; remember we are getting off here."

"By the way what time is our first lecture, I would like to go to the library before class, to extend the period of the physiology book."

"Let me accompany you my friend, our first lecture will start at 8h45," said Linda as they walk toward the direction of the library.

Chapter 4

"Freddy, can you take this envelope with a check to Mrs. Mabandla, tell her that I am very sorry to send it so late, I wasn't feeling well. While you are there make an appointment for me for next week Friday at 10h00. Tell her I will come to the salon, she doesn't have to come here," said Salome Phillips as she handed the check to her son.

"Mom! Have you seen that this check is written cash? Did you do that deliberately?" asked Freddy.

"Yes, my son I have seen it and I wrote it so," said Mrs. Phillips shaking her head.

"Is she still operating where she was before mom?"

"Yes, my child she hasn't moved."

"Mom can I use your ML? Daniel is still washing my car and Daddy has gone to work with his already?"

"That's fine as long as you will be back by 12h30 because I have an appointment with the doctor for 13h00."

"Does your doctor not take lunch? Why is he seeing patient at lunch time?"

"He does. This is a special arrangement because he is fully booked for today. He is sacrificing his lunch to see me."

"Wow mom, it is good to be known. Even doctors can sacrifice their lunches for Mrs. Phillips," commented Freddy as he grabbed the ML keys and moved toward the door.

"Freddy, I know you can be gone the whole day with my car, just remember I can't drive that small thing of yours it's a manual, that's the reason why I want the bigger car, make sure you are back on time."

"But Mom, I always come back on time, don't I?"

"Just go and stop talking nonsense here," said Mrs. Phillips with a cough, she continues "Martha!! Where is my medication? Isn't it ready yet?"

"It's coming ma'am," responded Martha with a soft voice.

The squeaking sound of tires outside drew the attention of everyone inside as the car parked outside the salon. Freddy stepped out of the car and swung the salon door wide open. Standing at the door he asked with a loud voice "Where is Mrs. Mabandla?" Freddy used to co came to the salon to pick up his mom before she got very sick, but he has never been inside the salon.

"Who are you? Coming in here swinging doors wide open without greeting. Where are your manners young man? What are you going to do with Mrs. Mabandla?" asked Sarah.

"My name is Freddy, and I am Mrs. Phillips's son. I am here to give Mrs. Mabandla this envelope from my mom."

"That is why you behave like this? you are Mrs. Phillip's son. Go to that office," she continued. "You will find a young lady and give her the envelope and explain to her where it is coming from."

Freddy proceeded to the office and found the door closed and he knocked. A sweet voice responded, "come in". This time Freddy was careful, he gently opened the door with his eyes wide open to see who was inside. He was expecting to deliver the envelope to an old Mrs. Mabandla. He walked in while the lady was looking down, she was deeply involved in what she was doing, and to his surprise the lady was looking very young to be Mrs. Mabandla.

"Good morning," he said softly.

Thandi lifted her head to look at the stranger in the office and got up on her feet to greet him. When her eyes met Freddy's eyes, he nearly collapsed; Freddy had never seen such beauty in his whole life. He gasped with his lips far apart leaving his mouth wide open and his eyes almost popping out. He was in complete shock.

"Good morning, sir," she responded.

There was no response from Freddy's side. He stood there extremely mesmerized by everything about this lady. Freddy was spellbound by the beautiful figure, the smoothness of the mixed complexion skin and dark slightly oily hair.

This is a piece of beautiful artwork that God took time to create and craft, he thought to himself.

Realizing that Freddy was still charmed by her, the lady continued with a sympathetic smile that slightly produced her shallow dimples on both side of her correctly fitting cheeks.

"My name is Thandi, Thandi Khumalo. How can I help you sir?"

Still looking very spellbound Freddy ultimately managed to say something.

"I am here for your mother Mrs. Mabandla."

"You mean my grandmother."

"Yes, no, no, no, your mother Mrs. Mabandla the owner of the salon."

"My grandmother, she is not in today, how can I help you sir?" Before she could finish the sentence, Freddy took a hundred and-eighty degrees turn and bolted out of the door without a word. He bumped one of the ladies on his way to the door as he was rushing out of the salon. He got into the car and drove off.

Thandi ran after him and calling him to come back. He did not hear a single word from her.

"What did you do to the young man Thandi? It's like he has seen a ghost," commented Sarah who had been working for her grandmother for more than ten years now.

"What was he looking for and who is he?" asked Thandi

"Didn't you guys talk? He had an envelope with him for your grandmother," said Sarah looking perplexed.

"Who is he?" continued Thandi with a surprised voice.

"Thandi, don't you know who that young man is?"

"I don't. In fact, I am seeing him for the first time."

"He is the son of one of the richest men in this town, and your grandmother's richest client Mrs. Phillips."

"Oh, is that the famous Freddy Phillips that every girl talks about in town."

"Yes, my dear that's the young man that all young ladies in town would like to date," echoed one of the ladies. (A)

"When did he come back from USA? I heard he went there to do an MBA and that his father is grooming him to take over the company," another lady chipped in. (B)

"My son studied with him from primary school, and he said he was a genius, he passed with A's all the way to the university. The boy is extremely intelligent," said another lady. (C)

"Why does God give rich people everything? That boy got all the bursaries even though his father could afford to take him to any university in the world." (B)

"They said he didn't have life at university, he always had his head in his books." (C)

"Some said he didn't even have a girlfriend, my daughter told me that other girls said he has never even kissed a girl," said (D).

"I wonder who is that lucky woman, who will have that boy as son-in-law, she will be swimming in money, with very spoiled grandchildren." (C)

"Thandi did he give you the envelope?" asked Sarah.

"No, he had it in his hand and went away with it," responded Thandi

"Are you sure you did not say anything wrong to the man that made him upset?" said Sarah.

"He did not even shake my hand, nor did he tell me his name, he just asked for Mrs. Mabandla and when I told him she was not in today he bolted out of the door before I could even finish my sentence."

Thandi went back to the office. Picked up the phone to call her grandmother to tell her about what has just happened, but a small voice in her said no, the man might comeback when he realized that he did not hand in the envelope.

"Guys do you know that Mrs. Phillips is dying a slow death?" (D)

"What are you talking about?" (A)

"Apparently she's got a cervical cancer stage 4." (D)

"Who told you that?" (B)

"I got it from my friend who heard it from her friend who is a friend to Mrs. Phillip's doctor wife." (D)

"Oh, that is why she is walking like a recently castrated bull." (C)

"This is where you see that money cannot buy everything." (B)

"Let her die I will be the first person to be Ruth to that man." (D)

"What do you mean when you say you will be Ruth to her husband?" (A)

"I will be an uninvited guest in his bedroom." (D)

"Who is this Ruth anyway? Who becomes an uninvited guest in men's bedrooms, I will beat the hell out of her if she comes to my man's bedroom invited or not invited. Where does she stay? Is she you friend Jane? You must be careful with friends like those." (A)

The others all laughed at (A).

"You can see that (A) has no clue of the bible; she hardly goes to church." (B)

"No, you should be like Tamar to Judah and be smart, Ruth got nothing that night, and she only went away with barley. Tamar got it all girls and even more than what she had bargained for, she got twins." (C).

"You are right. She was even lucky to have twins. I will give Phillips triplets in just one night." (D)

"Okay guys its lunch hour now, I am closing the doors and Thandi will stay behind because she is busy with month end reconciliation," said Sarah.

They all moved out and Sarah closed the door behind them and walked straight to Thandi's office.

"Thandi, can you tell me what is it that you have done to that young man?"

"Nothing, he was just startled and gazed at me as somebody who was seeing a ghost."

"Your beauty my child can do that to any young man, Thandi that's a catch my child, don't listen to any of what those ladies were saying. That boy has seen something he has never seen in this world; go for him he is going to inherit all what his father has. The man is extremely intelligent; he will give you brilliant kids, don't be like us, when we were young, we chose hunks. What have they done for us? They gave us kids and disappeared with other women who were not disfigured like us after giving birth. My child that boy is going to be rich, all girls and their mothers around town are talking about him. There is no girl your age here in this town who does not want to be with that boy and there is none of them that are as beautiful as you are my darling. That boy knows that and that is exactly what he has seen today."

"Call him and tell him you would like to see him; I have no doubt in my mind that boy has fallen in love with you."

"Sarah, how do I do that to a man that I don't know? To make things even worse, the man is extremely petrified of me. Guys like him needs to be given space. If it's me that he is interested to, he will come back I don't have to chase him."

"No dear he is not petrified of you, it's your beauty my darling that mystified him. Will you call him and talk to him? I don't want you to lose him. He is a big catch."

"No Sarah. That will be like exposing myself to a stranger. If Freddy is attracted to me, he will find his way back to this saloon," said Thandi.

As they were talking, there was a knock at the door.

Chapter 5

Freddy was 28 years old 1,79cm tall and slightly bulky and handsome. He was always dressed in smart casual clothing.

Freddy parked the car underneath the tree in front of the main door and rushed to his room. He grabbed a towel and went straight for the shower. He took the quickest shower of his lifetime. After drying himself he went to his dressing room and took out his red and white Nike sneakers, white Lacoste T-shirt, and a pair of white Jordan jeans. Though he was slightly bulky, he looked very smart in the outfit, and it made him look very funky and youthful. He drowned himself with one of his most expensive perfumes that his mother bought for him when she went to Paris. He took out the expensive watch that his dad gave to him when he passed grade 12.

He stood in front of the large mirror to check which part of the body or clothes might embarrass him. His hair needed a bit of attention; he quickly ran to Daniel and asked him if he could shave his hair properly and give him a nice haircut. Daniel told him that he was once a barber he could try. Freddy ran back to his room took off the T-shirt and brought a dry towel to Daniel. He asked Martha to bring the large mirror so that he could look at himself as Daniel was cutting his hair. Daniel wanted to know from him why he needed a haircut and why he was in such a hurry. "I saw the most beautiful angel in my whole life, if I don't hurry to catch her, she might fly back to heaven or disappear. I want to grab her before she is out of my sight," said Freddy panting heavily because of running up and down.

"What are you talking about Freddy?" asked Martha surprised "Where did you see an angel?"

"He is referring to a girl Martha," responded Daniel

"Does your mom know that you are chasing girls?" asked Martha

"He is not a child any longer Martha. He is a man now."

Daniel did a very good job with Freddy's head.

He stood in front of the mirror and tugged his stomach in to conceal the slightly protruding parts. He flexed his muscles and gave himself an acknowledged smile.

When he came out of the house his mom was gone with the car and the envelope was still lying on the front passenger seat. He was worried that his mom would see the envelope and know that he did not go to Mrs. Mabandla's salon.

Sarah quickly rushed to the door to tell the person that the salon was closed for lunch. She looked at the person standing by the door. The body was that of Freddy the boy who was there earlier on, but the face and the dress code was completely different.

"Thandi! He is here," said Sarah rushing back to the office

"Who Sarah?" asked Thandi as she was going out to meet Sarah

"It's him," she said Sarah as they meet at the door of the office.

"It's him!"

Who Sarah?" asked Thandi as she goes out of the office to see who Sarah was talking about. "Wow you are right, he is back. What do I do?" she asked as she was running back to the office with hands on her head.

"Quickly go and refresh yourself, he is coming to pick you up, I will keep him busy until you are done."

"How do you know that he is here for me?"

"There is no time for those questions now, just go and fresh-up quickly."

Sarah went back to the main door and opened it. She asked the young man if he had come to the salon.

"No ma'am I am here to see the young lady."

"Which young lady are you talking about young man?"

"The one who is working in the office."

"Does the lady not have name?"

"She does ma'am, and I forgot her name now though she told me," replied Freddy with his eyes on the floor, trying to avoid contact with Sarah.

"Well, how am I going to know which young lady you are looking for. There are a lot of young ladies working here."

Freddy was wordless because he doesn't know how many young girls were working there. It was his first visit to the saloon.

To ease a pressure from her Sarah continued "Do you have an appointment with her?"

"No ma'am."

"Is she expecting you?"

"No mam, I don't even think she knew that I was coming back."

"So, you were here. Are you the one who left here unceremoniously? What kind of a young man are you, who does not make an appointment to see a lady?"

"I am very sorry ma'am."

The lady's door opened and Thandi came out looking as beautiful as ever, as she was approaching Sarah and the young man, Sarah gave way. Freddy's eyes were glued to Thandi as she was approaching him.

When she was closer Freddy stretched out his hand to greet Thandi and bowed his head slightly as he touched her hand.

"Good day ma'am."

"Good day sir, call me Thandi, Thandi Khumalo."

"My name is Freddy Phillips. I am here to see you. Can I have a word with you?"

"Of course, yes Mr. Phillips."

"Can you please call me Freddy? Is it possible to talk to you in private?"

"Yes Freddy. Shall we go into the office then?"

"No ma'am. Can we go and talk somewhere not here in your office please?"

"Call me Thandi, please. Where do you want to go?"

"Can we go to my car if you don't mind Thandi."

"Can I quickly grab my bag then?" asked Thandi as she went back to her office to get her bag.

He opened the salon door to allow Thandi to walk out first, after closing the door behind him he quickly rushed to the Mini Cooper that was parked next to the salon and opened the passenger door for Thandi to step in. Before Thandi could step inside the car, she took a last look at Sarah and winked at her with her left eye and smiled. Sarah returned everything by waving her hand and giving her thumbs up with a wide smile.

"I am very sorry for what happened earlier on. It is just that I was seeing you for the first time and did not expect to find you there but your mother," continued Freddy with the conversation.

"Mrs. Mabandla is not my mother; she is my maternal grandmother."

"So, you work for your grandmother?"

"I am on school holidays. She is not feeling well that's why you found me in her office doing books for her."

"What are you studying if I may ask?" continued Freddy.

"I am doing my Master's in Business Economics with Rhodes University."

"And you? What are you doing?"

"I came back from USA some few months ago. I have just completed my MBA with Harvard University; I did my junior degree with UCT. Where would you like to go for lunch? I am starving," said Freddy

"Let's drive to Camps Bay there are some nice restaurants that sell very delicious seafood. We can sit down and have a good lunch. After lunch, we can take a walk along the beach. That's if you don't mind of course," suggested Thandi.

"That sounds great. Are you not supposed to go back to work after lunch?" asked Freddy

"Sarah will take care of things if I am late; I am supposed to be on holiday after all."

They had lunch in one of the restaurants in which Freddy paid for.

After lunch, Thandi asked to buy some sweets in one of the shops. "Shall we go and take a walk along the beach?" asked Thandi

"Yes, let's go. I will have to take my shoes off then," said Freddy as he was taking off his shoes and socks. "Can I carry yours?"

Thandi took off her sandals and gave them to Freddy and dipped her feet into the water. "Wow the water is cold!" exclaimed Thandi. "Let's go to those rocks up there."

Sitting on one of the rocks at Camp's Bay beach, Thandi turned and looked at Freddy. "Mr. Phillips can you tell me about yourself."

"I told you my name is Freddy, and I will appreciate if you can address me as such Miss Khumalo."

"I will do so sir, now tell me all about yourself."

"What do you want to know about me?" ask Freddy.

"Everything, if we are going to be friends, we need to know each other very well."

Freddy looked Thandi in the eyes and said "I am the only child to Mr. and Mrs. Phillips. I was born here in Cape Town, and I did all my school levels here and went to UCT for my junior degree. I got a bursary to go to the USA to do an MBA at Harvard University. My mother started her life as a professional nurse before she met my dad. My dad is a very rich businessman in town, and we stay just outside town. That is all I can say. What about you Thandi?" asked Freddy.

Thandi pushed her hair backward with both hands and rolled her eyes upwards, as she looked at Freddy and said, "okay shy guy, as I have told you that Mrs. Mabandla is my grandmother. My mother got married to my father when she was 18 years old. My mom and my dad were from the same school. She got pregnant when she was doing her first year at the university and they then decided to get married. My mother had complications after delivery, and she passed on three days after I was born. My father asked my maternal grandmother to take care of me while he continued with his degree in-law. When he qualified as an attorney, he took me back to stay with him. So, I left Cape Town for East London when I was six years old. My father got married again to an extremely good and wonderful woman who loved me like I was her own. She had two boys with my father. I went to school in East London and joined Rhodes University after my matric, where I am currently doing Master's in Business Economics. The reason why I am here now is that my grandmother is not feeling well, and I am here to help her with her salon business, which she wants me to take over. That's why you found me there when you were looking for Mrs. Mabandla."

Freddy looked at her and said, "you have said a mouthful. My father is a qualified engineer. After he graduated from UCT he started working for Bayern Steels as the company was called then, and it was owned by a German guy. After 12 years with the company the owner became very sick, and he had to go back to Germany. He left my father as the Chief Operating Officer. When he passed on after a year my father bought the company from his wife who was in Germany and had no interest in the company at all. My father changed the company name to Community Steels. I did an MBA because my father wants me to take over the management of the company as Chief Executive Officer soon."

Thandi noticed that there was a bit of sand from the beach on Freddy's forehead. She took out a tissue from her purse and wiped Freddy's forehead very gently. She quickly remembered what Sarah said to her about Freddy's father being rich. She leaned forward and slowly closed her eyes as she was moving closer to Freddy's lips. She gave him a motherly kiss on the lips.

Freddy did not know how to respond to this. He looked at Thandi without a word. Freddy had never been kissed by a girl before. When Thandi opened her eyes, she found Freddy's eyes wide open with his lower lip hanging and completely bamboozled by what had happened. She quickly remembered that Freddy was a shy guy who might have never kissed a girl before. To avoid any further embarrassment for him, Thandi opened her mouth and gave him a good passionate kiss. To her surprise Freddy responded to that positively. They were then absorbed in each other's kiss for a while. By now Freddy's heart was about to leave him as it was racing abnormally.

He held Thandi's head with both hands and looked her straight in her eyes and said, "I have never done this with any girl before; this is the first time a girl kisses me. The first time I saw you Thandi I was drawn by your beauty and now you have encapsulated me with your kiss and love. Would you allow me to say to you, 'I LOVE YOU THANDI' I have never loved any one before. I loved you the very first time I lay my eyes on you. I was paralyzed by your beauty from the onset."

Thandi's smile was an indication of saying, "You have done it girl, he is yours now don't ever make a mistake of losing him ever". With her pointing finger, she closed Freddy's mouth and gave him a passionate kiss again.

At this stage Freddy was completely paralyzed by the kisses. His arms were as tight around Thandi's body as the bear's claws holding a fish in fast moving stream. Every part of his body was telling him that he is a man. He felt a sense of happiness that he has never felt in his life. She slowly released herself from Freddy's mouth with her eyes looking down. She noticed how Freddy's manhood was as hard as a Cuban cigar.

She felt great because everything worked according to her plans.

"The wind is becoming stronger now Freddy, can we go somewhere else?" asked Thandi jokingly. There was no response from Freddy as his mind was still wandering somewhere in cloud nine. Thandi took out two sweets and put one in her mouth and the second one she put it in his mouth just to bring him back. "Open your mouth and eat this." Freddy quickly realized that he had to come back to reality. He grabbed Thandi's hand and opened his mouth to take the sweet. Thandi stood up and looked at Freddy and stretched her hands to assist him to be on his feet.

"I am the one who is supposed to do that to you, you are a lady remember," said Freddy with a smile. Thandi did not respond to that because she knew that she was in a mission of sinking her hooks as deep as possible into this prey, so that no other girl should think of changing his mind. Her fear was that she was going back to university to complete her degree and she would leave him with all the other sharks that are gunning for his body and money.

As they were walking along the beach, Thandi took Freddy's right arm and put it around her neck and stretched out her left arm and wrapped it around Freddy's waist and held him tight. They dipped their feet in cold water as they strolled at a snail's pace along the beach talking to each other as young lovers. There was laughter here and there as they walked back to the car. For Freddy, it was mission accomplished. He was the happiest man on earth. On their way back Thandi was doing most of the talking and Freddy was wearing the widest smile that any man would wear after he had successfully won the woman of his dreams.

Freddy stopped the car in front of the salon and quickly jumped out to open Thandi's door. Not only was Freddy in cloud nine so was Thandi. This was the biggest fish that every girl in town wanted to catch. She got out of the car and gave Freddy a kiss and said goodbye.

"When will I see you again Thandi?" asked Freddy with a begging tone.

"Freddy you now know where I am, and you can call me at any time if you want us to go out. Promise me that you will not be scarce."

"I will call you later for a movie at Canal Walk."

"That's great I will wait for your call."

Freddy got into his Mini Cooper and drove off. As Thandi was opening the salon door with a smile on her face, Sarah was standing there with her mouth open as if she was saying "And then young lady, what happed?"

"Sarah! You don't want to know what happed."

"Tell, me all girl, I want to know from here and back I want to hear all the details as they happened. Don't miss a thing."

Chapter 6

It was 07h30 am on a Friday morning. Jeffery Phillips was on his way to work. He had a budget meeting with his senior management and the union representative. His mind was fully occupied by the budget presentation he had to give that was not completed.

He was rushing to the office to complete the budget before 10:00 a.m. which was the time for the meeting. His concentration was not on the road that he was traveling.

He was brought back to his senses when he heard a bang from the front. He quickly raised up his eyes and he realized that he had smashed into a car that was reversing into the road.

Jeffery Phillips has smashed into a car that was reversing out of the yard. His mind was pre-occupied by the budget presentation he had been working on the previous night, that was lying open on the passenger's seat. His eyes were more on the presentation than on the road. He wanted to tie all the knots of the budget before the flight to Johannesburg 12:15 p.m. He quickly jumped out of his car to check what the problem was. It was an old Zodiac car driven by a gentleman. He smashed the car from the driver's side, and the Zodiac was badly damaged. The driver of the car hit his head on the door and there was blood coming out of his ear and a cut on his forehead. Mr. Phillips Mercedes Benz was not badly damaged, and he was also not affected by the accident. He took out his mobile phone to call the police and report the accident.

"Is that the police station?" Jeffrey asked,

"Yes sir."

"Is Captain Mayo there?"

"Yes sir."

"May I have a word with him please?"

"Yes sir. May I ask whose is calling?"

"It's Jeffrey Phillips."

"Hold on sir."

The captain phone rings. "Captain Mayo here, good morning."

"Captain Mayo this is constable Dlamini. I have Mr. Phillips on the line and he would like to talk to you."

"Put him through. Good morning Mr. Phillips. How are you doing sir? How can I help you this morning?"

"Good morning, Captain. Captain I had an accident just outside on the road. I collided with another car. The driver of the car seems to have sustained some injuries. I have called the ambulance already. I would like your guys to come to the scene as soon as possible. I am rushing for a meeting in Johannesburg."

"I will be there soon with my guys. Are you fine? How is your car? The other driver, do you know him? How critical is he?"

"I am fine, and my car is not badly damaged. The other driver seems to be critical, and I don't know the fellow," continued Phillips.

"I am on my way Mr. Phillips."

Jeffry decided to call his wife at work. "Darling I just had an accident on my way to work not very far from home. I am fine and the car is not badly damaged. The other driver seems to be critical."

"Oh darling, do you want me to come there? Are you sure nothing happened to you? Are you not feeling any pains?" asked the wife with great concern.

"I am fine my love. Can you do me a favor? When this gentleman gets there at the hospital, you take care of him. His car is smashed beyond repairs and it is also a very old car. Right now, I don't have his details I am waiting for the police to identify him and give me his details. He is not a young gentleman; he might be in his early fifties."

"Will do so my love," responded the wife

The paramedics arrived and later the cops. After all accident procedures were done, Captain came to Mr. Phillips and said "The gentleman is going to the hospital and his name is Daniel Maseko. He is from Gugulethu and one of the self- employed taxi owners. One of my guys knows him very well."

"Thank you, Captain. What is the next step now?"

"Mr. Phillips you can continue with your day's work I will talk to you during the course of the day. You have a great day sir."

"Thank you, Captain, same to you."

Daniel's car was declared a write-off there and then.

Chapter 7

Linda was woken up by a loud knock at the door very early on Monday morning. "Coming in," she said as she put on her gown and moved toward the door. When she opened the door, two policemen were standing by the door.

"Good morning, ma'am. Are you Miss. Linda Sibeko?" asked the constable.

"Yes sir," responded Linda

"Are your parents Mr. and Mrs. Sibeko?"

Linda knew there and then that there was something wrong. "Are they okay constable, where are they?"

"I am sorry ma'am. Your parents were involved in a car accident near Harrismith two hours ago, and they both died on the spot."

Linda threw her hands in the air and screamed very loudly with a very high-pitched voice that woke the whole neighborhood. Her next-door neighbor Mrs. Pillay was the first to come out and rushed to hold Linda.

"What happened?" she asked the policeman who was standing next to the door.

"Her parents Mr. and Mrs. Sibeko were involved in a car accident about two hours ago and they both died on the spot. They collided with an oncoming truck that lost control and moved to their side of the road. It was a head-on collision. The road was heavy with mist. We assume that they did not see the truck coming and then they collided."

Mrs. Pillay invited Linda to come and sleep in her room. Linda declined and said she would like to be alone.

In the morning Linda did not wake up. She didn't have courage to meet Joyce or to attend lectures. She decided to send Joyce a message that she was not feeling well, and she won't make it to school. She slept on her bed and with a very low voice she was groaning. Her eyes were flooded with tears and the pillow that she was cuddling was totally soaked.

"Lord how could this happen to me now? Why both my parents? What am I going to do now? How am I going to finish my degree? Who is going to pay for my university fees? Is this the end of my medical future?" All these questions brought more tears to her eyes as there were no answers for them.

Two months after Linda buried her parents, she was called by the bank manager.

Linda was at the bank early in the morning so that she could attend lectures after the meeting with the bank manager.

"Good morning, sir, I am here to see the bank manager," said Linda.

"Do you have an appointment ma'am?" asked a man on the other side of the table.

"Yes sir."

"Who shall I say is here?"

"Tell him it's Linda Sibeko."

"Will do so once he is done on the phone, please have a seat in the meantime ma'am."

"Thank you."

"Sir, Miss. Sibeko is here to see you she says she has an appointment with you."

"That's correct, where is she?" asked the manager as he stood up to go and meet Linda.

"Good morning, Miss. Sibeko, you are very early. I didn't expect you to arrive so early. Come let's go to my office."

"Morning sir, I had to come early because I want to go back to university, I have a 10h00 lecture that I don't want to miss."

"How are you, Miss Sibeko?"

"I am doing fine sir thanks, and how are you?"

"I am well thanks. Seeing that you are going back to the university Miss Sibeko, let's get down to business. Your father took a loan with a bank to buy the car he was driving, a loan for the flat and a loan to pay for your university studies, which he ceded with two of his Old Mutual policies. Your father's car was unfortunately not insured. If I look at what we can recover from the two policies and what your father owed the bank, it will be able to pay for your university fees for this year and the car but not for the flat. Your university fees we have already paid for the whole year."

As the bank manager was talking Linda's mind was not there. She was thinking about her future medical career that she had to kiss goodbye. She was thinking about her parents that left her with nothing.

"Miss Sibeko will you be in a position to pay for the flat."

There was no response from Linda. She was gaping at the ceiling with tears creating a pool around her eyes which she was trying to hold. When she tilted her head down to look at the bank manager a deluge of tears flowed down her cheeks.

"Miss Sibeko I would like to help you, but I am bound by the bank's policy. Will you be able to pay for the flat Miss Sibeko?"

With tears still streaming down her eyes, Linda shook her head to indicate that she wouldn't be able to do so.

"I am sorry Miss Sibeko there is nothing I can do," said the manager

"For how long am I allowed to stay in the flat?" she asked

"Up to the end of this month Miss Sibeko if you can't pay for the mortgage."

She picked up her bag with books and walked out of the office. She looked for the closest lady's room. She occupied one of the small rooms and started crying with a low voice. When she got out of the small room Linda washed her face and she headed for the park instead of university.

Chapter 8

It was the end of the month and Sipho and his crew were coming from the night shift. This morning they came out late from work because of a union meeting that they had attended. Most of them had some commitments in town so they left Sipho to walk home alone. He walked back home all by himself and spent this time thinking about his future with the company and the type of business that he is saving his money for. He opened the main door and went up the stairs. As he was climbing up the stairs, he heard something like a person crying with a low voice. He stopped and looked around. At the corner of the bottom floor there was a lady covered with a small blanket and with two suitcases next to her. Sipho looked at the lady with hesitation. "Should I go and ask her what her problem is or not," he whispered to himself. He continued climbing up the stairs but something in him was telling him to go back to try and find out from the lady what was wrong and who she was. He continued walking to his room. Insert the key in the keyhole and turned it, he stood for a while before opening the door and listened to the groaning that was coming from downstairs. He left the key at half opened door and dropped his bag inside by the door and went back to talk to the lady. Halfway down the stairs he turned back again to his room. "What if that person does not need my help? Why was she not helped by others before they left for work?" he whispered to himself. As he was walking back to his room the groaning became louder. He took a hundred and eighty degrees turn and walked back fast down the stairs. "Ma'am can I help you? What is wrong and who are you?"

The lady uncovered herself and looked up to see who was talking to her.

"Linda!! What's wrong? Why are you here? Why are you crying?" This was the first time Sipho had ever talked to the young lady. He used to see her from the distance and the fact that she was a university student made things worse. Sipho knelt with his right leg and holding Linda on both shoulders, he looked at her and asked again "tell me what has happened? Why are you sitting here?"

"I was evicted out of the flat by the sheriff of the court this morning for non-payment of the rental and I have nowhere to go. I can't go to my friend Joyce's place because there is no space there, she lives with some of her cousins from the Eastern Cape and their house is full. Sipho, I really don't know what to do," she said this as her voice was growing louder and tears flowing down her cheeks.

Sipho was astonished that the lady knew his name. He never thought that she would know people like him. Instinctively Sipho pulled Linda close to his chest and held her head tight to his shoulder and said "It's going to be alright. Come stand up let's go to my room, you can't be sitting here the whole day." He helped her on her feet and put his hand around her waist to assist her going up the stairs with one of the suitcases in the other hand. He kicked his door open wider and assisted the lady to the chair. "Can you sit down here I am quickly going to collect what is left downstairs?" He left her in the room. Immediately Sipho was out of the room, Linda lifted her eyes to inspect the room. She was shocked to see the cleanliness and tidiness of the room. Everything was neatly placed. Behind her was a single bed with colorful bedspread. The room looked small for the two of them. She was wondering where the hell she was going to sleep. What comforted here was when she saw a small couch.

"He is mad if he thinks I am going to share a bed with him. He is inviting me here and there is only one single bed and a small couch. Oh, by the way he works night shift. He will be at work when I am sleeping." When she heard Sipho footsteps she pretended to be looking down.

"Linda, were you not supposed to be at university today?"

"Yes, I was but I could not go because I had nowhere to put my stuff and I also don't have money for transport."

"How many lectures are you supposed to attend today? Can you still catch up on what is left?"

"I have already missed a lecture but there is still another three more." She looked at her watch. "The next one is due in an hour's time."

"Why don't you take a quick shower and prepare yourself for school, I will wait for you downstairs. Do you need anything to be ironed?"

"All my clothes are fine they don't need any ironing but where am I going to get the money for the transport and lunch?"

"Don't worry about that I will provide you with transport and pocket money, just get ready, you don't want to be late for the next class, do you?" Sipho closed the door behind him and waited for Linda by the stairs. "Sipho wake up. I am done and the lecture is going to start in 30minutes. I would like to catch the 10h30 bus to university."

Sipho woke up and took out his wallet and asked Linda how much she wanted.

"One hundred rand will be enough for the bus and food. What time are you leaving for work tonight?"

"I will be leaving here at 17h45 because I have a meeting with my crew. What time are you coming back?"

"I will be back very late I want to go to the library to do some of the assignments that are outstanding. Joyce and I will be attending a movie with her boyfriend later. What are you going to do with the key?"

"I will leave the key just above the door frame. Will you be able to reach up there?"

"Come on Sipho I am not that short I will," they both laughed. Linda left to catch the bus.

Sipho decided to go to the mall to do a bit of grocery for Linda to find something to eat before taking a nap. He woke up at 16h00 and took out clean linen and made up the bed. "People like Linda are university students, they wouldn't like to sleep in linen that slept backward people like me," he talked to himself. After cocking Sipho ate and washed his dishes and packed his bag for work. He took out a R100 note and put it on top of the table. He left Linda a note telling her about the food and the money for her transport and meals for the following day.

It was five minutes before the start of the Histology lecture when Linda alighted from the bus and Joyce was already sitting inside the lecture hall. Linda rushed to the lecture hall because she wanted to secure a seat next to her friend.

"Wow where have you been? You missed the morning lecture. Are you well?"

"Yes, girl I am. I overslept because I didn't sleep well at night. That is why my eyes are puffed up, I am feeling very tired. How was the Neurology class? Any tutorial questions?"

"Prof was not in today the class was handled by Dr. Clifford. He didn't cover that much because he spent time talking about himself, so you did not miss much really!"

"Oh, that's great, I was really worried."

When Linda arrived at home Sipho was gone already. She was welcomed by a pleasant aroma of food that filled the whole room. "Mhh! that smells nice, I wonder what is it that he cooked?" She found a note on the table addressed to her, slowly she moved toward the table and stretched her hand to the note with caution and opened it, and a R100 note fell from it. She read the note and smiled. "Any way I am finishing next year, and I will pay you all your money Sipho," she said to herself.

She looked at the R100 note in her hand. A thought came to her about the university fees for the following year. "Where am I going to get the money for next year to complete my degree? Is it possible for Sipho to get a loan from the bank and pay for my studies and I pay him back? Any way people like Sipho are not educated and it will be easy to convince him to lend me money to complete my degree. I should be able to pay him back within the first year of my salary."

She dished up for herself, ate and took a shower and then went straight to bed. "Mhh! this linen smells fresh." She heaved the blankets close to her body, switched off the light and dozed off.

Chapter 9

Salome dismounted from her car with a lot of difficulty, she was in pain and she was trying hard to hide it. She pushed the salon door wide open and headed straight to the counter where Sarah was waiting for her.

"Good afternoon Mrs. Phillips. How are you this afternoon?"

"Afternoon Sarah, can you find me a chair to sit please? Is Mary in?"

"Mrs. Mabandla is not in today she is not feeling well ma'am, but Thandi is here. Can I call her for you?" said Sarah as she was offering Salome a chair to seat on.

"What is wrong with Mary?"

"I really don't know Mrs. Phillips, but Thandi can tell you better. Should I call her to come and help you?"

"Who is Thandi?" she asked as she took out a handkerchief and coughed into it.

"She is Mrs. Mabandla's granddaughter have you forgotten her," said Sarah as she moved toward Thandi's office. She opened the office door and found Thandi on the phone and signaled to her that there is a person to see her.

Thandi quickly excused herself to the person on the phone to attend to the visitor. As she moved out of the office, she found Salome bent on the counter and coughing repeatedly with difficulty. "Good afternoon, ma'am," greeted Thandi

Salome lifted her head slowly to look at the person in front of her. "Wow, morning young lady. How are you and what's your name?"

"My name is Thandi Khumalo I am Mrs. Mabandla's granddaughter."

"You are Mary's granddaughter? Oh, I remember you now. Wow you have grown so much. The last time I saw you, you were still very young and beautiful. I didn't know that you have grown so much. Your grandmother always spoke about her own daughter that has passed on whom I suppose was your mother, but not you too much. You are such a beautiful young lady. Now I can see the resemblance, you look like your mom. How old are you now?"

"I am turning twenty-four this coming June."

"Do you know who I am?"

"No ma'am."

"My name is Salome but the whole town knows me as Mrs. Phillips. I am a very close friend to your grandmother. We've known each other for long. She has been doing my hair since the day this salon was opened. She sometimes comes to my house for a cup of coffee. Of late I haven't been at this salon for a very long time because of my health. I wasn't aware that your grandmother is not well either. How is she?"

"She is not well, but she is hanging in there."

"Is that why you are here, to look after your grandma?"

"I am on school vacation she has asked me to come and assist her with the business and to do her books as she is not feeling well," explained Thandi with her hands at the back and wearing a smile now that she realized that she was talking to Freddy's mom.

"What are you doing with yourself?"

"I am currently doing my master's degree in Business Economics with Rhodes University"

"When are you going back to school and what are you intending to do after your masters?"

"I will be going back in two weeks' time. As for what I will be doing after my masters I haven't thought about it."

"My girl, your grandmother is old, and she is running a very successful business here, this salon is always busy. Is that not so Sarah? She needs somebody like you to take over the running of this business. You cannot let her sell a family business. Is your father still running his law firm?"

"Yes ma'am, he still does."

"I came to give your grandmother this check for the work she has done for the past months. I sent my son to bring it earlier on, but today's kids don't listen. He went out with my car to his own places. He didn't even tell me that the envelop I gave him was not delivered. I just saw it on top of the passenger's seat as I was driving. I wasn't feeling well, and I promised to pay this long ago. Tell her I will pay her a visit tomorrow if I am well. Tell her to get well."

"I will do so ma'am," responded Thandi with a smile. She recognized the envelope as the one that was carried by Freddy the first time he came to her office.

"Goodbye Thandi I hope to see you again. Study hard and don't forget what I just told you about your grandmother's business," said Salome as she stood up and walked toward the door.

"Goodbye Mrs. Phillips."

She got into her car with difficulty and drove off. As she was driving something pre-occupied her mind, she found herself talking to herself.

"What a pretty well-mannered young lady. How I wish my son could meet her. I wouldn't mind a daughter in-law like her." She temporary closed her eyes and remembered the first time she met Jeffery during their graduation at UCT and how wonderful their wedding day was. How happy she was when she conceived her first child.

She remembered the abuse that followed, how her son witnessed the events, as his father physically and verbally abused her. She remembered how Freddy pointed a finger at her when he was fifteen and threatened to beat her in front of his father. The tears flooded her eyes as she was thinking about all this. "Even if my son were to marry Thandi, would he be able to look after her? She is such a beautiful innocent young lady. Will my son not abuse her?"

Salome arrived home without realizing that she was home already. Her eyes were still full of tears when Martha opened the car door and asked her why she was crying. The relationship between the two had grown beyond that of madam and servant but to friendship. They had been together for more than twenty years. Martha had witnessed all the abuse that Salome had gone through under Jeffery. Together they had shared many happy times and painful times. Martha has nursed her during difficult times. Martha has been with her during lonely painful times of Salome's pregnancy.

"I will be fine Martha."

"No, you are not going to be fine, madam. Why are you crying?"

"I came from Mary's salon and I met her granddaughter. She is such a beautiful young lady and -well-mannered. I was thinking if she would be a suitable wife for my son. I went back to my youth and life the first time I met his father at university and what I have gone through over the years. And now I am asking myself if Mary's granddaughter would not go through the same thing. Martha, I don't know if my son will be capable of taking care of such a beautiful and intelligent young lady. My main worry is that he has never shown interest in any girl in town. My son has seen his father's abusiveness to me, and I am wondering if he is not going to do the same to this young girl if I encourage him to propose to her."

"People are not the same ma'am. Freddy seems to be a gentleman and a fine young man. I should think he will be able to take care of her. I wonder whether if this is the same young girl that he spoke to Daniel about?"

"Where is he?"

"He has gone to see his father at work."

"Tell, him to come and see me when he comes back. Martha, help me up the stairs to my room please. I am not feeling well at all. Where is Daniel? I want him to go to the chemist to collect my treatment."

Chapter 10

It's been eight months since Thandi left for university. Sarah has been running the salon and Mary is in and out of the hospital and very few occasions at the salon.

Mary called Sarah to her office. "Sarah as you can see that I am struggling with my health. Thandi has just graduated with her Masters. I don't think I have long to live. As I told you before that I want Thandi to take over this business. You have served me well and for a long time. I am not asking you to stay and work for Thandi if you don't feel like it, but I will appreciate if you could stay and help her at the beginning on the operation side. She will do the books and all other things. I will leave a letter for her if I don't wake up one day then you can give the letter to her, or I will put it on my dressing cardboard next to my bed."

"No, ma'am I will not leave my work. Thandi is a nice person. We have already established a bond between the two of us. I don't think she will have a problem working with me. Besides that, I have nowhere to go. I can't go out there and start a new job with a new employer."

"I am glad to hear that, Sarah. Then at least I know that my granddaughter is in the hands of a person I trust," responded Mary

"Ma'am it looks like you are in pains. Don't you want me to drive you home?" asked Sarah.

"If you are going to drive me home, how are you going to get home?"

"The way you look like today, I don't think it will be wise for me to leave you alone in that big house. I will stay at your place tonight, then if you are better tomorrow, I can go home after work."

Sarah helped Mary with her bag and some few things she was supposed to carry to her car.

They got into the car and Sarah drove her home.

At home, Sarah helped Mary up the staircase to her bedroom. She asked Sarah to prepare a cup of coffee and some few scones and bring them to her bedroom.

Sarah went down to the kitchen and prepared the coffee and scones then went up the stairs back to Mary's bedroom. When she opened the bedroom door, there was Mary on the floor passed out. Sarah checked her pulse, and it was there but she was hyperventilating. She quickly went to the phone and called the ambulance. She went back to Mary. She took one of the pillows and put it under Mary's head and took off her shoes. She started pacing up and down in the room waiting for the ambulance.

In no time there was a siren of an approaching ambulance. Sarah ran downstairs to meet the paramedics. After checking all the vitals, the ambulance raced to the private hospital with Sarah inside.

After admission Sarah went to a call box and called Thandi.

The phone rang on the other side. Thandi's father picked up the phone.

"Khumalo's resident here. How can I help you?"

"Good evening, sir. My name is Sarah. I work for Mrs. Mabandla. Can I talk to Thandi please?"

"Oh yes, let me call her. Thandi phone for you."

"Who is it dad?"

"She said her name is Sarah, working for your grandmother."

"Ok, I'm coming."

"Hold on, she is coming," said Lesley

"Hi Sarah. How are you doing? How is my grandmother?" It was quiet for some few second. "Sarah are you there?"

"Yes, I am."

"Why are you quiet than?"

"Mary is very sick Thandi. She been admitted at Mediclinic now."

"What happened?"

"She was not feeling well at work. I decided to drive her home. I took her to her bedroom, after that I went downstairs to prepare her coffee. When I went back to her room, I found her on the floor passed out. I called the ambulance. She is now here at Mediclinic."

"How is she now?" asked Thandi

"I don't know but at work she was not looking good at all. That is why I decided to drive her home. Thandi, you must come here as soon as possible. I am afraid, it looks like something is going to happen with her."

"What do you mean something is going to happen?"

"The way she was talking about you and the business. Please Thandi you have to be here by tomorrow."

"Ok, let me talk to my dad. Hang in there and keep me posted please Sarah."

After talking with her father, Thandi and Lesley decided to take the earliest flight the following day. They drove straight to Mary's house and find Sarah ready waiting for them.

"Before we drive to the hospital, Thandi there is a letter in your grandmother's bedroom. She wrote it for you. Just grab it before we go."

When they enter Mary's ward, they found her on a ventilating machine.

Thandi sat next to her grandmother's bed side and her eyes full of tears. Her grandmother's blood pressure was low, the sugar level was high, and her liver was not doing well at all. Two years back she went through left toe amputation due to uncontrolled diabetes.

Thandi was fully aware that her grandmother might not survive the attack, but she was hoping that she could go on for a few years. Age was not on her side to fight the attack and she was very weak. Mary's eyes were closed she did not want to see the pain from her granddaughter. She tightened her grip on Thandi's hand and slowly opened her eyes. "Would you please leave me alone with Thandi," she asked Lesley who was standing behind his daughter. He was there to give his daughter moral support. Mary looked Thandi in her eyes and drew out a heavy breath. "You know that you are my only grandchild to my only child, and that I love you more than anything in this world? You represent your mother to me. I want you to listen to me carefully. Stop crying now because what I am going to tell you is very important."

"In this purse are all my house keys. Everything I have, I have changed it to your name. I have asked Mr. Thomas Morgan my lawyer to come and talk to you about all my investments. The salon is also yours if you don't want to run it, please give it over to Sarah, she has been working for me for over 12 years now and knows the business very well. I have two properties in town that I bought cash, there is a double story house where you are staying now and a flat. The flat is rented out. Mr. Morgan will explain everything to you. If you need more cash for whatever you want to do, feel free to sell some of the properties and cash in on some of the investments. I have left you with enough money to start any business you would like."

"Yes, grandma thank you for everything, I will do as you say. Why are you telling me all this? You are not going to die, are you? Grandma! You are not going to leave me now" responded Thandi with tears.

"I leave all these things for you my grandchild so that your life should be easy, but material things my child will not give you ultimate satisfaction in life. I want you to find a good man and get married and have children of your own. Live life with your husband and raise your children in the fear of the Lord. Enjoy life with your family. Wealth without sound family relationships is not a fulfilling life to any woman. As a woman when you get older, wealth means nothing as compared to the joy of seeing your children and grandchildren growing in front of you. You have given me joy more than anything in this world since I lost your mother. I have lived my life around you. You were my source of joy. I have always looked forward to your visits; I have loved you more than everything I have. Your presence in my life has given me the reason to live. Never live life for material things but live life for love and relationships with your husband and your children. Those are the things that God has given you as a woman. Find love my child with somebody that will give you love, a family and good life. It doesn't have to be an expensive life, but life based on sound family values and love. I don't know whether your father told you about my life when I was still young?"

"He did tell me some grandma, but I don't think he told me all, because whatever he told me he said he got it from my mom, and it left me with a lot of question marks. I have been hesitating to pry you with questions about your youth. Do you mind relaying the story to me now granny?"

"When I met your grandfather, I was at high school. My mother had just passed on due to lung cancer. I stayed with my father who was an academic. Your grandfather and I were very good in sport, we met at the school athletics meeting. I was 100 meters and 200 meters sprinter, and your grandfather was good in long distance running. To cut the long story short, we got married when I was going to start my second year at university, and he was working for government as a clerk. By the time we got married I was three months pregnant. My main aim in life was to become a lecturer in Psychology and ultimately to be a professor. For me to do that I had to finish my degree, do honors, masters and Ph.D. in Psychology."

"And then, what happened after that," asked Thandi

"After giving birth to your mom, I wanted to go back to university, but your grandfather refused and said I must stay at home at least for two years and look after your mother. This I refused because I saw it as something that was going to prevent me from achieving my goals in life and I also thought that your grandfather was jealous of me. I loved your grandfather because he was a very good man. He tried to make my life more comfortable. He provided for his family and gave us a good life. The problem was with me. I was not satisfied with what I had, I needed more than what your grandfather could provide. I needed academic recognition and financial independence."

"Why didn't you study further then grandmother?"

"After discussing this with my father your great grandfather who was a professor in Economics in the same University, I was torn between what my father was encouraging me to do and what my husband was suggesting. Because I was a very ambitious woman, I took my father advice. I divorced my husband and pursued my academic life. I left your grandfather and completed my undergraduate degree. When I was about to start with my honors degree, your mom got very sick. She was in and out of hospital. That exhausted all the financial resources that I had saved. Your grandfather was no longer in the same town. He left with his new wife that he had got married to. He took your mom out of his medical aid when they had their first child. That forced me to temporarily leave studies and focus on your mom's well- being. My father kept on pushing me to take your mom to your great-grandmother so that I could focus on my studies. He was not prepared to pay for your mom's medical bills. I felt that if I neglected my own child because of my academic ambitions, I might regret this later in life. I stopped schooling and I found a temporary job in a local salon that was owned by a white lady," continued Mary.

"Oh, grandmother you would have been called doctor Mabandla if you did you PhD," responded Thandi.

"Something I realized later in life my child was that, when women meet in a group and talk about life, most of their conversation is about their married life, their husbands, their children and grandchildren. Women hardly ever talk about their academic achievements and their careers unless it is a group of disgruntled women who never got married because of certain things in life and drowned themselves in studies or careers. Life is about relationships my child."

"What if those women never wanted to have kids?"

"My child it is entrenched into the heart of almost every woman to be married at some stage and have children of her own in her lifetime. Don't commit the same mistake I made in my life, get a good man for yourself, get married and have kids, just like your mom did. Try and make the best out of your marriage."

"I hope a rich Mr. Right will come my way grandmother. I will not get married for the sake of marrying."

"I am not saying you should do that. Good married life my child does not mean living an expensive life with a filthy rich husband or highly educated man. No, a good married life is about finding a man that will love you, respect your womanhood, treat you as if you are the only woman that lives on this earth and be able to provide an honest living for his family."

"Grandma, how do I find a good man that will love me and give me a good life?"

"If you pray and be patient enough my child, that man will come"

Thandi stood up from the chair to give her grandmother a hug. She gave her a kiss. "I love you grandma," she said

"I love you too my grandchild. You can call your father now I would like to talk to him before you guys go."

Thandi came back holding her father in her hand. She was wearing a smile and looked happy.

"When I left that room, you were crying your eyes out, now you look happy, and you are even wearing a smile. What happened?"

"Grandma would like to talk to you. Is she going to die Daddy?" Thandi's face changed there and then after asking her father this question. He quickly noticed that and gave Thandi a soft reply that would not hurt her feelings.

"I am sure she will be fine. Your granny is a fighter she will get through this," said Lesley to console his daughter. Deep down inside him, he knew that there was no way Mary would go through this because she looked very weak, and she had given up the hope to live.

When they walked into the room, they found Mary looking on the other side of the window. She did not hear them walking in. Thandi ran to her. "Granny daddy is here," she said that with an excited voice. Mary turned around and signaled to Lesley to sit down. When she turned around, Lesley could see that Mary was not going to make it to the following day.

"Lesley, I called you here to tell you that I left everything of mine with Thandi. There is a lawyer in town with the name of Thomas Morgan. I don't know whether you know him?"

"Yes, I do know him Mary he was my colleague at Wits."

"He is the one who has been handling all my legal and investment matters. I told Thandi that in my purse there are keys for the house and there is an envelope in one of the drawers in my bedroom. It is addressed to Thandi. Please do help her she will require your assistance in dealing with Thomas. He is a good and a trustworthy person I am sure he will be able to help Thandi with all that she needs to know. I am not going to go through all what I have discussed with Thandi, she will tell you herself if she wants you to hear it. One thing I will ask from you Lesley is that please assist her but also allow her to take her own decision and let her have the final word in whatever she wants to do. Guide her but do not decide for her. I know she is your child but one thing you must know is that her interests may not be the same as your interests. She is not Lesley she is Thandi, her aspirations are different from yours. I am asking you Mr. Khumalo to allow her to be what she wants to be and to be whom she chooses to be with your guidance."

"I will do so Mary."

"Thandi, will you pay me a visit tomorrow? Come in the afternoon after you have spoken to Thomas, I would like to get feedback from your discussion with him."

"Thank you, Mary. I will surely help Thandi with anything she would like to be assisted with. As far as deciding for her, she knows that I don't interfere in her life. She chooses wants she wants to do because she is an adult now. Thandi is very lucky to have you as her grandma. I am sure what you left with her she will be able to look well after it. Although I do have some investments for her it is not that much because she now has two brothers from her stepmom to share with. What her mother left for her is what we used to pay for her varsity education, so this will surely go a long way in helping her start up and in building her future. I can never thank you enough Mary. I will always be grateful to you for what you have done for my child. I will accompany her to Thomas tomorrow if that is what she wants, but I will not be able to come tomorrow since I must fly back to East London for a meeting. Goodbye Mary. You get well," said Lesley though he could see that he was saying those words for the last time to Mary. This he could not tell his daughter who had the hopes of seeing her grandmother the following day. Lesley walked out of the room to give Thandi the last chance with her grandmother.

"Grandma you know how much I love you. I will come and see you tomorrow. What do you want me to bring for you? Should I buy your favorite toffees?" said Thandi

Mary squeezed a smile out of her body to please her granddaughter. She stretched her hand to hold Thandi's hand and squeezed tightly. She pulled Thandi toward her to give her a kiss. "Anything that will please your heart my grandchild anything." Tears started to roll down on her side of her face as she was looking at her granddaughter who could not comprehend the difficulty of her breathing and still had hope in her grandmother's survival.

"Don't cry I promise I will come and see you tomorrow, I promise," responded Thandi with tears on her face. She bent down again to give her grandmother a hug. She squeezed her tighter and looked her in her eyes and said goodbye. Without a word her granny nodded her head.

Thandi walked out of the room to join her father who was busy on the phone talking to Thomas making arrangement for an appointment.

"I just spoke to Thomas, and he said he is available tomorrow, and he can see you in the morning at nine thirty if that is fine with you."

"That's fine with me. Are you not coming with me to see Mr. Morgan? I want you to be there," asked Thandi

"I told him that I might accompany you if it's fine with you. I also told him that you are coming to talk about your grandmother's investments. I told him so that he could prepare himself. He knows about everything, he told me that your grandmother had already warned him about your visit to him."

Chapter 11

At 09h30 Thandi and her father walked into Mr. Morgan's office. "Good morning, ma'am," greeted Thandi

"Good morning young lady. How can I help you?" asked the lady behind the desk.

"My name is Thandi Khumalo, and I am here with my father to see Mr. Morgan. My father spoke to him over the phone, and he said we can come and see him at nine thirty today. Is he in?"

"Yes, young lady he is in, and he told me about the appointment. Let me tell him that you are here already,"

Mr. Morgan's personal assistant stood up and knocked at her boss's door. "Miss Khumalo and her father are here for their appointment."

"Thanks, I am coming. Did you take out Mrs. Mabandla's file?"

"Yes sir, I put all of them in your last drawer."

Thomas stood up and followed his PA to the reception area. "Good morning, Miss Khumalo. How do you do?" he asked as he was stretching out his hand to greet the young lady.

"Good morning Mr. Morgan. I am well thanks, and how are you?" responded Thandi while shaking Thomas's hand.

"I am well thanks."

Thomas turned around and looked at Thandi's father and they hugged each other. "Hey Lesley, it's been quite some time we haven't seen each other. The last time I saw you is about five years back in Johannesburg when we were attending the soccer match. How are you doing and where are you now?"

"Yes, it's been quite some time Thomas, I am doing well thanks and I am still in East London. This is my daughter Thandi that I told you about. I wasn't aware that you are the person that my mother-in-law always talked about when I visited her," said Lesley

"You have a beautiful girl. When your mother-in-law told me about Thandi Khumalo as a beneficiary to all her estate, it never occurred to me that she was talking about your daughter, though she did indicate that it is her granddaughter. Shall we go into my office?"

"Can you offer Miss and Mr. Khumalo something to drink please?" he said to his PA.

"Thanks, for me I am fine," responded Lesley.

"I will like a glass of cold water please," said Thandi.

"Mis Khumalo what are you currently doing if I may ask?"

"I have just completed my masters with Rhodes university."

"Miss Khumalo you are a very fortunate woman. I wish I had a grandmother like Mrs. Mabandla," said Thomas as he bent down to take out files from his bottom drawer. "Mrs. Mabandla has been my client for the past fifteen years. I have never heard her talking about anybody else either than her granddaughter Thandi. I guess you took your mother's place in her heart. Every time she visits me, she would say 'Mr. Morgan I don't want my granddaughter to struggle in life.' She left everything for you Thandi. Everything that is hers is yours now."

Thomas opened the top file and handed it over to Thandi. The top sheet was the mirror image of the sheet that Thandi found in her grandmother's bedroom in an envelope that was addressed to her. The signature at the bottom was the same. Both sheets were reflecting what her grandmother was handing over to her. The total value of the assets was not reflected.

"As you can see Miss Khumalo that there is no value attached to all that is on that page. Here is a file that details the individual values of all your assets. In this file, you will see the value and where the assets are kept."

Thandi's hands were shaking as she took the file and handed it over to her father. "Daddy can you open this for me please. My hands are shaking, and I am feeling very nervous. Spare me the individual details, I just want to know what the amount is."

Lesley opened the file and he stared at it for a while with his mouth half opened and his eyes wide open. Lesley could not believe his eyes.

"What is it daddy?" asked his daughter. He put the file on the table and turned around to hug his daughter sitting next to him.

"What is it daddy?" she asked again.

"Your grandmother has left you with assets with the total value of three and a half million."

"What!!! Are you sure daddy?" asked Thandi as she picked up the file to check for herself. After she saw the amount, she fell on her knees and thanked the Lord for her grandmother.

She stood up and took her chair again next to her father who was in tears because of joy. "Are all these assets here in town Mr. Morgan?"

"Yes, they are ma'am, all your grandmother's properties are paid up, and the double story house she is living in, the flat she rented out, the salon building and all the others she paid them cash. That is not all that will be for you, in her private bank account she has about R350 000. She said this is for your private use". Thomas bent down again and came out with a small box from the drawer. The box was locked with a small padlock. "All her cards and the banking details of her private accounts are here in this box and the key is with her, she is wearing it around her neck as a necklace."

"Do you want to tell me that small key that my granny is wearing around her neck as necklace is worth that much?" asked Thandi.

"Miss Khumalo these are all your files. You can take them and do whatever you would like to do with them. I was your grandmother's lawyer not yours. You have a choice to choose whom you want as your estate lawyer," said Thomas.

"If it is fine with my father, I wouldn't like to change lawyers, since you have proved to be loyal to my grandmother, I would like to stay with you. What do you think daddy?" she asked.

"As I said to your granny that Thomas and I we were colleagues at university I know him as a man of integrity. I will strongly advise you to stick with him if that is what you want. The final decision is yours."

"Thank you very much Miss Khumalo for entrusting your investments with me, I promise to give you an excellent and professional service. Lastly Miss Khumalo here is a letter from your grandmother. I don't know what the contents are. She gave it to me sealed and said I must give it to you when you are visiting me. She said I must tell you that it is for your eyes only. Please do call me at any time if you want clarity on anything."

"Thank you, Mr. Morgan. I will read the letter in front of her at the hospital. I am visiting her now. Can we be excused now Mr. Morgan? I can't wait to go and see my grandmother and thank her. Shall we go now daddy?"

They both shook Thomas's hand and left the office. "Daddy! Thank you for accompanying me. I appreciate it a lot. Can you please do me a favor? Take all that you have invested for me and share it among my two brothers. I have enough money to see me through my lifetime and the salon to keep me going. I know you are making enough money but let that be for you and mom to live on. You gave me an education as a very good investment. Surely, from now onwards I will never struggle in life. Thank you so much, I love you daddy. I know you have to drive to the airport now and I am also rushing to the hospital to see granny and read this letter with her."

"Thank you, my girl. If you feel that you don't need your investment that we have for you, and you would like me to divide it between your two brothers that is well and good for me. Thank you for being so considerate. Give my greetings to your granny and pass my sincere gratitude for her generosity. I am so sorry that I am rushing for my appointment back home otherwise I would come with you to the hospital. I love you, my baby. You take care of yourself. Goodbye for now," he kissed his daughter on her cheek.

"Goodbye daddy."

On her way to the hospital, she stopped at the market to buy flowers for her granny. She opened the hospital doors and headed straight to the ward where her granny was admitted. She opened the ward doors wide with a smile to surprise her granny with her favorite lovely bunch of flowers. She found her granny's bed empty and the whole room had been cleaned up. She turned around to check if there is no hospital staff nearby. She saw the hospital matron walking toward her.

"Are you Mrs. Mabandla's granddaughter?" asked the matron
"Yes, I am ma'am. Where is my grandmother?"
"Can you come with me please?"
"Where have you taken her to? Why did you remove her from there?"
"What's your name young lady?"
"Thandi Khumalo. Where is she ma'am please tell me now?"
"I am very sorry Thandi your grandmother…." She didn't even finish what she was going to say. Thandi dropped the jar of flowers on the hospital passage and broke it as she screamed uncontrollably. As she was about to collapse the matron quickly grabbed her before she could hit the floor with her knees for the fear of the broken pieces of glass on the floor that might cut her.

The matron took Thandi to her office and tried to console her. After some time, she kept quiet. "When did she pass on?" she asked

"Yesterday in the evening, but she told us not to tell you because you promised her to come back today to see her. She said she didn't want you to be disturbed because you had a very important meeting today with your lawyer. Come with me let me give you all her stuff that she left behind. She said everything must be given to you."

"Matron can you allow me to go to the room where she was sleeping, please?"

"Yes, my dear you can. Should we give you a chair?"

"No, I would like to sit on top of the bed."

"Okay. Come and see me when you are done to give you the rest of her stuff."

Thandi went back to the room where her granny had been sleeping for the last time. She walked in and closed the door behind her. She sat down on the bed and took out the letter that her granny left with the lawyer and read it:

> *My dearly beloved granddaughter,*
>
> *Thandi since your mother died, I have loved you like my own child. You have been a source of hope in my life. I cherished and appreciated each minute I stayed with you. By the time you read this letter I might be gone.*

Please my lovely grandchild, do not cry. I have been sick for some time now, but I never wanted to tell you that.

I would like you to cremate my body when I die, I do not want you to incur any funeral costs. Please put my ashes in a box not in a glass bottle and see to it that my ashes are buried.

I have loved you and I will always love you as my little angel.

Please my grandchild live life to its fullest. Do not spare what I have left with. Use it to enjoy life.

I LOVE YOU

Your grandmother Mary

By the time she finished reading the letter her eyes were brimming with tears. After wiping her tears, she went back to the matron's office. "Thank you, matron I should be going now. I will have to inform my parents."

"Your grandmother gave me this necklace and her ring. She insisted that I must give them to you."

"Thank you, matron" When Thandi looked at the necklace she remembered the small box that Thomas gave her. She quickly realized that the necklace was the key that Thomas spoke about.

Chapter 12

Linda knew that she could not hide the fact that she was staying with Sipho to her friend Joyce forever. The question was, how was she going to tell Joyce, that she is hosted by Sipho in his flat. How was she going to tell Joyce that Sipho was the one who was currently paying for her transport and food cost? How was she going to tell her that she was intending to ask Sipho to raise a loan with the bank to enable her to pay for her final year studies?

As they were coming out of the Histology lecture Linda felt a need to be level with Joyce, but her pride was preventing her.

"Joyce, can we go and sit underneath that tree, there is something I would like us to talk about," said Linda.

"Oh, what is it girl? You sound so serious. Are you pregnant?"

"Pregnant me, are you kidding. There was only one Mary and if I remember very well, she was in the bible," said Linda jokingly "My friend, it is much more serious than that, it's about my financial situation. When my parents died, I was called by the bank to tell me how much money my parents left for me. They just left enough money for the payment of my fees for this year and next year. They left enough money for me to live for the next two years. The only problem is that the flat is not fully paid up. When I did my calculations, I realized that if I keep on staying in it, I will exhaust my saving before I complete my studies. I decided to give the flat over to the bank and find a cheaper place for to stay. Mrs. Pillay our neighbor has agreed to host me for now, I am currently staying with her."

"You made the right choice my friend, and I am glad Mrs. Pillay agreed to host you," responded Joyce with a smile.

"Hey friend, do you know that guy called Sipho who stays in our block, the technician. He is always with the guys that we sometimes meet in the morning coming from night shift."

"Yes, I know him, that quiet guy at your flats. What about him?" asked Joyce.

"I am sure the guy wants me. He is always looking at me of late."

"Sipho, wants you! That guy who can't even look at a woman. Are you sure we are talking about the same Sipho?"

"Definitely sure girl," said Linda.

"Any way as far as I know you, Sipho is not your type of a guy. He is not the sophisticated, educated and moneyed guy that you are looking for in life. Sipho is just an ordinary technician working for living."

"He is definitely not my type," said Linda with a lot of emphasis.

"Why don't you expunge him from your list because you have always said that all those guys do not have what you want from a man? Is Sipho aware that he cannot afford you? You better tell him. Don't make a fool of that poor guy he is too good to be messed around by you."

"Not so fast my friend, I think he is not bad for a start, and he looks like a good milking cow for the mean time. I can use a man like him; he can support me while I am still at university. When I qualify, I will not be fiddling with small fish like him I will be catching big ones. I need a sheep that is going to supplement for my traveling and toiletries without bleating for any sexual favors in return. He looks just like that kind of a guy; he is the perfect man for the job. My friend this world does not have mercy for sheep who give themselves up for slaughter like Sipho. If he wants me, he must know that I don't come cheap. I will milk him dry, but he must know I am not going to open up my thighs for nincompoop like him. I am too expensive for simple technician like him."

"Why then do you want to do this to him? Why don't you go and look for some rich old man for yourself? Somebody who is going to pay for all of this without asking any questions."

"No, my friend, those sugar daddies come with a price. You don't get their money without opening up. The other thing they hate using condoms. I am still a virgin. I don't want some old man breaking my virginity. I would rather catch Sipho whom I know is not going to bother me with sex."

"How do you know that he will not demand sex in future?"

"No, not that one. He is too innocent and naïve in that field. I don't think he has ever touched a teat of a woman."

"Okay, you can do whatever suits you my friend, but be careful and know one thing, what goes around, comes around."

Linda and Joyce both had passed their exams and were now going for the final year. It was four weeks to the re-opening of the university for another academic year, which was their last year. She knew that she needed money for registration for her to complete her degree. Linda woke up early and prepared breakfast for Sipho, she knew Sipho was the only possible solution for her plight, and she had to approach him soon so that she could know if he is going to be able to finance her studies or not. Linda looked at her watch and the time was 07h30. She knew that Sipho would be in within the next 30 minutes. She quickly took off her night dress and went for a shower. Within minutes she was done, and she put on her make-up and clean clothes and then sat down to have a cup of coffee. At 07h55 there was a knock at the door, Linda stood up to unlock the door. It was Sipho.

"Good morning Sipho. How was your shift? You look tired."

"Morning Linda! The shift was not heavy at all. Did you sleep well? I am sorry for yesterday. I left some of my clothes on the bed I was very late. What time did you and Joyce come back from university yesterday?"

"Not to worry Sipho, I put everything in the washing basket I assumed it was dirty, I hope that's ok with you. Joyce and I came back very late. After the lectures we went for diner with Joyce's boyfriend. He treated us to some ice cream, we had lots of fun. I have cocked some food can I dish for you or are you going to wash first?" she asked

"I am not tired. Thanks, I am not hungry at all I just want to wash to refresh myself. I also want to go to the bank before I sleep."

Linda's heart started to beat fast when she heard Sipho mentioning the bank. "I wonder what he is going to do at the bank. Does he have financial problems," whispered Linda to herself as she was preparing the shower for Sipho.

"When is the university opening?" he asked

"In four weeks', time."

"That's soon, are you ready?"

"Yes, it is soon, time flies." Linda decided that it was a good opportunity for her to talk to Sipho about her registration fees. "It looks like I will not be able to go back to university this year," she said that with a low voice and putting her hand on Sipho's shoulder and the other holding one of Sipho's hand.

"Why so?" asked Sipho with a concerned face looking at Linda.

"My father paid my fees up to the end of last year. This year was not paid for. I am currently penniless and have no money to pay for my studies this year. I don't know where am I going to get money from to finish my studies. Sipho is it possible for you to raise a loan with your bank for my registration? This is my last year and next year I will be doing my internship and we are getting paid for that. I will be able to pay you back all the money that I will be owing you, including all the pocket and travelling money that you have given me for last year and this year. Please just help me for this year. It's my final year, I will pay back every cent, I promise," pleaded Linda with tears in her eyes.

"How much are your fees for this year? Do not include the traveling and pocket money that I have been giving you."

"The total fees including all the books that I will need for this year is R55 000," she responded.

"I will discuss this with my bank manager today and come back to you later. As for the traveling and pocket money that I am giving to you, you need not to worry about paying that back. I am just being hospitable and for hospitality one requires no payment really. Linda it is only this R55 000 that you need to worry about so that I can repay the bank loan. It's by the grace of God that I am able to help somebody to achieve her dreams and I am grateful for the opportunity to assist."

"No Sipho, I want to pay you back everything I will be owing you. I will be working as a doctor and I will be paid a lot of money, then I can pay you back whatever I will be owing you, the pocket money, traveling, accommodation and your food."

"As I have said Linda that the only money, I would like you to pay back is the R55 000 loan that I am going to discuss with the bank. The rest no payment please."

"You can take a shower while I am out, I want to take a walk to the shops to buy some soft drinks for you. I will be glad if you can give me more money I have run out of toiletries. Do you think the loan will be approved within next two to three weeks or is it going to take longer?"

"I don't think it will take long. I have never tried to raise such a large amount in the past. It shouldn't be a problem because there is more than that in my account. When this is approved, what do I do with it? Do you want it in cash or a bank guaranteed check?"

"Please make it a bank guaranteed check addressed to the university. Here is my student number because it may be required as reference and for proof of payment."

Chapter 13

Thandi managed to pick up the phone and call her stepmother. She couldn't call her father because he was still in the air.

"Mummy. It's me Thandi."

"Hi Thandi. Why are you crying dear? What's wrong?"

"Grandma has passed on. She died yesterday evening. Tell daddy when he arrives. He must give me a call, there are some few things I want to discuss with him. Mom I will have to hang around here for a while. Granny has left the business in my care."

"Will you be fine alone there dear?"

"Yes mom, Sarah is here, she will help me, and she has agreed to stay with me. Bye for now."

After dropping the phone Thandi thought of Freddy. "Sarah, do you think it's wise for me to inform Freddy?"

"How is your relationship with him?"

"We have talked to each other over the phone since he left here. Our relationship is very healthy."

"Call him dear. He deserves to know what is happening in your life. It looks like he is going to be part of your life for long. Does he know that you are here?" asked Sarah

"The last time I spoke to him I did indicate the seriousness of my granny's health and that I might have to come back here. He won't be surprised to learn that I am here."

She called Freddy on his cell phone. The phone rang and later it went to voice mail. She left a message that Freddy should give her a call as soon as he gets the message. Later Thandi's phone rang, and it was Freddy on the line. "Hi, I missed your call. My dad and I were in a meeting. I am in Johannesburg now. How are you?"

"I am sorry for disturbing you in a meeting. I am not doing well at all. My grandmother has passed on. I am trying to organize for her body to be cremated she said she doesn't want to be buried. When are you coming back from Johannesburg?"

"Oh Thandi, I am very sorry my love. When did this happen? We will be flying out from here tomorrow in the afternoon. We have two meetings tomorrow morning. Is there something I can ask Daniel to assist with for the time being?"

"Yes, my love. If he is not busy, can he help driving me around because I don't have energy to drive myself?"

"Okay my love let me talk to him I will come back to you. When you meet Daniel, please tell him not to tell my mother about your grandmother's death. She is very sick now Thandi, anything that can affect her emotions will be detrimental to her health. I will ask my father to find a way of letting her know. They were friends we cannot hide it forever from her. When is the cremation date?"

"I am waiting for my father to land and call me. As soon as I discuss with him, and we finalize I will let you know."

"Is the salon closed?"

"No, Sarah is there, and she is prepared to work meanwhile I am arranging the funeral."

"Let's talk tomorrow then. Where will you be when I land?" asked Freddy.

"I am not exactly sure. Give me a call when you land then I will come and pick you up and Daniel can take your father home."

"No, my darling I will go with my father home. I need to see my mother first then I will come to you later. Is that fine with you?"

"Yes, my love. That's fine with me. Where is she now? And how is she doing?" asked Thandi.

"She is at home in bed, and she is really struggling. Her doctor said the cancer has metastasized into most parts of her body. She is refusing to go for chemotherapy. I will arrange that the two of us see her before anything happens to her. I don't want a situation like the one with your grandmother. I have never met her. I would like my mother to see you before she departs. The sad thing is that I haven't mentioned your name to her nor to my father, the only person who knows about you is Daniel. I think I talk to Daniel about things like this more than I talk to my parents. The beauty with Daniel is that he is open-minded, and he gives me a lot of advice about relationships. My dad does not have an interest in my personal life though there are days I wish I could talk to him. He is only interested in making me a good businessperson. I am very sorry my love I shouldn't bother you about my family life. Can we talk when I come back?"

"That's fine baby let's talk when you are back," she dropped the call.

Thandi started pacing up and down the room digesting what her boyfriend had just said to her. She kept on talking to herself.

"I wonder why is it always so difficult for fathers to talk to their sons about relationships? In as much as our mothers as girls will always talk to us about the importance of marriage, and how we should take care of our husbands when we get married, I think young men should also go through this. When girls are about to get married there is always what women call a bridal shower. In these bridal-showers married women will educate their daughters about married life and how to be a good wife," she continued.

"How come there is nothing like this for men? I wish it was very easy for fathers to talk to their sons about the importance of marriage and how to take good care of their wives. I wish they could teach them how to be a good father to their families. Why can't elderly men who have been married for years educate their young men about the dos and don'ts of marriage. Why can't they have their own groom-shower instead of bachelor's party that does not serve any purpose? Everyone knows that in most cases it is not women who are the cause of unhealthy marriages but man. It is commonly men who will execute abuse in a home."

She decided to stop pacing and she took a seat. Thoughts started to flood her brain. She was thinking about what if Freddy's father does not accept her as his daughter in law. What if he wants another girl for his son? She was sure in her mind that Freddy's mother liked her though she was not aware of their relationship. Then she realized that this was not about Freddy's parents but about what Freddy wanted.

Chapter 14

Sipho was on his way to work when he was joined by Thabo and Seth. He had his headphones on when he heard somebody patting him on the shoulder. Took his headphones off and greeted his colleagues with a smile "How you guys doing?"

"I'm grand my man. You dude?" asked Thabo.

"I'm also grand my bra," responded Seth.

"No complaints my brothers, was just enjoying my sound. Where are the other guys?"

"Themba called me and said his wife will drop him at work and John is not feeling well," responded Thabo.

"You look like you are in a good mood today dude. What's up? Did you win a lotto my bra?" asked Seth.

"Yes, he is wearing this sarcastic smile, tell us dude. Is there an angel in your life?" asked Thabo

"Don't be silly Thabo, why are you saying such a nasty thing to me?" asked Sipho.

Ever since Sipho started accommodating Linda in his house, he had never talked about it to his friends. He didn't know how to start it. Something was telling him that he had to disclose it, especially that now that he had this exciting feeling about Linda. He knew that he was starting to fall for her. In fact, he loves her.

"Okay let me start this from the beginning." Sipho relayed the whole story to them of how he met Linda one day when he was from work, and how he eventually ended up hosting her and supporting her.

"Sipho! How come you have never told us about this dude? Are you keeping secrets now? Woo!!! Women can change guys overnight," said Seth.

"I thought it was going to be for a short period but now it is taking longer than I had anticipated, actually I am gradually falling in love with this woman every day and I think she feels the same way too. One morning I was from work, and I knocked to check if she was awake. She said come in and the door was not locked, I opened the door and there she was standing wearing only panty and bra."

"Wow! Wow! And what did you do dude?" asked Thabo excitedly and clapping his hands with laughter.

"I took a sharp U-turn my bra and I closed the door behind me."

"No, Sipho man! Why my bra. Linda's body is the most perfect body of any woman I know. Sipho I will die to see that body in a frog suit my bra," said Seth with hands on his head walking slightly away from Sipho.

"You right Seth. She has an exquisite body. And the boot my bra kuyafiwa (perfect)," said Sipho with a slight smile showing a sense of happiness in him.

"But Sipho, she knew it was you and she deliberately said come in when she was half-naked," said Thabo as he was stepping hard on the ground and shaking his head facing down and walking away from Sipho. On the other side Seth threw his hands up in the air and shook his head and said,

"Wow I can't believe this, Sipho you've got to wake up and smell the coffee my bra. Tell me, are you man enough? Does a half-naked woman mean anything to you?"

"Guys you must know one thing, there are fundamental things that my father taught me when I was young, and one of them is to respect a woman. A half-naked woman does not mean anything more especially if she is not yours. A real man will either look away or get out of sight."

"No Sipho no. Not for an open invitation like that. You and your fundamentals are wrong. Your father taught you the wrong thing. Well, that is why you will never have a woman in your life," said Seth

"That's not true," said Thabo. "Sipho was still telling us why he is feeling happy. He just said he is falling for Linda. Are you then going to propose her?" continued Thabo.

"I am not sure what exactly I must do. All I know is that I love that woman a lot. I am afraid that if I tell her she might just decide to leave my place which is something I wouldn't like to happen right now," responded Sipho

"You Sipho falling for an educated woman, didn't you say last time that Linda is high society woman? Life has got its funny ways of dealing with human beings," commented Thabo

"You know what dude, you really need to tell her how you feel, and the sooner you do it the better. Let's plan for tomorrow afternoon, ok, what time does she normally come back from university?" asked Seth

"Sometimes she comes back a few minutes before I leave or just after I have left."

"Okay then, leave a note for her tomorrow and tell her that there is something you would like to discuss with her, she must try to be back an hour before you leave for work. Then you can tell her how you feel about her. After you have done that, you take your stuff and leave for work. If she is game, she will wait for you the following morning."

"And then what do I do if I find her home?" asked Sipho.

"Dude you've got to be kidding, it's obvious what follows next," responded Thabo.

Chapter 15

Linda was standing at the bus stop waiting for the bus, she did not have a lecture on that day, but she was going to the library to study. She was nicely dressed as usual. Her thoughts were suddenly disturbed by a red convertible Mercedes Benz with a snow-white interior that had just stopped at the bus stop in front of her. The car was driven by a very handsome gentleman in his forties who was wearing sunglasses. Because of warm temperatures that morning the roof of the car was opened. Linda came back from where she was with a "Wow, what a beautiful machine."

"Good morning young lady. Where are you off too? Can I have the pleasure of offering you a lift to your destination?" asked the man who was driving the convertible as he switched off the car and jump out to open the passenger's door to usher the lady inside the car.

Highly impressed, Linda looked at the gentleman from the bottom up analyzing each and everything the man was wearing. Being label conscious, Linda could see just Gucci all over the guy. His shoes were a Gucci crocodile penny loafer, pants G denim, and a light brown G T-shirt that was hanging over the denim. He was wearing a G leather baseball hat with G golden plated aviator sunglasses resting on the hat. When she came closer to the guy, she was intoxicated by the expensive perfume he was wearing. Without a word, Linda found herself on the passenger seat with the seat belt around her. Still taken by the beauty of the car, the handsomeness of the driver, the cologne and the attire she had just witness, Linda found herself off to town with a stranger before knowing the man's name.

"My name is Eric, and what's yours my lady?" asked the gentleman.

Linda did not respond to the introduction. Her head was resting on the headrest and eyes closed. Her mind was somewhere. The wonderful breeze from the convertible is something that she had always been dreaming about. Here she was today having the ride of her life, this was like manna from heaven, a car that she always dreamt about with the most handsome man on earth. With her eyes still closed, she was thinking to herself that this must be a very rich and highly educated man. She was brought back from her dreams by a pat on the shoulder from the driver. "Lady, I said my name is Eric and what's yours?"

"Oh, I am very sorry sir I have a slight headache that is why I closed my eyes. My name is Linda Sibeko. You said your name is Eric. Eric who?"

"It would be easier for you my lady to just call me Eric. I won't have problems with that Linda, if you don't mind me using your first name," by this time the glasses were back on his face. "Do you mind if we drive to town first to the pharmacy to get some pain killers for your headache?"

"No, I will be fine sir. In fact, I was on my way to the university to study."

"Will you call me Eric please Linda? Oh, are you a student at Wits? I got my degree there and I went overseas to do my masters and doctorate. What are you studying there?"

"It's my last year in MBChB."

"And what would that be baby?" asked Eric.

"I am in my last year of my medical degree. Next year I would be doing an internship as a medical doctor. You said you have a doctorate, it's a doctorate in what?"

"It's a doctorate in Psychology, with the Lake Ford University. Seeing that you want to go and study, can we go for a light breakfast at the mall first, after which I will take you to the university". Linda felt that she could not resist such an offer with the hunk next to her.

"Breakfast! I am in. Where shall we go?" she asked

"Shall we try Killarney mall, then from there the university is not far."

"Fine with me, as long as you promise that by 13h30 I will be at the university."

"I Promise," said Eric.

They sat down in one of the coffee shops at the mall. "Apart from being Eric who is driving this beautiful car and wearing very expensive clothes, what else do you do in life?" asked Linda

"When I came back from overseas, I was employed as a senior lecturer at the University of Johannesburg for ten years. My father was a very successful farmer and he used to export a lot of his produce. When my parents passed on, I had to inherit the farm, but I didn't like farm life, so I sold everything. I took the money from the farm and my pension fund I started my own business. I am currently self- employed."

"What is your line of business that seems to be doing so well?"

"I buy stuff like exotic cars and lady's goodies from overseas and sell to the local market, I don't sell direct to end users, but I have a chain of stores that I am working with. Now back to you, after finishing your medical degree what are you going to do, are you going to work, or do you plan to further your studies?" asked Eric to cut Linda short from asking a lot of questions about him.

"I am intending to specialize as a pediatrician."

"And what's that baby?"

"It's a doctor who specialized in dealing with children."

"Is it like Dr. Judy? The lady I always take my daughter to in the mall?"

"Yes, like her, but I will not be working privately I will work for the government in the public hospital. Do you have kids?"

"Yes, I do."

"How many?"

"Just one, it's a girl."

"Where is she now?"

"She is with her mom in Mpumalanga. She does come and visit me occasionally. Her mom and I are divorced," explained Eric to prevent further questions from Linda.

"How old is she if I may ask."

"She is turning ten years next month."

"Oh, that's great," responded Linda.

It was almost 12h30 when Linda looked at her watch and said, "I think we should drive to the university now."

Eric held Linda's hand and said, "Linda I was still enjoying talking to you. Are you really in a hurry? Can't we go to Zoo Lake and just take a walk there before you go to the university? I know you want to study but you have the whole afternoon to do that. I am still admiring your beauty and enjoying the lovely conversation."

"You know what; the problem is I can't stay till late at the library because I will not have a transport home. That is why I must go and study now so that by 16h30 when the last bus leaves I can catch it," this she said trying to check how flexible Eric was.

"My baby, transport is not a problem, you can just call me when you are done with you studies and I will come and pick you up," responded Eric to assess if the fish will take the bait.

"Really! In that case then we can go to the Zoo Lake if I will be at the library by 15h00," responded Linda with a tilted head and gentle smile on her face as if she was saying I got you.

Chapter 16

This morning Sipho came back very late from work because of a Union meeting. The meeting had dragged for long. As he was climbing up the stairs to his flat, he met Joyce on her way coming down. "Good morning Sipho. My name is Joyce I am Linda's friend," she said as she was stretching her hand toward Sipho.

Sipho was surprised that the lady knows his name "Good morning, Joyce, and how are you this morning?" he asked shyly.

"I'm fine thanks, how are you?" asked Joyce with excitement.

"I'm good, thanks. Are you not at school today?"

"No, we don't have lectures today. In fact, I am from Mrs. Pillay's flat, and I am looking for Linda. Have you seen her?"

"No, I am just arriving from work. Is she not in the room?"

"No. Mrs. Pillay doesn't know where she is; in fact, she said Linda does not stay with her."

"She's right. Linda should be in my room. She stays with me," said Sipho looking puzzled.

"What do you mean when you say Linda stays with you, since when?" asked Joyce with amazement.

"Ever since her parents died and the flat was taken away from by the bank, I thought she told you. Linda has been staying with me," Sipho innocently told Joyce the whole story from the beginning.

"Can we quickly check Linda in your room please?" asked Joyce with a very perplexed facial expression

They both walked toward Sipho's room and Sipho knocked at the door and there was no response. He knocked harder and called Linda by name. There was still no response. He tried to open the door and the door was locked. He quickly checked the key above the door and the key was there. He opened the door the room was empty. They both walked in and Sipho showed Joyce Linda's clothes and some of her books from the university. By this time Joyce's mouth was wide open with shock. "Why is Linda so devious? Why is she hiding things from me? I thought she was my best friend. Thank you Sipho, let me go to the university I am sure I will find her there."

"Can you do me a favor, please don't tell Linda what I have just told you. I don't want her to be angry with me. She might decide to pack her bags and leave me," said Sipho sadly after realizing that Joyce knew nothing.

"I promise you Sipho I won't say a word; even if I do, I don't think she has anywhere to go. She will not leave you. You have done more for Linda than what she has done for you. Believe me Sipho Linda would be nothing without you. If she packs, her bags and leaves you that would be the end of her academic future. Linda is using you Sipho and that makes me very angry."

"What do you mean by that Joyce? One other thing that you must know is that I love Linda and I have no intentions of hurting her."

"What? Did you say you love Linda, or you are in love with her?"

"No, I am not in love with her, but I love her. I have not yet told her that I don't think she knows about it."

"Sipho forget about Linda. Linda is not your type of a woman." She took her school bag that she put on top of the table. "Let me go to school. Bye Sipho." She walked out and closed the door behind her, leaving Sipho standing there thinking about what Joyce had just said.

"Why would she say things like that about her friend? If Linda can hear things like those from her best friend, I don't think she would be happy. I know Linda loves me, I think Joyce is jealous of the relationship between Linda and I."

Joyce was standing at the bus stop waiting for a bus to the campus, within a short time it arrived and took her to the university. She was tapping the base of the bus with her right foot and her lips tightly and slightly squeezed with anger. She was wondering how Linda can do this to her. She asked herself, "Why is she so mendacious? She should have told me that she is staying with Sipho. Can they be in love? Is Linda sleeping with Sipho or is she using him like she said? How do they sleep in that bed and in that room if they are not in love? Linda said she is still a virgin and Sipho said he loves Linda and Linda does not know about it. If Linda is not sleeping with Sipho, she is doing what she said she was going to do, that's milking him, which means she is very devious. I feel pity for the poor guy. I don't think he knows that Linda is playing a fool of him. He is such a gentleman."

Joyce's thoughts were interrupted by the bus opening the door and the driver indicating the destination. She got off the bus and walked toward library. She then decided not to go to the library because she would not be able to study with the amount of anger that she had. She changed her direction to the university cafeteria to have a late breakfast. As she was sitting there, she was joined by some of her classmates, and they started talking about schoolwork and some other things that took her thoughts away from Linda and Sipho.

It was 16h15 and Joyce was on her way to the bus stop to catch a bus back home. She was not in a hurry at all. The next bus was going to arrive at about 16h30. The distance from the library to the bus stop was less than 100 meters. She had her headphones listening to music and deeply absorbed in the song that was playing. She was disturbed by a hooting car that was next to her and a familiar voice that was screaming her name. Her first reaction to the car was a wow! And then she noticed Linda inside the car.

"Wow! What a car!" said Joyce with her eyes wide opened.

"Joyce! Come jump in my friend," said Linda as she was getting out of the car to allow Joyce to occupy the back seat in the two doors convertible car.

"Eric this is my friend Joyce that I told you about. We are in the same class we stay in the same neighborhood." She then turned around and looked at Joyce who was busy inspecting the car. "Joyce this is Eric my boyfriend. Eric has a doctorate in Psychology and a businessman."

"Hi Joyce, how are you?" asked Eric

"Fine thanks and you?"

"I'm fine my lady"

"You have a beautiful car sir." commented Joyce

"Oh, thanks. Call me Eric please ma'am."

Joyce turned to Linda.

"Linda where have you been, I have been looking for you the whole day?" asked Joyce sitting at the edge of the seat with her upper body leaning between the two front seats with her back on Eric.

"My friend it's a long story. It will require us to talk about it when we are sitting down but not here in the car. What were you up to the whole day?" asked Linda wearing a very broad smile.

The question quickly changed Joyce's mood because she started thinking about Sipho and how he feels about this deceitful friend of hers. She looked at her friend's excitement for being in such a beautiful car with a hunk like Eric, she compared that with the gloominess that is always on her face when she talks about Sipho. The man that is paying her university fees and who had allowed her to stay at his place for free when she had nowhere to go. The man who was feeding her, paying for her transport and giving pocket money every day for her daily expenses. She could feel the anger rising from deep in her stomach coming up to her shoulders. She immediately felt a slight headache. She was not sure whether to tell her the truth in front of Eric or to reserve it for later. Something at the back of her mind told her not to rock the boat and leave it for later. She changed from gloominess and brought a smile on her face to ease the pain from her. She said, "I woke up did some few errands in town then I went to the library. I have been there most of the day. Your lips are shinning my friend what did you put on?"

"Eric bought me this new lip gloss from the pharmacy in town," replied Linda as she was scratching from her school bag looking for it. "I am seeing it for the first time. I should think it is new in the market. Eric is importing exotic cars from overseas and selling them, he also imports some lady's cosmetics and sells them to the local market."

"Do you put on make-up Joyce?" asked Eric.

Joyce hesitated to respond because all along she was hoping that Eric would not talk to her. There was something that did not like Eric in her, but she didn't know why. "No, I don't. I am still too young to mess up my skin with make-up. The time will come when I have to use it, and the other thing I don't think I can afford it now that I am still at school."

"I can get some for you without you paying for it."

"No, thanks Eric I think I am fine without it. Can you stop in front of that shop please? There are few things I would like to buy before I get home. Thanks, Eric, for the lift. I hope we will meet again. My friend I will see you tomorrow at the bus stop. Enjoy the rest of your day."

Joyce hugged her friend and alighted from the car in front of the shop and waved goodbye to her friend and Eric. She waited for the car to disappear before she started her walk home. She requested to be dropped there because she didn't want her parents to see her getting out of a stranger's car.

"Your friend is not friendly at all. She looked angry. What's wrong with her?" asked Eric.

"She is not normally like that. I am sure there is something bothering her," answered Linda.

"I would like to take you somewhere before I drop you at your place if you don't mind?" said Eric.

"Do I have a choice?"

"No, you don't because I would like you to see this place."

"That's fine then as long as you will drop me at home after that."

"I promise I will."

Chapter 17

The time was 17h45 and Sipho was dressed up for work. He had prepared everything for the night shift. He was slowly pacing up and down in the room with a note pad on the table and a pen in his hand. He was supposed to write a note to Linda as per agreement with his friends. He was supposed to express his feelings for Linda before it was too late. Sipho had never proposed to a girl before as such he didn't know how to start penning his feelings. There were several papers on the floor already from the pad. He stopped and sat down, scribbled some few words, stood up and tore the pages off. "What do I say to her? What if she does not accept my proposal instead, she becomes angry and leaves? How I wish Thabo or Seth was here to help me with this. It's getting late I must write something." Sipho sat down and started writing. He went on and to the second page. He stood up with the pad in his hand he read what he had written to himself and nodded his head. He tore off the two pages put them in an envelope, sealed it and put it on top of the table.

He then took his work bag, locked the door behind him and off to work he went. All what Sipho was doing in his room took his time, by the time he finished writing the note it was late already. All his friends had already left for work. He walked to work alone that day.

Chapter 18

With a glass of red wine in her hand and tipsy Linda went to Eric and requested him to take her home. "Eric it is way past my bedtime now and I have lectures tomorrow. It's an Immunology and Histology lectures which I cannot afford to miss at all. Take me home please."

Earlier on Eric had driven Linda to a night club that he owned but he had told her that it belongs to a friend. He didn't want Linda to know the truth about the night club.

"Do you take wine Linda?" asked Eric as he was already opening a bottle of red wine, he took from the bar shelf.

"I would like a glass please but just a glass and nothing more because I have lectures tomorrow. How come you can just go to the shelves and take something without paying for it? Are your friends not going to fight with you for that?"

"As you are saying they are my friends we've known each other for long not to trust each other. I have chosen a very good wine for you, it's a 1982 red wine bottle," said Eric.

Linda was on her second glass when she asked for Eric to take her home. Eric was hoping to spend the night with Linda but seeing that she wanted to go home, he did not want to appear as a pushy person from the word go.

Linda was staggering to the car with Eric holding her on one side.

She got into the car and slept. Eric drove her off to her flat.

She got out of the car with difficulty after Eric opened the door for her. Eric helped her and walked her to the stairs of the building.

Eric said, "When will I see you again Linda?"

"Can we see each other next week? This week I am writing two tests and I would like to have time to study for them." she said with a sluggish voice.

"When next week baby?"

"In actual fact let it be Friday night because I am writing the second one on Friday and I will finish at about 20h00."

"Can I come and pick you up at 21h00?"

"Yes please."

"Is Joyce coming with you?"

"I don't know. I will have to ask her. If he will be coming. I think she will be with her boyfriend."

"That's fine then, we can go to the night club and chill out there.

Good night baby, talk to you some time. Sleep well," said Eric and gave her a kiss.

"You, too my love."

She walked up the stairs and took the room key where they kept it and opened the door and threw herself on top of the bed. Within seconds she was gone. When she woke up the next morning, she was ten minutes late. She rushed to the bathroom and washed and within few minutes she was out of the room rushing for the bus.

When Sipho came back from work that morning he was hoping to find Linda's response, he opened the room and threw his eyes on top of the table with a hope of seeing something addressed to him. To his disappointment he saw the letter he had written the previous night unopened on the table same spot where he left it. Linda's clothes were all over the room and the bathroom was a mess. He took the letter tore it into pieces and sluggishly started cleaning the room.

Chapter 19

It was two months after Mrs. Mabandla's cremation when Freddy came rushing into the Salon. He opened Thandi's office and with a concerned voice he said "My mother is admitted in hospital, and she is in ICU. Can you accompany me to the hospital?"

"Yes, for sure I will. When did this happen?" responded Thandi as she packed her bag and rushed to the ladies to quickly freshen up. When she came out of the ladies Freddy was already standing next to the car that was driven by Daniel. Freddy occupied the front seat with Daniel and ordered Thandi to sit at the back.

"What happened Freddy?"

"I really don't know. I got a call from my father's PA at about 10h30 saying that Martha called and told her that my mom was not doing well at all. She was requesting that daddy should come home. Unfortunately, my dad left this morning for a meeting in Plettenberg Bay. I was also busy in a meeting with the marketing team. I told the PA to tell Martha to monitor the situation and if it gets out of hand to call me. The next thing after an hour she came back to tell me that my mother collapsed, and Martha had to call an ambulance to take her to the hospital."

"Are you from the hospital now?" asked Thandi with a great concern because it was after 14h00 and his mother was taken to the hospital at about 11h30. "Why is he going to the hospital now? What was he doing all along?" she whispered to herself.

"No, Thandi," responded Freddy with great annoyance. "I told you that I was busy with the marketing team. We had a serious problem in the factory, and I also did not go because I didn't know what I was going to do there. That is why I am fetching you to accompany me. I know mom is in her terminal stage, she can die in anytime."

Thandi leaned forward and put both her hands on Freddy's shoulders and rubbed them to calm him down. "It's okay it will be fine darling," said Thandi with a soft voice trying to cool Freddy's anger down and consoling him. She had gone through this with her grandmother and understands clearly how he was feeling.

Daniel stopped the car in front the hospital's main entrance to allow them to get off, so that he can proceed to the car park. They both went to the information desk and asked about Mrs. Phillips ward. They were told that she was in ICU, and her doctor had ordered to be called when there are people who would like to see her. The nurse called her doctor who came immediately.

"Good day lady and gentleman," greeted the doctor as he stretched his hands to shake Thandi then Freddy's hands. "I am the oncologist, Mrs. Phillips's doctor."

"Good day doctor. I am Freddy Phillips, and this is Thandi Khumalo my girlfriend. We are here to see my mom. How is she doing? Can we see her?"

"She is in less pain now and her condition has stabilized. I sedated her and I wouldn't like her to be disturbed today, she needs time for the morphine to kick in for speedy recovery. Is it possible for you guys to come and see her tomorrow? She really needs some rest now."

"Is tomorrow not too late doctor? Why can't I see her now?" asked Freddy

"She is still heavily sedated now and will not be able to hear you. You can visit her at any time tomorrow because she will be out of ICU, and she will be in female medical section in a private ward. Your mother is a fighter Mr. Phillips I admire her."

The following day Freddy called Thandi and asked her if she could pay her mom a visit "How busy are you today? I don't think I will be able to go with you to the hospital because my father drove to Port Elizabeth last night and he has a meeting today the whole day and there are some things I must take care of in the office and there are also some documents that he wants today for his meeting in Port Elizabeth. I will be busy the whole day. Can you check on mom for me please? I will ask Daniel to drive you to the hospital"

Thandi was quiet for a while and then she said "Yes, Freddy I will. Sarah will look after the salon. Your mother only knows me as Mary's grandchild. What do I say to her? Is she not going to ask me why I am visiting her?"

"Tell, my mom that you are my girlfriend, that's all. She will have to accept that. I will call Daniel to come and pick you up. What time do you want him to pick you up?"

"Tell, him to be here at 13h00. I would like to start at work first then go to the florist to get some flowers for her. Freddy! Is your father aware of your mother's condition? Did you tell him yesterday?"

"Yes, my father is aware I explained to him everything that happed with my mom's condition at the hospital. Pass my regards to her and tell her I will come and see her tonight or tomorrow morning." Freddy dropped the phone.

After dropping the phone Thandi sat on the chair, and she stared at the ceiling. She whispered to herself "What kind of family is this one? Freddy's mother is dying in hospital and his father is busy with business meetings far from his dying wife. Freddy does not have time to visit his dying mother because of business commitments. To them life is all about business and making more money."

Daniel arrived with the car. He drove Thandi to the hospital. "How long have you been working for the Phillips's, Daniel?"

"This is my seventeenth-year ma'am," responded Daniel.

"Please don't call me ma'am, my name is Thandi. Okay Daniel?"

"Yes ma'am."

"Where is your family?"

"I never got married ma'am."

"Danie, I told you that my name is Thandi not ma'am. Do you mind if I ask why?"

"I was disappointed by a lady I loved and intended to marry. She left for another man."

"Why didn't you look for another woman then? There are so many beautiful ladies out there."

"I lost interest in anything wearing a dress."

"How are you surviving now?"

"I eventually changed my mind and now I have a girlfriend."

"I am glad to hear that. Don't forget I will have to go to the flower market in town first."

"Ma'am, where would you like me to drop you?"

"At the car park Daniel. I will walk to the market."

After buying flowers Daniel drove Thandi to the hospital. She arrived at the hospital about 13h30. She proceeded straight to the female medical section and look at the board for Mrs. Phillips ward. In the ward she found a nurse who was checking the vitals.

"Good afternoon sister. Is she sleeping? How is she doing?" she asked with very low voice.

The nurse indicated to Thandi that they should talk outside the ward because Salome was sleeping.

"Good afternoon, ma'am. I cannot tell, it is only the doctor that knows her condition."

"Am I allowed to sit and talk to her when she wakes up?"

"Yes, the doctor said we should allow the family only to see and talk to her when she wakes up."

Thandi put her flowers next to the flower jar that had flowers. She pulled her chair close to the bed and sat down and looked at Mrs. Phillips. She said a short prayer from inside. She looked at Mrs. Phillips hand which was on her side of the bed. Realizing that she was still sedated Thandi started speaking softly. "The first time I saw you, you and I had a lovely talk. I was hoping that I will be able to see you soon. I thought your son was going to introduce me to you. You really looked and behave like a mother to me when I first met you. Strange enough I loved you from the first time I saw you. Your son was supposed to tell you about our affair, but he didn't. I am hoping that Freddy and I will get married one day so that you become my mother-in-law. How I would love a lady like you next to me as my mother-in-law." Thandi heard somebody making a very low groaning sound and she turned around but there was nobody. She quickly stood up to look at Salome and she realized that she was trying to open her eyes. "Mrs. Phillips! Mrs. Phillips!" She called her name softly. Slowly Salome opened her eyes and looked at Thandi, she then turned her head and looked on the other side and she saw the monitoring machine.

"Martha where am I?" she asked as she was turning her head back to Thandi. "Why am I in such pains? Is Jeffrey back? You are not Martha. Who are you and how did you get in here?" she asked as she was looking away from Thandi.

"Mrs. Phillips, I am Thandi, Mary's granddaughter. We met at Mary's salon one day and we talked. You are at the hospital."

Salome looked at Thandi and trying to recall. "Oh, I remember you now," she said with a slothful voice. "You are Mary's granddaughter. Why are you here and where is Mary?"

Thandi quickly remembered that when her grandmother died the Phillips family never wanted Mrs. Phillips to know about it because of her condition. She was never told about her grandmother's death. Thandi was not prepared to divulge that information to Salome because of her condition. She was very weak and struggling with her breathing. "My granny is at home. She said I must pass her greetings to you."

Salome put a smile on her face that just pushed her cheeks behind without exposing her teeth. She stretched her hand toward Thandi and hold Thandi's hand. She slowly pulled Thandi toward her and put both their hands on her chest. She looked Thandi in her face and said, "I heard everything you said when you were talking but I was hearing it from afar and I wasn't sure if it was a dream or not. Did I hear you properly when you said you are my son's girlfriend?" asked Salome as she is trying to squeeze Thandi's hand with her shaking hand. Thandi could feel the slight tremor from Mrs. Phillips hand. She looked Salome in her eyes and realized that there were tears coming out slowly. This touched Thandi because it reminded her of her grandmother when she was in a hospital.

"Yes ma'am, we have been seeing each other for long. Freddy was supposed to inform you and Mr. Phillips about it."

"Thandi, I loved you from the first time I saw you, I am very happy that my son has finally found a woman in his life. Are you prepared to marry my son if he can propose?"

"Yes Mrs. Phillips I love Freddy and would love to be his wife."

"Please my girl you must take care of my son, he does not understand the value of life. His father has trained him to be a businessperson and I don't think he knows what love is all about. I am expecting you Thandi to hold his hand and teach him and tolerate him where he has pitfalls. I might not live long to see your wedding, but you must know that you have all my blessing to marry my son and be Mrs. Phillips in my place. Don't be afraid to be who you are and be proud of yourself. Always stand by your husband no matter what happens. His strength is in your encouragement and his success is in your support."

"Will try and do so ma'am," responded Thandi.

"Please my child, never discuss your husband's weakness with other women no matter who they are, but always talk and boast about his strengths. I hope my son will give you a good life." By now Thandi was in tears and her head on top on Salome's chest. Thandi was not crying because of what was said to her, but she was thinking of the pain that Salome was going through. She was in hospital and facing her last days of her life. Both people that meant a lot to her, people that constitute what her family is, were not near her but busy attending to business. The man that she loved and supported from the early days of her life was far from her death bed. Her only husband, the father of her child was abandoning her on her last days to be with the business that they have built together when they were young and yet this was the time, she needs him next to her.

The son that she struggled to conceived and carry him for nine months is with the company that she helped her husband to purchase. Thandi cried because she never had an opportunity to close her grandmother's eyes.

"I am a stranger to this woman, I am not the one who was supposed to be here, Freddy is the one, this is his mother," mumbled Thandi to herself.

"Will you come with my son for the next visit? I would like to talk to the two of you before I depart. Thandi, I have gone through a lot in my marriage with Freddy's father. I hope and wish that you will not experience the same. I am praying that my son whom I struggled for year to conceive will treat you as a lady and be a man enough not to abuse you.

No matter what happens between you and my son please my child you should never quit. The Phillips family is a very rich family they will give you everything materially that you want in life and all I am asking from you is to teach my son how to love."

Thandi was now attentive. She looked Salome right in her eyes as she was talking. She had an idea of what Salome was talking about. She had witnessed Freddy's anger when he responded to her in the car but no abuse. The machine started bleeping to indicate a misnomer from Salome's system. As the machine was bleeping Salome started gasping and closing her eyes. Thandi went out screaming with a loud voice and calling for help. One of the professional nurses came running and went past Thandi to the ward.

Salome's heartbeat had dropped tremendously, and her blood pressure tumbled. She gasped desperately for air. The nurse went straight to her and when she realized that she was going, she rang the bell for extra medical help. By the time the doctor arrived Salome's heart had already stopped. They tried to resuscitate her, but all was in vain. Thandi was not allowed to enter the ward when the medical team was busy. When she saw the doctors and the other nursing staff come running, she realized that there was something seriously wrong with Salome.

The doctor came out of the ward and saw Thandi standing next the door.

"Good afternoon, lady. You are the one who came here yesterday with Freddy Phillips is that so?"

"Yes, doctor it's me. Is she alright?"

"Come with me. Where is Mr. Phillips? I must talk to him." The doctor asked Thandi to wait outside his office. He called Jeffrey's number and there was no response, he then tried Freddy's cell phone number.

"Freddy Phillips here how can I help you?"

"Freddy, this is doctor Kekana the oncologist. How are you sir?"

"I am well thanks for asking doc. How are you doing doc if I may ask?"

"I am also well."

"Any news about my mom?"

"Do you have a minute to talk sir?"

"Yes, doc I do. We can talk now."

"I have been trying to get hold of your father, but he is not answering his cell phone, do you know where he is?"

"I am sure he must be on his way flying back from Port Elizabeth. Is there something I can probably help you with doc?"

"Mr. Phillips I am very sorry to tell you this. Your mother has passed on this afternoon at about 14h10. The lady you came with yesterday is here outside my office and I have not informed her yet. Would you like me to tell her, or should I send her home so that you can brief her?"

"She is my fiancé doctor, and I don't think I will be able to tell her, I will appreciate if you can be the one who breaks the news to her. I will not be able to console her if she breaks down more specially that she also buried her grandmother some few months ago."

"Okay Mr. Phillips I will get our matron to do that for me. We will keep her until she recovers and can you get somebody to drive her home after that please."

"She is with somebody there. My drive Daniel is the one who brought her there."

The hospital matron called Thandi and broke the news to her. After the matron briefed her, she never broke into tears instead she just became numb. She saw it coming and she could not stop it. The question in her mind was that, is this not supposed to happen in the presence of Mr. Phillips or his son or is it because I am her future daughter in-law in waiting? "It was also good that I came, otherwise she would have died without me knowing how she felt about me," she murmured.

The two deaths she has witness within the few months has made Thandi strong. She knew now that losing somebody you love is not in anybody's hands but in the hands of some powers beyond human capabilities. She was hoping that when she marries Freddy his mother would still be alive, and she was planning to take care of her like her own mother. On her way to the car, she called Freddy. "Hey, how are you doing? Did the doctor call you?"

"Yes, he did. Where are you now? Can I meet you at the salon after work?"

"I am on my way to the car. I will wait for you then. Should I tell Daniel of what has happened? Or you will tell him?"

"Please my love, do tell him. I don't think I will have courage to tell him. My father landed ten minutes ago, and I asked his PA to convey the message to him."

"Where is he now?"

"He said he was going to wash and then go to the hospital."

"Why don't you join him then my love? Don't you want to see her?"

"Baby I am not good when it comes to death. I wouldn't like to see my mom who can't talk to me any longer. Besides I don't know how my father is going to behave when he gets there. Let him be alone."

Chapter 20

Linda came back from the lectures alone because Joyce did not attend, and she was not feeling well. She came back early so that she can catch Sipho before he leaves for work. On her way home her mind was already pre-occupied by the Friday's invitation. She couldn't wait to tell Joyce about it also invite her and her boyfriend. "I must find a beautiful dress for myself. I have heard that girls who are attending that night club dress to kill. They say Friday nights are competition nights for ladies. Where am I going to get the dress from?" she whispered to herself.

She knocked at the door and there was a response from inside indicating that the door was unlocked, and she can get in. She found Sipho siting at the table having a meal before he could hit the road to work.

"Hi Sipho, how are you? What smells so nice? I am starving. Is there enough food for me?"

"Good afternoon, Linda," responded Sipho as he stood up to allow Linda to occupy the seat so that he can take another one. "I cooked some mutton curry, vegetables and pap. There is enough for you for now and tomorrow before your lectures. Were you late this morning? I saw the way your clothes were all over the place and the bathroom not cleaned. Did you go somewhere last night?"

"Yes, I was late. Joyce and I studied till very late. I came to sleep at about 00.15 this morning. By the time I got up for my morning lecture I was already late because I didn't want to miss the lecture. I had to leave everything the way it was knowing I will sort it out now. I thought you were gone already." Linda pulled the chair that Sipho vacated and sat close to Sipho. She rested her elbow on Sipho's lap. "You know by now that I care about you. Sipho look at me. You are very quiet, and you are a gentleman. You know I appreciate everything that you have done for me. I told you that next year I will be working, and I will pay back all what I owed you. If it was not for you, my academic future would have been lost. There are things that I need, but I can't afford them because I don't have money. Will you be so kind and help me to buy those things? I will pay you back all your money."

Sipho's heart was racing very fast. He became nervous the minute Linda pulled the chair and sat next to him. When Linda started talking his head was slightly bowed down and his eyes were zoomed in the plate in front of him. The only time he lifted his eyes was when Linda asked him to look at her, but even then, he could not keep his eyes on her. "What are those things that you need money for? I told you that whatever you need you should tell me. How much do you want?"

"Joyce and I are invited to a function on Friday and Saturday night, I will have to have two dresses for both occasions. Will you be able to buy the dresses for me? I don't know the price of the dresses by now, but I will leave a note for you tomorrow so that when you come back from work you can get the money for me. I will ask Joyce to accompany me to town on Wednesday or else if you don't mind waking up on Wednesday afternoon, I can go with you to town," she said that but knowing it will not be possible for Sipho to accompany her. Linda stood up and took Sipho's plate because he had already indicated that he was full, and his food was almost finished. "What time are you leaving for work today? I would like to take you halfway."

"No, no, no, you don't have to do that. I will be walking with my friends, there are work related things we would like to discuss today," interjected Sipho with nervousness. He wouldn't like his colleagues to see him with Linda otherwise they will tease him all the way to work. "I will get the money for you tomorrow when I come back from work." He stood up and took his work bag and said goodbye to Linda. As he was going to the door Linda grabbed his arm and pulled him toward her and hugged him then gave him a kiss on his cheek. Sipho was completely startled his eyes were about to pop out of their sockets.

"Poor Sipho he is so meek. I will have to milk him as much as I can. He is going to buy the two dresses for me to attend the night club on Friday and Saturday. Oh! Eric will be proud of me. I will be so beautiful on both days he will hardly recognize me."

Chapter 21

Freddy's mother was buried on a Friday because his father was scheduled for a flight to Asia the following day. The funeral was well attended. Freddy attended the funeral in his mom's ML. He drove to the graveyard with Thandi in the car. His father was driven by Daniel to the cemetery. After the funeral when everybody was gone from the house except for Thandi who Freddy asked to remain behind. Freddy's father was sitting under the tree in the garden. He walked toward his father gingerly with both hands intertwined next to his chest and his head slightly bowed down.

"Excuse me daddy, can I disturb you for a minute please? I would like to introduce someone to you if you don't mind. Someone very special to me."

Jeffrey lifted his head and looked at his son. "No, you are not disturbing me. You can go ahead."

Freddy signaled with his hand to Thandi to come to him quickly. She walked toward Freddy hastily with her hands at the back. She came right in front of Jeffrey and stood next to Freddy with her face down and her eyes with no contact with Jeffrey's eyes. "Daddy this is Thandi Khumalo. Thandi is Mrs. Mabandla's granddaughter. Thandi this is my dad Mr. Phillips."

With slightly bent knees and bowed head Thandi said, "Good day sir."

"Oh, you are Mary's grandchild? I knew your grandmother very well. What are you doing with yourself? And what education background do you have?"

"I am currently running my grandmother's salon. I have a master's in Business Economics from Rhodes University".

Before Thandi could respond to that question Freddy quickly interposed and said "Thandi and I met at her grandmother's salon when she was on school vacation about year and half or two years ago, and we have known each other since then?"

"I am glad to know you Thandi."

"Thank you, sir so am I," said Thandi with a very polite voice.

"You can go back to the house now," said Freddy to Thandi. "I still want to talk to my dad about some few things."

When Thandi was gone Freddy turn to his father and said "Daddy I am intending to marry Thandi, what do you think of her? I love her daddy and she is the first woman I ever loved, and I would like to spend the rest of my life with her. She has never judged me for my weight. The first time I met her she didn't even know that I was from the Phillips family, unlike the girls here in town that are after me because of who I am. On top of that her father is a well-known lawyer in East London. She is well-mannered daddy, and she respects me a lot. I even asked her to pay mom a visit at the hospital just before mom passed on and she did."

"Is this Khumalo's daughter, the well-known lawyer from East London? If that is the case my son, she is from a fine family. Her father is one of the well-respected gentlemen I have ever met. Who you marry my son is your own choice? It is not me who is going to spend life with that woman but you. I just don't want you to marry a woman who is after your money but not your well-being. She must be able to love you despite and despite of who you are. One thing you shouldn't do, never take any nonsense from a woman. She must know her place and know that you are a man, and she is a woman. You are my son, and you are going to inherit everything I have. You are going to be a very wealthy young man. You don't bow to any woman; women must bow down to you Mr. Philips junior."

With the smile on his face Freddy bowed to his father and said "Thank you daddy. I hear you." He left his father and joined the anxious Thandi at the lounge. As Freddy walked in Thandi stood up and met him halfway. She wrapped her hands around his waist and with rolled eyes, her head slightly tilted to the left and a shallow smile she asked, "And so what does your father think of me Mr. Phillips?"

Freddy put his elbows on Thandi's shoulders and hold her head with both hands and pull her toward him such that their foreheads meet and rub his nose with hers and looked her in her eyes and smiled.

Chapter 22

"Joyce, do you remember Eric? My new boyfriend." asked Linda as they were waiting for their morning bus to the lectures.

"Yes, I remember him very well. The SLK guy," replied Joyce slightly unconcerned.

"He is a co-owner of the night club we spoke about at some stage. He has invited us this coming Friday. He said you can bring your boyfriend with you."

"My boyfriend and I we will be driving to Magaliesberg after the test on Friday. We will not be around. Linda my friend even if I was not going with my boyfriend, I don't think I was going to attend the club with you. I don't think I like what you are doing and the way you treat Sipho. I know it has nothing to do with me, but you are my friend, I should think I have the right to tell you where you are not doing right. I think that poor man loves you, it is just that Sipho is one of the guys who can't talk for themselves."

"Are you now proposing me on behalf of Sipho, I have told you time and again that Sipho is not my type? He can love me until he dies. He is not going to get me. Joyce, tell me my friend, why should I waste my time with people like Sipho when there are hunks like Eric. Men who have money, brains and know how to please a woman. Secondly, I don't think you have any right to tell me how to live my life. Because we are friends does not give you the right to interfere in my life. Eric is my man not that stupid Sipho, that's all," said Linda slightly agitated.

The bus arrived and they embarked. "Tomorrow can you accompany me to town I want to buy two dresses for the Friday and Saturday night club functions?"

"Why do you have to buy new dresses for night club?"

"Eric said I must look beautiful."

"Is he paying for that beauty?"

"Yes, he is my friend. He is going to give me R 2000 for the two dresses and some other things that I might need." Linda lied with the fear that if she can say it's Sipho, Joyce will eat her raw. She could see now how much Joyce cares about Sipho, so whatever she says to her must be correct.

"Does Sipho know that you are going out with Eric? Is he aware that on Friday and Saturday you won't be sleeping at home?"

"Where I am going is none of his business. I am an adult. Sipho cannot control me."

"I am sure you have forgotten that you are staying in Sipho's flat not yours. If you have that attitude, I wish Sipho kicks you out of his apartment and we shall see if your Eric will accommodate you," said Joyce angrily.

"Wow friend I wish you could have seen Eric's house, it's so beautiful and stylish. Well, if he kicks me out, I will gladly go out of that tin and go and stay with my lover in a spacious place with lots of bedrooms not that bachelor flat with just one room. I don't think you know that I am doing Sipho a favor by staying with him. At least people are starting to know him now and one of them is you."

"My friend, how sure are you that Eric loves you or he just wants to use you? Do you know how many girlfriends he has? What if you are one of his statistics?" asked Joyce

"Joyce my friend, you sound very jealous. How can you say such things about Eric and yet you do not know him? The man loves me, and I think that is all that is important now. The other things that you are talking about I will cross that bridge when I come to it. Eric can't be a crook. The man is highly educated Joyce. He has a doctorate in Psychology."

"Be careful my friend, crooks nowadays don't come wearing overalls but suits and ties. They don't come walking but driving beautiful big machines and they can sweet talk anyone. Let's talk later because I am running late for my appointment with the Dean of student's affairs."

"You will find me at the library. What about on Wednesday going to town? Are you going with me or not?" asked Linda.

"Let me rush for my appointment we will talk when I get back."

Chapter 23

It was a Friday after the test, Linda and Joyce were on their way home in the University bus with other classmates. They were all in a jovial mood because the test paper was not very difficult. Everybody felt like they had done well.

"This was a very good paper. Most of the questions were the tutorial questions," commented Linda just to break the silence that was there between the two of them.

"Yes, it was," responded Joyce without showing any signs of enthusiasm to the conversation.

Linda was determined to continue with the conversation because she had something she wanted to share with Joyce despite Joyce's reluctance to join in the conversation. Joyce knew that there is one thing that Linda is going to talk about and it's the club and Eric. This is the topic that bored Joyce to death.

"Did you manage to answer all the questions before time?" Linda kept on probing Joyce.

"I went through all questions before time, and I even had time to check my spelling mistakes" responded Joyce with a little bit of keenness. "How did you go?"

"You know that I am very slow. I did manage just in time, but I did not get time to cross check. Are you guys still driving up to Magaliesberg?" asked Linda

"Yes, we are going. He is going to pick me up at 21h30 from home. How are you going to get to the club this time alone?"

This is the question that Linda has been waiting for. "Eric will come and pick me up at 22h00. He said that is the time the club is starting to be alive. My friend, which one of the dresses do you think will be proper for tonight, considering that people will be seeing me for the first time in the club with Eric? I don't want to be an embarrassment to him on our first outing together."

"Any one of those dresses they are both very pretty. I am sure in any one of them you will look very beautiful enough to impress anybody. Oh, the bus has reached our destination already."

They disembark and wave to each other goodbye.

"Travel safe to Magaliesberg and pass my regards to your boyfriend," screamed Linda at Joyce as they were drifting apart to different directions.

"You do the same to Eric. Will see you on Monday morning," echoed Joyce.

At 22h00 Linda was not ready, and she was praying that Eric shouldn't arrive until she is fully prepared. She finished dressing up and putting on make-up at 22h10. When she looked at her wristwatch, it was 22h20. She decided to wait for Eric in the room than going outside as it was late already. She knew that Eric would call when he was outside. At 22h30 she decided to call him on his cell phone, the phone rang several times until it went to voice mail. She called again at 22h35, the same thing happened. She told herself she will give him time and call at 22h45. Linda made several calls after 22h45 and all of them were in vain.

She started crying at 23h15 because she realized that Eric will not be coming and she was thinking of how she is going to explain this to Joyce, such an embarrassment. "Did something happen with him? Why is he not answering his phone? Should I call a cab and go there? What if he is not there? Should I be patient most probably he is busy somewhere and he is still coming?" These questions were running in her head as the tears were spreading the make-up from her face and eyes, smudging it all over the face as she kept on wiping her eyes with the back of her hand. She gave up on waiting and went to bed at about 00h15.

When Sipho came back in the morning she found Linda sleeping. He tiptoed around the room all the time trying not to make noise. He quickly went to the shower and dressed up and left for town. When Sipho came back from town, he opened the door, Linda was awake, but she quickly turned herself and faced the wall as the door was opening. She pretended to be asleep all the time Sipho was in the room. She did not want to face him. She didn't want to explain yesterday's embarrassment and she also knew that her eyes were still puffed up from all the crying. Sipho might notice them and start asking questions.

Sipho took out some few things from the closet and went out to visit friends.

When Sipho was gone she woke up and dialed Eric's number, the number was engaged. She tried the number the whole day but all in vain. She wasn't sure whether to stay in bed or wake up wash and go to town. Ultimately, she decided that she will wake up and wash. Sipho came back when she had just finished dressing.

Before he tried to open the door Sipho knocked. There was a response from inside. "Oh, you are awake? How did you sleep? I didn't want to wake you up this morning."

"I slept well but not enough. Joyce and I came back early hours of the morning that is why my eyes are still puffed up. The way I feel so tired I am not sure if I will make it for to night's function. I will be going out soon to give you space and time to sleep."

"Where are you going?" asked Sipho

"I want to go to town. I will go to Joyce's place and ask her to accompany me."

"Do you have money for transport to town?"

"Yes, the change from the dresses though it's not a lot for the things I want to buy."

Sipho took out his wallet and gave Linda R1000. "I hope this will be enough for what you want to buy."

"It's more than enough. Thank you Sipho," said Linda and gave Sipho a kiss on his cheek. "Bye I will see you later." She went outside and stood at the pavement for a while thinking whether she should call a cab and go and check Eric at his place or should she go to town. She ultimately decided to call a cab and went to Eric's place. She pressed the bell several times but all in vain. She went back to the cab and requested the driver to drop her in town. When she was in town, she came across

Joyce and she was surprised because she didn't expect her there. The last time they spoke she was going out to Magaliesberg with her boyfriend. As she was moving toward Joyce, she had a lot of questions in her mind. "What happened? Did they break up? Did they fight? Or was she lying to me?" She opened her arms to hug her friend "Hi. How are you, my friend? Why are you here? I thought the two of you went to Magalies."

"We decided otherwise. We will go to Durban next weekend rather. How was your night lady? Did you enjoy yourself? Did you take pictures with the dress you were wearing? I would love to see you in one of them?"

"Oh, my friend! The night was splendid, and I looked stunning with the yellow one. Eric was very impressed, and most people were looking at me girl. Unfortunately, I didn't have time to take pictures the way I was so busy with Eric. We danced the whole night. I only came back early hours of this morning. I am still feeling tired."

"Why did you wake up early then? You were supposed to be still in bed," said Joyce with her eyes wide open with surprise.

"Sipho sent me here because he said he can't come he is feeling sick and tired from the night shift. I am here to do a bit of groceries."

"Let me leave you my friend because my boyfriend is waiting for me next to Woolworths. Enjoy your shopping."

"Why don't you wait for me to finish my shopping and give me a lift back home?" asked Linda

"No, we are on our way to Pretoria, and we will be back late this evening," said Joyce as she was leaving her friend.

"What are you guys going to do in Pretoria?" screamed Linda as Joyce was slightly far from her.

"I will tell you later. Bye now," replied Joyce as she was trotting and waving a hand to Linda.

Chapter 24

It was a Sunday morning, Thandi and Freddy were back from the local church. This was the second time that Freddy is seen in public with Thandi. They were the talk of the town. Most young girls of Thandi's age did not know Thandi well, very few knew her. Freddy's colleagues were very envious of him when they looked at Thandi and knowing that Freddy was a book worm at school that he never cared about girls and today he has the most beautiful girls in town.

"Can we go up the Table Mountain today?" asked Freddy.

"Love, you mean climb it?"

"No baby, we will take the cable car."

"That's fine with me and I also told Sarah not to work on Sunday any longer. What time do you want us to go there?" asked Thandi.

"Let's go before lunch so that we can go to the Waterfront for lunch. Are you going anywhere now otherwise I would suggest that we go there now before this weather changes?"

"Nope, but I want to change my clothes into denims and a light sweater."

"You fine as you are my love," emphasized Freddy.

Freddy took out a camera at the back of the car and they went to buy tickets and then stood in a queue to the cable car. This time Freddy was doing most of the talking. He kept Thandi laughing with a joke after a joke. When the cable car was a quarter way up, Freddy with a loud voice said to all who were there "Ladies and gentlemen my name is Freddy, and this is Thandi my girlfriend" to the attention of everybody and Thandi's amazement Freddy took out a purple box from his pocket. He knelt before Thandi with his left leg and opened the box and looked up to Thandi eyes and said "Thandi Khumalo will you marry me?" By this time Thandi was jumping up and down with both hands on her month not sure whether to cry or laugh. One young tourist screamed and said, "Say yes lady."

"Yes, yes, yes I will!!!" Responded Thandi with both arms oscillating, hands intertwined in front of her belly.

Freddy grabbed Thandi's left hand and slipped a 24-carat gold with round shape 0.5 carats, G color with VS2 clarity diamond stone into her finger. Everybody in the cable car clapped their hands when Freddy stood up and gave Thandi a passionate kiss. She wrapped her arms around his neck and said, "Thank you my love."

Two of the girls in the cable car came to Thandi and asked if they could have a look at the stone. Thandi agreed and extended her hand toward them.

"Wow you are so lucky, I won't mind having one like that, that's so cool and it looks very expensive lady," commented one of them. When they got on top of the mountain the whole crew in the cable car allowed Thandi and Freddy to disembark first as they were clapping hands for them. They spent some time walking around hand-in-hand, taking pictures and in most instances, asked people to take pictures of both standing together. Other times Freddy took pictures of Thandi alone.

Thandi's left hand became her mirror. She just couldn't stop looking at her ring with a smile. The words of Freddy's mother reverberated in her mind "I might not live long to see your wedding, but you must know that you have all my blessing to marry my son and be Mrs. Phillips in my place." After sight-seeing and photo shooting on top of the mountain the couple went to Waterfront for their lunch. After lunch they took the boat to Robben Island.

When Thandi arrived home, she picked up her land line and called her mother. "Mummy I am engaged. Freddy and I are getting married. He proposed to me today."

"Wow that's great I am happy for you, my child. I wasn't aware that this affair of yours with Freddy was that serious. Any way you have always spoken very passionately of him and the way you love him. Did you tell your dad?" When is the wedding day?"

"I don't know mom. We haven't discussed that. Where is daddy?"

"He is in the study. Would you like to talk to him?"

"Yes, mom please."

"Hold on. Pass my regards to Freddy. Here is your father. Goodbye now."

"Goodbye mom"

"Hello my baby. How are you?" asked Lesley.

"Hello daddy. I'm fine thanks. Daddy, guess what?"

"What baby?"

"I am engaged. Freddy proposed to me today in a cable car up to the mountain top."

"Wow that's wonderful my child, that is great news. Are you happy?"

"Of course, yes, I am very happy daddy. You know how much I love Freddy; I always tell you how I feel about him. What do you think dad?"

"As long as you are happy my child, so am I. All I want my child is for you to be happy with the choices you have made. You know me by now, I will support you in whatever decision you take as long that makes you happy and it's your own choice. When is that boy going to pay for the lobola?" asked her father jokingly.

"Well daddy that I don't know. That one is between you and his father it doesn't concern me. Do you want me to ask him?"

"No, no, no, you don't have to. I am sure his father will call me after they have talked about it. I am sure he had to proposed to you first and see if you will agree to his proposal before talking about lobola and wedding to his father."

"Oh, is that how it works?"

"Yes, baby. If he talks to his father about lobola and wedding before and then you decline his proposal it will be an embarrassment to him. When is the wedding my child?"

"I don't know dad we haven't talked about that yet. As soon as we finalize the date, I will let you know. Will you help us pay for our wedding dad?" she asked him joking.

"Your father-in-law is a very wealthy man; I am sure he can foot the whole bill."

"You dad from the bride side, with the lobola money you will have to come up with something."

"I am sure your future father-in-law will not like that. Okay my angel we will see then. Goodbye now."

"Goodbye daddy." After dropping the call to her father, she called Sarah. Sarah's phone rang for a while and there was no reply from her side. Thandi dropped the phone and decided that she will not be able to sleep without sharing the news with Sarah. She got into her car and drove to Sarah's place.

Chapter 25

The first Wednesday of every month Sarah knew that the morning session was for her friends. She normally gets a few extra hands to help her in the salon. Since Thandi started operating the salon as the manager, Sarah requested her to take the Wednesday off because of the commotion and the noise that the other girls make in the salon, and the fact that things they talked about sometimes would not be suitable for a young girl like Thandi. This Wednesday was no exception. At 10h00 the salon was full and buzzing. For this day Sarah ordered a lot of coffee for those who were waiting to keep themselves warm with a cup of coffee.

"The madam has ultimately kicked the bucket," said (A) with a smile on her face. "I wonder who is going to replace her," she continued.

"Who told you that Jeffrey wants to take another wife," asked (D) trying to turn around so that she can face the mirror.

"He will have to do that. Who is going to take care of him at his age?" responded (C). "I know the man has uncontrolled diabetes and he is going to die soon. Whoever is going to marry him it would be for his money nothing else because there is nobody there it is just a moving corpse."

"Since the wife died, he is going down very fast. I hardly see him at church nowadays," commented (B).

"That is where he is supposed to be if his health is deteriorating. This is the time that he needs Pastor by his side." (D)

"What is the Pastor going to do to him? Is he going to nurse him? Why doesn't he go to the hospital? Or else there is one Traditional Healer I know I can take care of him." (A)

"You always say stupid things. How does a man of his stature go to Traditional Healers? Don't you know that he goes to church?" asked (B)

"You will be surprised of how many men of his stature and those that go to church attend Traditional Healers." (A)

"Hay'suka wena. There is no such thing," screamed (D)

"Sarah, I saw Freddy together with your boss at the funeral. Is there something between the two of them?" asked (E)

"Thandi is too beautiful for that chubby rich boy. He must just go and get a girl that will suite his weight." (A).

"You're talking nonsense you. Freddy is very handsome and rich man. Why do you think every girl in this town wants him? Why should Thandi then be different from other young girls? If I was young, I would be around him like a fly on a rotten meat." (B)

"I wonder whether with that weight, how is the load in front. He mustn't starve the poor girl." (D)

"Hee! I am just wondering how their honeymoon is going to be like. Freddy has never had a girlfriend before, and I am wondering if he knows how to do it right." (C)

"Thandi is a beautiful girl she must have been around the block for some few times she will coach him how to do it." (B)

"Thandi is a virgin she has never slept with a man before. She had a boyfriend at school, but they have never slept. She got principles that govern her life and one of them is no sex before marriage," interjected Sarah.

"Wow!! That honeymoon is going to be a disaster. Both had never had sex before. Somebody has to show the boy how to do it." (A)

"Why the boy? Can't we then show Thandi how it is done?" (B)

"No, we cannot. Men are supposed to take a leading role when it comes to sex, otherwise if it is a woman, they perceive her to be a prostitute and a person who has been around the block several times. Men don't want to be taught by the woman when it comes to sexual issues, they interpret that in other way." (D)

"The problem is, this one doesn't know a thing. The poor kid will not enjoy her honeymoon and yet this is where the woman must taste the enjoyment of sex because this sets the bar for the beginning of your married life." (C)

"That's not a big deal. She will catch along the way." (A)

"You don't understand, if you start your sexual married life on a wrong foot, you better stay like that for the rest of your life not knowing any better. If down the line you can find out that there is another side of sexual life, it's going to be a disaster. That marriage will be heading for a divorce unless you have an open-minded partner, who is willing to talk about it and change. It must be right from the word go." (C)

"Hey these are newlyweds, what does sex means to them?" (A)

"Sex is an important aspect of the newlywed's life. That is why it must be on the correct footing from the word go. Otherwise, it will spell a disaster. I guess that is why God's honeymoon is a year and its specific to a man what to do. He must bring happiness to the bride. God knows that it is love making that will bring happiness to a woman. Women enjoy love making more than men." (C)

"Where is that in the bible? Don't come and talk nonsense here. Honeymoon comes from man" (A)

"You must go and borrow a bible from somebody because I know you don't have one at home and read from the book of Deuteronomy 24 verse 5." (C)

"How come you know the bible so much? I hope you are telling me the truth you not trying to impress the others here" (A)

"Don't elderly men talk to young unmarried guys about the dos and don'ts of the honeymoon. God orders a man to keep his wife happy during honeymoon." (C)

"You talk as if we do talk to young girls about these things. Our experiences as far as the honeymoon is concerned, remains a secret to most of us. No woman wants or would like to talk about her honeymoon experience." (B)

"Some women who kept themselves for that day don't want to talk about it at all." (D)

"How I wish that young men could know when you have kept yourself as a virgin for that day, that they be gentle, steady, caring, loving and prepare you properly before any act. When it's your first time as a woman, you don't know what to expect." (E)

"How are they going to know that?" (A)

"I wish you could listen to me before you start with your stupid questions." (E)

"Okay talk we are listening." (A)

"How I wish they could know that they are dealing with somebody who has never gone through this in her life. How I wish they could know that you are doing this for the very first time in your life and your expectations are high." (E)

"E is very right. You kept yourself for him." (B)

"As a woman you have no clue of what is going to happen. They should know that your future interest in sex depends on how and what you will be experiencing on the honeymoon day, especially if it's the very first time." (D)

"As a virgin you sometimes listen to girls who have been around talking about the different experiences with different guys. You sit there asking yourself about how yours will be." (C)

"Guys what I am going to tell you about might sound as a joke, but it is my personal experience." (D)

"What's that?" asked (A)

"Do you guys promise that you will not laugh at me." (D)

"Let us promise guys." (A)

"When I got married, I was a virgin. My boyfriend and I never had a passionate kiss. We had never been intimate before. We both agreed to spare ourselves for our honeymoon." (D)

"Do you want to tell me you went into marriage with your boyfriend without having kissed each other?" (A)

"Yes A. Can I continue?" (D)

"Continue" said (E).

By this time everybody had stopped doing what they were supposed to be doing and all concentrating on D.

"We had both agreed that on our first night we will be naked in font of each other before we engage into the act." (D)

"Did you strip in front of each other for the first time?" (A)

"Could you please stop asking stupid question A and allow her to continue," said Sarah

"On the first day of our honeymoon we got to this lodge. I told him that I should be the first one to take a bath. After taking a bath put on some body lotion and I wrapped myself with a towel and came to the bedroom. He went to take a shower. He came back with a towel around his waist. I was lying on top of the bed naked waiting for him. I should think by the time he finished washing he was already on. He stood by the side of the bed in front of me and removed his towel." (D)

"And then?" (A)

"Wow when I saw that thing, I was scared to death. I stood up and climbed on top of the dressing table screaming." (D)

The all laughed. "And then what happed?" asked (C).

"I will not go further than that. I just wanted to tell you that honeymoon sometimes is not always that rosy if you have no clue of what sex is all about specially if you have never seen your partner naked before" (D)

"Did you ultimately make love that night?" (A)

"I told you that I will not go further. Are you deaf?" (D)

"What I heard was that a couple went to a honeymoon and three months down the line the woman was still a virgin despite the fact that they claim to have engage in sex several times during and after the honeymoon." (B)

"You are lying B. Where have you heard that, that can't be true." (C)

"So, it means that the man never got to it," said (D) with a loud laughter and they all joined in.

"And then what happed to them?" (C)

"They went to the doctor to find out why she was not falling pregnant, after the doctor determined that she was a virgin he sent them back to the Pastor and told the Pastor to do a proper counselling. The Pastor had to demonstrate to the man how it is done by showing them a video." (B)

"Oh! Poor Pastor." (A)

"So, it means this thing is a problem on both sides. How can it be overcome?" asked Sarah with a concern. Her main concern was about Thandi and Freddy.

The time was almost 13h00 and it was time for lunch. Sarah emptied the salon and closed the doors for lunch. She went to a restaurant nearby. Took out her cell phone and called Thandi. "Hi Thandi. Where are you now?"

"I am in town, is there anything wrong? Are you ok Sarah?"

"Yes I am. Are you alone where you are?"

"Yes. Why are you asking?"

"I would like to talk to you."

"Fine Sarah, I am alone we can talk."

"No Thandi it is very important I would like to talk to you in person not over the phone. If it is possible today, please."

"Ok, I am done with what I was doing where can I find you now?" Thandi sensed uneasiness from Sarah's voice and then she felt that she had to see Sarah then.

"I am at the restaurant opposite the salon. You will find me there."

Thandi was there in no time. She parked her car next to the salon and walked over to the restaurant.

"Hi, how are you?" she asked Sarah.

"I'm good and you?"

"Fine thanks. What's up? You sounded very serious over the phone. Is there something wrong?"

"No, there is nothing wrong I just want to have an open chat with you."

"About what Sarah?"

"You remember that you came to me to tell me about your engagement to Freddy."

"Yes."

"Thandi you must know whatever I am going to talk to you about now, I am doing as a mother to her daughter. If your mom was still alive this conversation would have been done by her." Sarah started the conversation from what came out of salon from the girls.

Thandi was sitting there listening attentively. Her eyes were fixed straight to Sarah's eyes as if she didn't want to miss not an inch of it.

Chapter 26

It was almost a month since Eric had spoken to Linda. Linda was preparing herself for the morning lecture and Sipho was not back from work yet. After dressing up in a red dress that was sleeveless and a shallow cleavage, she called Joyce to check if she was done dressing. Joyce phone was ringing with no answer. She dropped the call and proceeded to the door; she went down the stairs to wait for the bus to the University. As she opened the main front door that led to the bus stop, there was Eric with a cigar in his mouth standing outside his car with the roof top of the car wide open and playing music very soft. Eric was obedient to the weather because he was dressed up in all white and the morning temperature was on the high side. When Linda saw this, her lips cracked wide pushing her soft cheeks to both side of her mouth without exposing her teeth. She stood at the door for a while with that smile looking at Eric. There is no doubt that Linda was highly impressed with what she was looking at. The anger that she had toward Eric, vanished instantaneously.

As Linda was approaching the car, Eric quickly killed the cigar, took off his hat and went to meet Linda halfway. He offered to help Linda with her school bag and then rushed back to the car before Linda got there. He opened the door for the lady and ushered her in with a slight bow and the hat at his chest.

"Good morning, Miss Sibeko," greeted Eric with a smile.

Linda slightly bowed her head back and greeted Eric "Good morning, sir," wearing a beautiful smile. She got into the car like a real lady. She sat on the seat first then swung both her legs into the car without having them part at all.

Linda was ecstatic with Eric's civility. To her Eric was demonstrating his apology for his absence. This lifted Linda's spirit and filled her heart with instant forgiveness even before Eric could ask for one.

"How are you this morning Miss Sibeko?" asked Eric as he turned the car's engine.

"Can you stop addressing me formally and call me by my name. I am fine thanks and how are you this morning Eric?"

"Thank you for asking I am fine too. Linda firstly I would like to apologize for my absence and for letting you down on our appointment for that night. I had an emergency I had to attend in Durban on that whole week. I could not call and let you know before time. When I came back, I got busy with a lot of things that took my mind from anything else than business. I am very sorry. I promise I will make it up to you. Are you in a hurry for your lecture?"

Linda turned around with a smile and looked at Eric. "You are forgiven. Can you do me a favor now? In future just drop me a message and I will be fine. I know you are a businessman, and you are very busy. I am not expecting you to be calling me at all times." She bent forward and gave Eric a kiss on his cheek. "I am going to a lecture, and I can't miss it. My last lecture for today is at 11h30. Can you pick me up at 12h30 next to the library? I will be waiting for you there."

"Can we make it at 13h30 because from 11h30 to 13h00 I will be having a business meeting with my partners? Please do not eat I will take you out for lunch at Mike's Kitchen." Eric dropped Linda at the main entrance of the campus and gave her a kiss.

She was on cloud nine when she got out of the car, feeling that her love with Eric was back on track. One of the things that were exciting her is that she's got news for Joyce about her relationship with Eric. When she got into the lecture hall Joyce was already sitting next to two colleagues and there was no space available in that row. She had to take a seat behind Joyce. After the first lecture there is ten minutes gap before the second lecture. Within that ten minutes Joyce heard all what took place in the morning between Eric and Linda something that she was trying to avoid, that is why she didn't pick up the phone when Linda called in the morning. "Are you going to join us? Eric and I are going for the lunch today?"

"No, I won't be joining you guys. My boyfriend is picking me up and we are going to magistrate court. Does Sipho know about your relationship with Eric?"

"My relationship with Eric has nothing to do with Sipho. He must take care of his own business."

"Well said young lady. Linda do you really know who Eric is and what kind of business is he into? Have you met his friends outside the club environment to know who they are in the society?"

"Why do I smell an element of jealousy here? Why are you asking all these questions? Are you doubting Eric? Does he look like a crook to you? Or is there something you know that I don't know of? You must tell me girl. We are friends you don't have to hide things from me."

"No, there is nothing. It's just that there is something I don't like about him I cannot put my finger on it."

"Oh. Is that why you are avoiding me of late and you don't want to be in his presence. Are you sure you don't fancy him? Eric is handsome and charming I won't be surprised if you do." responded Linda with a smile.

"The lecture is about to start, let's go inside the lecture hall," said Joyce with exasperation.

After the lecture Linda went to the cafeteria to wait for Eric. Eric arrived just some few minutes earlier than expected. Linda got into the car, and they drove off to the restaurant.

Chapter 27

By now Sipho was feeling his obsession toward Linda growing. He felt that he should express his feeling for her. He was battling in his head how he was going to approach the topic. He knew that the issue of leaving her a note is not going to work. She might just pretend as if she never saw or read it and throw it away without any response.

After dishing for himself he sat down to enjoy his meal. He temporarily closed his eyes and saw himself and Linda walking in a park hand-in-hand. This brought a smile on him. After finishing his food, he took a quick shower and went to bed. He did not take long to fall into deep sleep, and he had a dream. He dreamed as if he was living in this big house with his family of twins and his wife. He was so happily married. He saw himself as a manager in a big company. He could hear his twin boys calling him daddy and playing with them. He saw himself and the woman in the park with the boys playing and him chasing the woman in between the park trees. They were in a very happy mood. Laughing and rolling on the grass with each other hold close body to body. He woke up from the dream and he was sweating.

"Where was I?" he said to himself. He woke up and sat up straight on the bed. "This is a very strange dream. What is strange is the fact that the woman in my dream was not Linda. Who the hell was she? I am going to spend my life with Linda not with some woman I don't know of. Does this mean that Linda is going to mother me twins? Oh, my married life with Linda is going to be a wonderful life. I just can't wait for it." This brought a smile on his face. He put his head back on the pillow and he was gone again.

He was woken up by his alarm clock in the afternoon. He woke up and washed himself and prepared for work. To his surprise Linda was not back yet. This time he was not bothered as the dream was still fresh in his mind. Sipho was convinced that the woman in his dream was Linda and that both will have a wonderful married life. He felt that he is not going to rush her into marriage as he was sure now that the dream was showing him his future with Linda. He felt very happy, and he was in a very jovial mood and ready for work.

On his way to work he had his headset on and playing music louder than normal. As he was walking to work, he would now and then stop and dance to the music.

"Why are you in such a joyful mood today, Dude?" asked Thabo.

Sipho's mood was brought down by Thabo's question who was with Seth. He took off his headset and switched his music off. "Wow how are you guys?" asked Sipho. "Feeling like I am on cloud nine."

"I saw you dance alone and moving your body. What has happened? Did you ultimately propose to her?" asked Seth

"Where are the other guys?" asked Sipho.

"I am sure they are on the way coming. I should think the three of us are early today. Tell me dude why are you in such a jolly mood today?" ask Thabo

"Dude I had a wonderful dream. I dreamed that Linda and I had a family, and I was managing a very big company and it was ours."

"You did what? You dreamed about Linda and you being a family? Is that why you are in such a jovial mood?" Seth asked with his eyes wide open and looking at Sipho with surprise.

"Yes, don't you think that's wonderful?" asked Sipho

"Are you crazy dude? You are happy because of a stupid dream!" followed Thabo with the question.

"Is there anything wrong in there?" asked Sipho

"Dude I give up on you. You will never have a woman in your life as long as you still entertain dreams," said Seth.

"Forget about Linda in your life and I didn't think you will ever get married. You so petrified of women. I don't know how you think you will ever get married" added Thabo.

"Will see you guys' tomorrow, enjoy your shift," said Seth as he was leaving the two still talking.

Chapter 28

It was a lovely Spring Saturday morning. The whole town was alive, and people were talking about the wedding of the year. Sarah opened the salon at 05h00 and it has been busy since yesterday and even that morning the salon was filled up to the brim with people waiting for their hair to be done.

A kilometer away from Spier where the wedding was going to take place, the roadway was fully decorated up to the venue. The walkway which was about 50 meters to the altar was carpeted in red.

There were ten horse carts for the bride and her bridesmaid fully decorated. In front of the carts were drum majorettes with colorful attire waiting for the bride. All the marshals were dressed up in the same attire and the same colors. Waiters were also dress in the same colors.

The wedding started at 09h45 exactly with the arrival of the bridegroom and his groomsman in a convoy of ten different types of exotic vintage hired cars. The drivers of the cars were dressed in white, in each car including the first car where the groom was, were groomsmen, they were sitting at the back seat wearing black suit, white shirt and red bowtie. The cars were all convertibles. They all got off and stood on one side of the altar on the red carpet next to Freddy's dad.

At 10h30 the bride with her entourage of bridesmaids and two flower girls arrived in all white Mercedes Benz up to the carts. They got off from the cars and rode on horse carts lead by the majorettes to the entrance of the wedding venue. The bride and the flower girls were on the last cart. When the bridesmaids arrived at the venue, they all proceeded to the altar and stood opposite facing groomsmen.

The bride was brought to the altar by her father who was wearing a white suit, a red shirt and white bowtie. Thandi's face was covered with a veil that completely concealed her face. As they were moving to the altar the bridal choir was singing a song that says "Uzumphathe kakuhle mfowethu umakoti wethu." meaning "You must treat the bride well brother."

The celebrant for the ceremony was the Methodist priest where Freddy and Thandi attended church.

Mr. Khumalo handed his daughter to Freddy Phillips, he then proceeded to sit next to his wife. When the priest asked Freddy to remove the veil, he was amazed how beautiful Thandi was.

On the other side of the carpet was Freddy's father sitting in a wheelchair and next to him was Daniel who was assisting him with everything he required.

After the wedding proceeding and Freddy kissing the bride, the couple turned around and faced the people. Thandi looked at her father-in-law and smiled. Jeffrey smiled back and saw how happy Thandi was; tears started streaming down his cheeks. Thandi left Freddy and went to her father-in-law and gave him a kiss on his cheek and wipe the tears from his eyes with her white gloves. She whispered in his ear and said, "It is going to be alright daddy it is going to be alright."

The wedding proceedings took almost 45 minutes. The bride and the groom led the pack with the dance and followed by bridesmaids with groomsmen out of the church for the photo shoot session.

Sarah stood up from her front seat and went to the back in one of the corners. She started crying silently with her face covered with a handkerchief.

Martha was sitting not far from Sarah. She saw her standing up and she followed her. She realized that there was something wrong with her friend. They have known each other through the friendship of Mrs. Mabandla and Freddy's mom. She put her left hand on Sarah shoulder and comfort her.

"Let's go outside. There are too many people inside to talk," said Martha.

"It's painful Martha, it is very painful. How I wish at least Thandi's grandmother was here."

"I know, I know Sarah. I am also hurt that this boy's mother is not here to witness her son getting married to such a beautiful young lady.

At least she was going to have a daughter in-law that was going to nurse her better and with love that she deserved."

Daniel was sitting next to his boss holding his boss walking stick. He saw Martha following Sarah. He turned and looked at his boss to check if he saw Martha following Sarah.

Daniel notice that his boss was holding back tears with his eyelids.

"Sir is there something wrong? Are you feeling any pains?" asked Daniel to his boss.

"No, there is nothing wrong Daniel. I am looking at how beautiful Thandi is, she reminded me of Freddy's mom when we got married."

"Yes, sir she looks very beautiful," responded Daniel

"I am worried about the fact that I never spent time with my son to teach him how to love and treat a woman. He has only seen the negative side of me".

"What do you mean sir?" asked Daniel though he knew exactly what he meant because he had witnessed Mr. Phillips abuse to his wife.

"My fear Daniel is that my son is going to treat this beautiful little girl like an object, just like I treated his mom. I have taught him the importance of business not that of love and relationships."

"But he will be fine sir."

"No Daniel, he won't be fine. I see more of myself in him, the lack of compassion, no sense of relationship, the pride, lack of respect for his mate and love of business. This is what my son is. This is what I taught him."

"Thandi might change him sir. She has a very strong character," added Daniel

"Freddy's mom was just like Thandi. She was a woman with a very strong character, endurance, patience, respectful, obedient and full of love. Did that change me? Not at all. I never returned her with any one of those instead I gave her hell. I was married to my business more than her. I loved the business more than her. I gave my clients and customers more respect than my own wife."

"At least sir you were building a future for your family," responded Daniel sarcastically.

"Where is that family now Daniel? That business has destroyed the humanity in me. My wife died when I was busy with this company.

(Tears started to drip from his eyes) I never had a chance to close her eyes when she died. What kind of husband am I to my family? I am now dying without my wife next to me. You and I know that my business kept me busy, and I never had time for my family. My son doesn't have time for me. That boy Daniel has never visited me when I was hospitalized not even a single day, because he is busy with the very same things that kept me busy when I was young. Freddy doesn't care about me; he cares about the business. There is just no relationship between the two of us. Do I blame him. No! I planted that seed in him. Now I am reaping the fruits of my own plant."

"He is running the company that you have taken time to build very well. This is what you have been emphasized to him from childhood. Is that bad?" asked Daniel

"That boy Daniel has never showed any love for me, do you know why? It is because as the father I have never planted a seed of love in him. What is the use of all the money I have accumulated now to me? You see, I am sitting in a wheelchair dying with all that money in the bank. It is now not the money that I need the most but it's for that boy to show me some love. I am not going to live long Daniel. My son and I we hardly talk to each other."

"What do you mean by that sir? You have built a very successful business for him," said Daniel

"Yes, I have but I have failed to teach him basic things in life that a father is supposed to impart to his son, and that is love for the family. The father's inner fulfillment is supposed to be loving his wife, family and being loved by his family. Is that not what God is to us and is that not what He requires from us? Why should then us human beings be different from Him? The millions that I have in my bank account cannot bring my wife back nor can they take me out of this wheelchair. They can't give me any inner fulfillment. I am dying empty in me. It is true that as a man you reap what you sow in your family."

"Is Freddy not trying to maintain or better the standard of the company you have left with him? If he hangs around you, who is going to manage the business?" asked Daniel

"That is exact where the problem is Daniel. When I was young, I kept myself busy building up my company and had no relationship with my family. I taught my son the same sickness, now I am old, and I need him, he is too busy for my attention."

"Your son is doing a very good job in building what you gave him sir," responded Daniel.

"There are times I would like to talk to him as father and son, but he just doesn't have time for me. Do you know that Thandi spent more time talking and caring for me than my own flesh and blood? It is that girl who paid me a visit every day when I was hospitalized. That daughter-in-law of mine brings joy to me more than anything I have in this life. I guess this is what my wife was trying to do for the past 40 years of our marriage, and I failed to grasp it. Wheel me to the dining hall please, I would like to talk to Thandi before I leave for home."

There was food galore. Everybody was catered for. There were different types of dishes on the menu. Everything was well marked so that people would know what to find and where to find it. There was a section for vegetarian, halal, white and red meat, a section for fruits, salads and variety of desserts.

When the newlyweds and their entourage came back from the photo shoot session, there were some words to the couple by a few people and the food was served. During mealtime as the bride and the groom were intermingling with the guests, Daniel went to Thandi and told her that Freddy's father is in the car, and he would like to talk to her.

Thandi quickly followed Daniel to the car. Jeffery was sitting at the back and Thandi got in and sat next to him. "Hi daddy, why are you sitting here alone? Why are you not inside? Are you not feeling well?"

"No, there is nothing wrong my child. I am feeling fine. I just want to talk to you before I leave for home."

"Why do you want to leave now? Are you not going to join us for a meal? Is there something serious? Shouldn't I call Freddy so that you can talk to the two of us?"

"No, my child, you are the one I want to talk too."

"Ok, I am listening, daddy," responded Thandi with concern.

"The few times I have spent with you, and every time you visited me at the hospital, I have appreciated it a lot. Thandi my child I can see how much you love my son. Please Thandi, no matter what happens between you and Freddy never leave him. My child, I have no doubt in my mind that he will not be able to give you what you have for him. Do not allow him to do what I have done to him, not give his children love if you guys will have any. At the same time allow him to be who he wants to be as a man, husband and the father."

"I promise daddy that I will stay with him through thick and thin. About our kids I also promise that I will see to it that he does show them love."

"There are things that I have done to his mother in front of him. I pray that he will never do those things to you, my child."

"Freddy will be fine daddy. He is a grown-up man and I have no doubt that he will be able to take care of me. Don't worry yourself."

"Thank you for taking care of me and for all the visits when I was hospitalized. You are now the only Mrs. Phillips alive. You are a member of the Phillips family. Community Steel is part of this family. I have worked hard to build that company Thandi. It has cost me my family time. Please whatever happens, do not allow your husband to sell it to anybody. It must remain within the family for the years to come. Let my grandchildren be part of what I have built for them."

Thandi looked at her father-in-law and she felt tears coming but held them back. She bent forward and gave her father-in-law a kiss on his cheek and said "Thank you daddy and I love you. I must go now. I will see you later just before we leave for our honeymoon."

Jeffery wanted to respond and say, "I love you too Thandi" but the words stuck onto his throat and could not come out. She opened the door and got out. When she was about to close it behind her, she heard Jeffrey say, "I love you too Thandi and May God bless you, my child."

It was the first time Jeffrey used these words to a person in his life. Not to his wife or his son. He had never shown any emotions to his family at all except displaying his anger for small mishaps that his wife or his son had done.

After saying this he felt like a very heavy load had been removed from his shoulder. He started hyper ventilating and he called Daniel who was standing just outside the car when he was talking to Thandi. When Daniel opened the rear door, he realized that there was a problem with the old man. "Should I call Thandi back?" he asked.

"No, this is her special day. Drive me to the hospital. I will try and get my doctor ready for the time being. After the call I would like to sleep while you are driving." Jeffrey pretended as if he was calling his doctor and took off the safety belt and put his head down and he was gone. Daniel drove fast to the hospital without knowing that he was already driving a corpse. When he arrived at the hospital Jeffrey was certified dead.

Chapter 29

Linda and Eric had their lunch at Mike's Kitchen in Parktown. Linda was not in a mood of taking any alcohol, but Eric persuaded her to take some red wine. He told her that red wine was good for cholesterol. She started with a sip and then took a full mouth and then went on finishing her glass. As they were talking and laughing Eric filled her glass again. She gulped more glasses of wine during her meal. By the time they had to go her knees were wobbling already. Eric helped her to the car, drove her to his house and took her straight to his bed.

By the time Linda woke up she was at her flat next to the stairs and the time was 03h20 in the morning. She looked around to check where she was. After realizing that she was at familiar environment she stood up, "How the hell did I get here? And where is Eric?" She asked herself. As she was trying to move around, she kicked her school bag. Picked it up and headed for the stairs to her room. She reached out for the key and opened the door. All this time she had not fully recovered and did not know what had happened to her. She slept on top of the bed without taking her clothes off.

When she woke up in the morning fully recovered, she was surprised that she was at her room. "How did I get here? I wonder what happened to Eric." When she tried to pick up her head from the pillow, she could feel the heaviness. She ultimately turned around and tried to stand. When she moved her legs, she realized that her inner thighs had a slight pain, and that little Linda was feeling uncomfortable and a slight pain. Walking was not easy. She shuffled to the bathroom. The urine was burning little Linda. She realized then something had happened. She took her small mirror to examine little Linda and she realized that she had some small bruises and there were some small blood stains on her inner thighs next to little Linda.

She went for her cell phone and tried to call Eric. Eric's cell phone rang unanswered. She started panicking. "Is it possible that Eric raped me? If it is so why dump me here unceremoniously?" These were the questions that came out of her month. She decided that she was going to wash and consult the doctor.

The doctor confirmed that there was forced entry that broke her virginity and some bruising at the entrance of little Linda. Linda was completely devastated and worried about pregnancy. The doctor suggested a morning after pill and Linda was bit doubtful to take it, thinking that Eric might want the kid and if they get married late, they will have one child already.

Her only concern was why did Eric force himself on her instead of asking her nicely for sex and why did he dumped her at her flat instead of keeping her at his house. She took out her cell phone and call Eric again. There was no response from him again. On her way back home, she was thinking about what had happened. All she could remember was Mike's Kitchen restaurant and her drinking red wine. What happened after that she couldn't recall.

Linda tried to avoid Joyce for that entire week. She told Sipho that she was not feeling well, and she would not want to be disturbed. She kept on trying Eric's cell- phone number but it was constantly unavailable. This compounded her misery and left her in the middle of the road. She was not sure whether Eric was deserting her for what he had done, or he did not want her any longer. "Did I behave improper during our diner time?" she asked herself.

It was Friday morning and Linda was preparing to attend morning lectures. Her phone rang and she picked it up. It was Eric. "Hi!" answered Linda with a low depressed voice.

"Good morning, Linda! How are you doing?" asked Eric with a lively excited voice.

Linda was fully aware that Eric sounded excited, and she did not know how to respond to his excitement. She wanted to play it as cool as possible though inside she was happy to hear his voice again. "I am fine thanks. How are you?" responded Linda with little enthusiasm.

"I am very well thanks for asking. Are you not attending lectures today?"

"I am. I am just about to leave my room now. Why are you asking?"

"Well, if that is the case I am at your service. I am waiting for you outside."

She quickly jumped with excitement grabbed her schoolbag and dashed for the door. She locked the door behind her and rushed down the stairs. As she was approaching the main door, she slowed down so that she doesn't show him that she was excited to see him. When she opened the door there was Eric standing next to a red X6 BMW. He was dressed in all white except for the shoes, belt and the hat that were black. This melted Linda's heart, and she was forced to smile as Eric was opening the passenger door for her. He grabbed the school bag from Linda and allowed her to get into the car. He closed the door and put the bag at the back seat. "It's good to see you again Ms. Sibeko how was your week after the dinner?"

This question infuriated Linda. She did not expect him to start their conversation like that. She expected an apology for what he had done to her. All the smile and the excitement that she had quickly vanished, and she put on an angry face, turned around, looked at Eric with eyes that were slightly closed, and the nose slightly raised with nostrils wide opened like a horse after the race. "How do you think it was after you raped me and dumped me at my flat unceremoniously? After that you disappeared for a week without a word of apology or explanation. Then the next thing you rock-up at my place with a new fancy car and think that I will be impressed."

There is one thing that Linda did not know about Eric. Eric is the mastermind of lies, conniving and manipulative. He always turns every nasty situation to suit him. He never loses his cool in a violent situation. He has been in this game of playing around with girls for too long to be cornered by Linda for what he has done. He jumped from his seat and threw his hands in the air. "Hold on ma'am, what are you talking about? Me. Raping you? What a hell are you talking about Linda. Are you accusing me of rape heh? Linda, do I look like a rapist to you? What are taking for girl? After our diner you were so drunk that you could hardly stand. As I was taking you to the car you insisted to go to your flat. I told you that you were not in the right frame of mind why not to my place and then I take you home the following day? You said to me you want to go home. So, I took you home. At you flat you didn't want me to accompany you inside, you said you will manage. So, then I allowed you to be alone and I drove off."

"What do you mean when you said I did not want you to take me inside, you have just said I could hardly walk? So, you left without checking if I was safe?" asked Linda

"No, I waited for you to open the main door and walked in, then I drove off because I realized that you were safe. What happened after that, I have no idea. I will never rape you I am not that cheap. Hold on. What do you mean by rape? When did that happened? How do you know that you were raped? I dropped you at the door and I waited for you to get in the building, and you did. If you were raped, then it must have happened inside the building."

"I woke up early hours of the morning next to the stairs with my school bag next to me. I did not realize by then that there was something wrong. I went to my flat and slept again. It is only when I recovered that I realized that there was a discomfort in my walk, I checked and I saw some blood and bruises underneath," said Linda.

"What did you do? Did you report that to the police?" asked Eric with concern.

"No, I went to see a doctor and he confirmed that there was a forced entry, I am bruised and there was also some semen still coming out."

"And what did the doctor said?" he asked with his eyes wide opened.

"He wanted to give me a morning after pill and suggested that I should open up a rape case, but I refused."

"What is a morning after pill?"

"It's a pill that you take after having unprotected sex and you don't want to fall pregnant."

"May I ask why you didn't take it?"

"I thought it was you and I didn't want to kill the pregnancy if it is there. I love you Eric I won't mind having your baby."

Eric's eyes were now wide open, and he pulled the car aside and looked Linda straight in her eyes and said, "Woman I would never do such a thing to you. I would strongly suggest that you terminate that pregnancy. I don't know who has done that to you. I am sure you don't want to keep a pregnancy of somebody you don't know. I love and respect you a lot Linda to do such a stupid thing to you." Eric was now scared that if Linda carries the child and the child comes out and look like him Linda would know that he was lying. His intention was to use Linda in the future for her profession in his business.

Eric's response quickly dampened her anger and she looked apologetic. She was convinced that it really could not be him. "Eric is too much of the gentleman to do such things" she whispered. Her concern now was who could have done this in their building and that person will never reveal himself. Linda was a very principled person. The fact that she kept her virginity for that long, she will have to make a major decision about the pregnancy if she was at all pregnant.

Eric decided that he would not go a long way with her. His mission of getting her to understand that he was not the one who had rape her that night had been accomplished. He dropped her at the University and promised to see her later during the week.

Linda gave Eric a kiss and got off to the lecture rooms. For the first time after some few days of avoiding Joyce she felt that she would like to talk to her. She would like to tell her about the different feelings that she had for Eric and Sipho. She was not attracted to Sipho but does sympathize with him and yet she loves Eric. Sipho does not have the status that Eric is carrying. Sipho does not appeal to her, but Eric is a different person. Eric has a persona that Sipho does not have. Eric dresses in style while Sipho is a very simple guy.

Chapter 30

"Wow what a wedding. What a gown. It must have cost fortune. She was the most beautiful bride I have ever seen in my life. She reminded me of Esther when she was prepared for King Xerxes. Needless to say, the groom was far from being a King," said (A).

"Wow, listen who is quoting from the bible here. When did you start reading the Bible wena? Nevertheless, whatever you are saying it's absolutely right. Whoever designed that gown is the master designer. It was a beautiful mermaid/trumpet wedding dress with a very long cape. The glittering beads that surround the cape crowned it all. The girl looked stunning. She was out of this world. None of the girls in this town would match that. That was beauty at its best. I don't care who says what, the girl is beautiful, jealous down. Everything with that girl on Saturday was like it was made for her from heaven," commented (C).

"Sarah, who did that girl's hair? Was it you? Though I doubt it could be you," asked (B).

"No, it was not me. I sent her to Jon in town to do her," replied Sarah

"Can you see what money can do? It can bring heaven down to earth. Those horse wagons and the horses, the flowers on the roadside and the walkway to the altar were all out of this world," continued (A).

"It's like I was somewhere where I don't even know myself. I swear I was like in a dreamland," interjected (E).

"Sarah! Who was the wedding planner? I am sure you should know about that. Did your boss tell you where she was from?" asked (B).

"She came from Johannesburg. She was organized by Freddy," replied Sarah

"All of those bridesmaids are not local. Who were they Sarah? Where are they coming from?" asked (E)

"They were from East London they were all her school mates from high school to University," responded Sarah.

"Yah! You could see the way they walk in those stilettos that they are educated ladies," responded (B)

"What are stilettos? Don't come and use words that we don't here," commented (A)

The rest of them laughed at A.

"Stilettos are high heels my friend. Ignore these ones who are laughing at you," (C)

"Their entrance dance was something else. You could see that they took time to practice for it," said (B)

"My son is so crazy about the one who was slightly bulky and beautiful. Apparently, they spoke. Yesterday he was telling me that he wants to visit the lady in Graham's Town." (C)

"Does he know what the girl is doing? Doesn't she have a boyfriend where she is coming from?" asked (A)

"I don't know but it is the agreement between the two of them and the girl is a junior lecturer at Rhodes University." (C)

"Well in that case it means she doesn't have one. Is your son aware that the girl is of high status? He has only gone up to grade 12 and working for Freddy as machine operator with mine. How is he going to cope with a lecturer?" (A)

"Ai, a man's capability in a relationship is not determined by his level of education. His love toward a woman that is all that the bible requires from man. A man that loves his woman unconditionally is far better than the one who will shower her with precious gifts without love. What is important is the fact that he loves the woman, and he can also provide for the basic households needs," commented (C)

"That's nonsense. To me a man must show his love by spoiling me with gifts, before he gives me that nonsense called love which I don't understand. I am not going to eat, wear love." (A)

"That is why you are still single even today. I am worried that you will die a spinster with that attitude," interjected (C)

"Humm!! Thandi's father is a hunk, did you guys see him? I can see now where her looks are coming from," commented (D)

"Yes, you are right. Her stepmom is also a very beautiful woman, but they said her biological mother was a fine morning star. Sarah can tell you." (B)

"Wow, that woman is gifted in speech. What she said to her stepdaughter on Saturday very few mothers can say wonderful words like those to their daughters, let alone a stepdaughter." (D)

"What did she say because I was outside when she spoke?" (C)

"She said a lot of constructive things but what touched me the most was when she told her daughter that the power of a woman lies in her influence over her husband. She said this was set from the Garden of Eden. She said when man is inflexible only his wife can make him pliable. She told her stepdaughter that her influence in the marriage must be to build and support her husband in a positive manner." (D)

"I liked her when she said to her daughter 'You are the wife to your husband only and your husband is your husband to you only. Do not expect any other man to treat you as his wife and do not expect any other woman to treat your husband as her husband. Your husband must take priority in your life. He must be number one in your life nobody else. Protect what is yours. You are the only Mrs. Phillips that is alive now.'" (B)

"No, no, no B you have skipped something which I think was powerful. Before she talked about protect what is yours, she said to her 'Do you see that man sitting there and she was pointing to her husband. He comes first to me not to you. He is your daddy but my husband. Freddy is your husband from today onwards and your number one. You must learn to protect and defend him all the time," said (C) with excitement.

"She continued and said to her stepdaughter. 'You must always look at your husband's faults and failures with your third eyes. That eye that sees dim. That eye that will never say I told you when he fails, or he stumbles on something you talked about. Always encourages him not to give up," continued (D)

"She was good," commented (C)

"Guys it's getting late I have to go to town now, but before I go, I would like to take this opportunity and extended my deepest gratitude to Sarah for inviting us all to that spectacular wedding. I am sure most of us if she didn't invite us, we would go six feet under without having witness such a wedding. Thank you, Sarah," said (A)

They all turned around and thanked Sarah.

"You guys must thank Thandi. She is the one who said I must invite you guys. I am not the one who was making the invites, she was," said Sarah.

They all looked surprised.

"What is your boss going to do with this salon? She has bigger things to do than running such a small business," asked (C)

"Most probably she will sell it. She can't be looking after such things when she has a mansion to manage." (B)

"I guess Sarah will be doing her hair from home now, no longer at this salon." (C)

"Why so?" (D)

"She is now the most famous Mrs. Phillips. She will be driven around by that handsome old man called Daniel who was Mr. Phillips chauffeur." (A).

"That girl has a very good heart, and she does not appear to be a greedy person." (C)

"What are you trying to say?" asked Sarah

"Let's wait and see," said (C) as she stood up and headed for the door and the others following her.

"Goodbye Sarah." they said as they were now all leaving.

Chapter 31

Linda came from the doctor and the doctor had confirmed that she was four weeks pregnant. She was pacing up and down the University grounds not knowing what to do. What was bothering her was, whose baby was it that she was carrying? If Eric did not sleep or rape her, then who did? She was not prepared to abort the baby because that was against her principles. She is going to be a doctor and her duty is to save lives not to take them. That is why she became a doctor and that is why she was not going to terminate the pregnancy no matter what the cost. "I've got to make a plan. I cannot be a single mother. I don't' even think that Eric is prepared to marry me with this baby. The way he talked shows that he doesn't like children," she whispered to herself. "How am I going to bring up a child alone without a father? What do I tell Joyce, that I was raped by somebody I don't know? When she asks me how did it happen, what am I going to say? She will never believe me if I tell her that I was drunk. She knows that I don't drink. Nobody will believe my story. Who is this cruel person who goes around raping innocent women?" As she was pacing the strides became slower and she stopped and with a louder voice she said, "Yes, I know what I will do."

She picked up her school bag and went to the bus stop. She boarded a bus that was headed for town. She went to a Pharmacy and spoke to one of the pharmacists, a lady that she knew from high school, and she was her classmate. They spoke for a while. The pharmacist went at the back and brought a container with few tables and gave to her. She paid for the drugs and went home.

By the time she got home, Sipho had gone to work. When she opened the door, she saw a note on top of the table. She took the note and read it.

Dear Linda.

I will be glad if you can wait for me tomorrow morning, there is something I would like to discuss with you that has been burning in me for a long time now. I should think I cannot go on longer than this without telling you. I will appreciate if you could give me a chance to talk to you tomorrow morning.

Yours Sipho

After reading the note Linda smiled at herself. "Things seemed to fall into place all by themself. It's like my plan is going to be very easy. Do I drug him or not? Sipho is a very principled man. He will never sleep with me before we get married. I cannot wait for that because by then this pregnancy would be showing. I think it is better for me to continue with my plan." Linda went to bed determined that she was going to continue with her original plan. Under normal circumstances when Linda goes to bed, she puts on a full non-transparent nightdress because she sometimes wakes up in Sipho's presence. She never wanted anything that was going to be a temptation to him, but the following morning of that night was going to be a different morning. Temptation or not her plan has to work. She went to bed with a very short red transparent nightdress that was fully open in front, with a red and black G-string.

She woke up early the following morning and quickly freshened up and put on very light make up and went back to bed. She took a magazine and start reading. Not long there was a knock at the door and Sipho put in his key which he had just cut from the locksmith to open the door. Linda quickly dropped the magazine turned to face the wall and pretended as if she was sleeping.

Realizing that Linda was still sleeping Sipho silently took off his jacket and some of his clothes and went for a quick shower. He wanted to fresh-up and wait for Linda to wake up. When he was done with the shower Linda was long awake and boiling water in the kitchen. Sipho came out of the shower with a towel around his waist. Still dressed in her night dress Linda came straight to Sipho. He inspected her from top to the bottom. When he saw what she was wearing, something springs up from him and his heart started pounding fast and his hands were shaking. He had never seen this before.

Linda came very close to him and gave him a slight kiss on his lips.

By now Sipho was as hard as a fresh carrot and about to collapse.

She had already prepared two glasses of juice that were on the table by the time Sipho finished taking a shower. Sipho opened his mouth to say something. She closed his mouth with a finger and picked up the glass close to him and took it straight to his mouth without a word. Like a lamb to the slaughterhouse, Sipho became obedient. He opened his mouth to take a sip and the next and next until the glass was empty. The sight of Linda with a sexy outfit made him very thirsty.

She removed Sipho's towel and kissed him. When he tried to push her away from him to say something, the temptation was overwhelming. His manhood was saying contrary to what his mouth wanted to say. His sexual feelings overpowered his sense of reasoning. She took off her night dress and took both Sipho's hands and put them on her breast. Every time Sipho wanted to say something she would prevent him with a kiss.

By this time Sipho was gradually losing power and his eyes were becoming heavy. He could feel his head spinning but he had no power to do anything. When Linda realized that Sipho was losing strength she took his hand and lead him to bed. She gently helped him to lie on the bed naked and she was on top of him. Ultimately Sipho was sleeping.

Linda took out a syringe from her bag and drew a small amount of blood from her. Took off her underwear and threw it on the floor, sprayed some droplets of blood on the bottom sheet, some on her inner thighs and a few on Sipho's organ. She wiped the syringe with the toilet paper, put it back in her bag and went into bed. She lifted Sipho's leg to be on top of hers and his arm around her neck. Part of Sipho's body was halfway on her. She made it a point that part of the blood on the sheet was underneath her.

The drug she used was not heavy but an effective one. It was not going to keep Sipho sleeping for long. She knew that. When Sipho was struggling to wake up she pretended as if she was sleeping. Ultimately, he woke up and realized that he was sleeping on top of Linda. He quickly jumped out of bed and looked for something to cover himself. He grabbed the towel that was on the floor. When he saw the blood on him and some on the sheets he started panicking and woke Linda up.

"Linda, Linda, wake up," he said with a panicking voice and very concerned.

Linda pretended that she was in a deep sleep. She opened her eyes and looked at Sipho and asked him, "What? I am still sleeping."

"Look what has happened. You are bleeding. The sheets have blood what happened?"

Linda sat up straight and looked at herself and the sheets and started crying and said to him "You raped me Sipho, you raped me! Look at me, I am bleeding."

"How did it happen? I don't remember a thing."

"You remember we had a little romance after you took a shower?"

"Yes, I do, but that was it. After that I cannot recall what happened."

"You forced yourself on top of me and you took off my underwear by force and you penetrated me. I tried to stop you, but you overpowered me. You broke my virginity Sipho, you raped me."

"But how Linda? You know I will never do such a thing."

Still crying crocodile's tears Linda showed Sipho the blood on her inner thighs and on him. "I will have to report this to the police right now I don' know how much of your semen is in me."

"Please Linda don't, please don't, we can talk about this. I am prepared to do anything but please don't go and report this," said Sipho thinking about the embarrassment and his friends.

"What if you have impregnated me Sipho? What am I going to do with that? What is going to happen with my degree?" asked Linda pretending to be frustrated.

"Linda, you know that I took care of you. I will still take care of you. If you are pregnant, I will take care of the child also, but please do not do anything funny. I promise I will look after you until you complete your degree," said Sipho as he sat down next to Linda and holding her and pressing her toward his shoulder.

"If I am pregnant Sipho, how am I going to bring up a child without a father?"

"What do you want me to do Linda?"

"I can't bring up a child as a single parent, not at all." "What do you want me to do?"

"I don't know Sipho I just told you what I am not prepared to do."

"Will you marry me then, so that we can bring the child up together?" asked Sipho

"If you are sure, you think that is what you want. I don't want you to think I am pressurizing you to something against your will and your future plans."

"No, no, no, no, Linda I have no problems in marrying you, not at all. You are not pressuring me at all. As long as you are comfortable with that. It's just that I wouldn't like my child grew up not knowing his/her father."

"Ok, I will marry you provided we will agree on certain terms."

"What terms are those?" ask Sipho

"When we get married, I will keep my surname, no ring on my finger until I complete my studies and you must also promise me that you will not force me into sex again."

"I don't have any problem with that. I am very sorry for what I have done to you. I never intended to do such a thing; I don't know how it happened. Believe me, it is not like me at all."

She stood up and went to the loo. As she was walking toward the loo, she smiled to herself, her plan has achieved its intended purpose. She was very happy now that she would be able to tell people who the father of her child is. She knew that Sipho was a disciplined man, and he would not explain to people how he became the father of the child.

Knowing how men are, he would not even count the number of weeks of her pregnancy.

After a week Linda bought a pregnancy test kit and brought it home. She came home early before Sipho was out for work. She explained to Sipho how it works. She tested her urine sample, and the test was positive. She jumped high and hugged Sipho and said to him "Congratulations Mr. Mokoena you are a father now, I am pregnant." Sipho did not look excited at all. He was still in a state of shock and was wondering how all this had happened.

"Sipho, you don't look happy? Don't you want this baby? You must tell me if you don't want the child. I will just terminate this pregnancy."

"No, no, I didn't say I don't want the child. You know I cannot allow you to terminate that pregnancy. I have told you that I will take the responsibility for my actions and look after this child. I cannot abandon my own blood."

"Now that the pregnancy test is positive, we need to go to the magistrate and sign. When can we do that?" asked Linda.

"When would you like us to do it? How much is this going to cost us?"

Chapter 32

A week after Thandi and Freddy came back from their honeymoon, Thandi called her father in the morning. The phone rang on the other side. Her mom picked up the phone and said "Khumalo's residence can I help you?"

"Hi mom, how are you?"

"Oh! Good morning my baby. Are you guys back from your honeymoon already?

"Yes, mom it's almost a week now."

"I hope you enjoyed it. How is Freddy?"

"I think he is fine mom. He has gone back to work now; you know Freddy and his work. How is everybody at home?"

"Everybody is fine except for your little brother who had tonsillitis last week and he stayed at home for a day and then went back to school. Would you like to talk to your dad?"

"Yes mom. Is he around?"

"Yes, he is. He is just busy outside in the garden. I will pass the phone to him. You have a great day. I love you."

"I love you too mom."

"Hi my baby! You guys are back already? I thought you will take the whole month. People who have money normally extend their holidays. I am joking my baby. How are you doing?"

"I am doing just fine daddy thanks, and you?"

"I am fine baby thanks. How is Freddy doing? Has he gone back to work already?"

"He is well daddy, and he has gone back to work. The reason I am calling you I first want to say thanks for everything that you and mom have done for me and my husband. I will forever be grateful to you and mom."

"You are welcome my baby. If your biological mom was still alive, I know she would be proud of you like your stepmom is."

"Daddy, Freddy wants me to move into the big house with him as soon as possible."

"What are you waiting for I thought you have moved in long time ago. You cannot expect him to stay in that big house alone now that he is married."

"Of course, yes dad. I am supposed to move in before the weekend."

"And what's your problem my child?"

"Freddy does not want me to continue with the salon and he wants me to stay at home."

"And my child, do you have a problem with that?"

"No daddy I don't. Will it be fine with you if I give the salon to Sarah and give her R500 000 that will allow her to stay afloat for six months to a year?"

"Baby, Sarah has served your grandmother very well and for a very long time. She has been loyal to both of you in that business. Personally, I don't see any reason why you should not do what you want to do for her. What is your husband saying?"

"He said I must do what my heart tells me, all he wants is to see me at home not running some small salons."

"What are you going to do with the house?"

"I will rent it out and the money from it I will open up an account for my two brothers and it will wait for them when they are old enough to start their own businesses."

"Did you tell him about your other investments?"

"Yes, I did, and he is not interested in them. He said I should keep that money for rainy days or spend it on anything I like."

"I would strongly suggest that you invest it somewhere for the real rainy days. Talk to Thomas about that."

"Thanks dad. I will call Sarah and talk to her."

Chapter 33

It was three months after Linda and Sipho had signed at the magistrate. Linda was losing weight and she was highly frustrated because Eric was not responding to any of her calls. It was the third month without her talking or seeing him. The frustration resulted in her losing the pregnancy, but she never informed Sipho about the loss. Her losing weight was of great concern to her friend Joyce. Joyce wasn't happy about the explanation she was getting from Linda about her missing her parents because it was just over a year they passed on. She suspected that whatever was happening had something to do with Eric. She was aware that her friend hadn't seen him for some time. She suspected that there was more to it than what Linda was telling her. It was getting toward examination time and Joyce did not want her friend to fail after so many years of hard work. She wanted to get to the bottom of this about her friend. One day she stayed away from lectures and waited for Linda to go to the lectures. She told herself that she was going to wait for Sipho and ask if he knows anything. Joyce hadn't spoken to Sipho ever since the last time. In fact, they hadn't met since then.

Joyce stood at a position that was convenient for her to see Linda when she was leaving for lectures. She saw her taking the bus to university. She waited for Sipho by the main entrance to the flat. About 30 minutes after Linda left, Sipho appeared with his friends from work.

"Hi Joyce! How are you? I haven't seen you for quite some time. Where are you hiding yourself?"

"I am fine thanks for asking. I haven't been hiding myself at all Sipho. The workload from university is keeping me very busy. How are you doing?"

"I'm good thanks. Are you waiting for Linda?"

"No, I am here to see you, in actual fact to talk to you," responded Joyce.

"Do you want to talk here or inside the room?"

"I will prefer we talk inside."

"You guys are getting closer to exam time. How are the nerves?"

"Nervousness will always be there when you are going to write exams. Nobody ever gets used to writing examinations, but we are working hard because this is our last year at medical school. Next year we will be doing our first year of internship."

"I guess you guys can't wait to finish," echoed Sipho as he was opening the door and allowed Joyce to step inside. "You may take a seat Joyce."

"Sipho I am not going to stay long with you. I just came to find out if Linda is still staying with you? And if you have noticed any changes in her behavior?"

"Yes, she is still staying here. Are you and Linda still friends?"

"Yes, we still are that is why I am here."

"How come then you are here to ask me questions like the ones you are asking me?"

"What do you mean?" asked Joyce

"Did Linda not tell you that we are now married, and she is carrying my child?"

"What!" responded Joyce with her eyes wide opened "You must be joking Sipho. That would never happen. Linda marry you! You are a daydreamer, Sipho you are definitely dreaming."

"I can't believe this. Do you want to tell me that Linda has never said anything to you about our marriage?"

"Sipho I am not here for jokes. My friend is not feeling well. I want to know if she is still staying here and if she does, what have you done to her or what has she done to herself that she is losing so much weight?"

"Joyce, I told you there is nothing that anybody has done to Linda. She is pregnant and I think she has pregnancy moods that's what she told me."

"Sipho are you serious about what you are telling me, that you and Linda are married, and she is carrying your baby?"

"Yes, Joyce. How can I joke with such a thing? This is now the fourth month in our marriage and her being pregnant."

"What are you telling me is that Linda is four months pregnant?" asked Joyce with a lot of suspicions.

"If I count properly yes, she is."

"Sipho, can I ask you a very personal question. If you are not comfortable answering it please feel free to say so, I will not feel offended."

"You can ask Joyce. I will say anything to you because I trust you."

"When did this affair between you and Linda start? The last time I spoke to you there was nothing between the two of you," asked Joyce.

"I can't tell you when it started. All I know is that Linda and I are now in love and we are expecting a child."

"How did this thing happen that you and Linda get married and have a child so soon? Did you guys plan the marriage and the pregnancy?"

"Let me be honest with you and tell you how this all started. It started on the morning I was coming from work after I left a note for her the previous night," he went on to tell the whole story.

As Sipho was talking Joyce was listening attentively. She did not interrupt Sipho not even with a single question. When he was done then Joyce asked him if she can ask questions. "Yes, you can I will try and answer them all if it is possible," said Sipho.

"When you came from work that morning and Linda poured juice for you. Where were you when she was pouring the juice in the glass?"

"When I came out of the shower the juice was in the glass on the table already," explained Sipho

"Was it your glass only or did she also pour some for her?"

"There were two glasses with juice. Though I don't remember her drinking hers."

"So, you are saying after you drank the juice you don't know what happened to you? You don't remember at all making love or raping Linda that day?"

"As I have said I don't remember what happened after I drank that juice, all I could remember was her trying to kiss me non-stop and she did not give me a chance to talk."

"Was it the first time you sleep with a woman the day you slept with Linda. I am sorry for asking you such personal questions."

Joyce had to ask these questions because she could see how naïve Sipho was and knowing how devious her friend is, anything was possible with her. She suspected that Linda manipulated Sipho into this. The question in her head was that, was this all true.

"I don't think you expect me to answer that question."

"Please do. It is important for me to know. I promise you that whatever we talk about now will remain within these four walls, but I must get an answer so that I can establish the truth."

"Yes, it was. I have told myself that the first time I will sleep with a woman it will be my wife in our honeymoon."

"My second question. Why is Linda not wearing a ring if you guys are married? Has she said anything about changing her surname?"

"Oh, I forgot. She made me promise not to change her surname, wear a ring and that I will never force her into sex again."

"You guys have not made love again since then?"

"No. She said it is not good for the baby and the doctor told her it will damage the baby."

"Thank you Sipho. I really don't know how you got to associate yourself with such a perfidious woman. You are such a kind and honest man, and you deserve much better than this. Goodbye."

"Please Joyce don't tell Linda that I told you all this, she will get very upset, and I don't want her to lose the baby."

"Don't mind Sipho she will never know, and she won't lose the baby. (I don't think the baby is there in any way)," she said the last part when she was already on her way and Sipho did not catch it.

On her way to the bus stop Joyce was extremely angry with her friend for playing a fool of Sipho. Joyce was sure that the baby was Eric's child and that he might have forced himself on her. "Why is she doing this to Sipho? How am I going to approach her with this whole thing without getting Sipho into trouble?" she whispered.

Chapter 34

It was after the graduation both Linda and Joyce had graduated. Both girls were looking forward to their year of internship. Linda got accepted at Vereeniging hospital and Joyce was going to Baragwanath hospital for internship.

Joyce never got to tell Linda about her conversation with Sipho. She kept it to herself, and she never asked Linda either about her pregnancy and her marriage to Sipho. She felt that if Linda was a good and honest friend, she would tell her when the time comes.

Linda did tell Sipho after some time about the miscarriage. This is after Sipho wanted to know how the pregnancy was going on.

Sipho was very hurt when Linda told him.

Like all other internship students, Linda and Joyce got accommodation within the hospital premises. Linda decided that it would be better for Sipho to remain in the flat while she is residing at the hospital premises. She promised to visit him every time she was not on call.

It was Linda's third month at the hospital without her coming back home. Sipho was calling her almost every day. Some other time she would not respond to his calls for a week. When she eventually did, she would make excuses telling him about a busy schedule and tight calls. One Saturday afternoon when she was on call, she got a message from one of her colleagues that there was somebody at the residence that was looking for her. When the lady described the person, she knew it was Eric. She dropped everything and rushed to the residence. When Eric saw her coming walking high, he ran to her to meet her halfway. Linda threw herself on him and started kissing Eric all over. They held each other for a while without any words but with Linda sobbing. She ultimately said "I have missed you. I have missed you where have you been?" She gave Eric a long passionate kiss.

"Okay, okay that's enough." He put her down and looked at her and said:

"I missed you too my love. I was out of the country, and I am very sorry that I could not tell you."

"How did you know where I was? You missed my graduation and I wanted you to be there. How are you? You look so handsome. I am sure the girls where you have been must have been crazy about you."

"What are you doing? Can we go to Johannesburg, and I will bring you back tomorrow?"

"I am on call my love and it's a weekend call."

"Can't you make a plan? Get one of your friends to take your call and do hers later."

"Unfortunately, everybody by now is gone. Those that are here are all committed in one way or another. Why don't I see you next week? I will take public transport and come to you."

"Can you come through on Friday mid-day? We will drive down to Durban for the weekend."

"That sounds fine with me. Baby, can I go back to work now? I was still busy with something." She gave Eric a kiss and left.

When Linda was doing her community service, she moved from Vereeniging to Helen Joseph Hospital in Johannesburg. To cut costs she decided that she was going to rent a flat not far from the hospital. She discussed this with Sipho, and he agreed. Eric had disappeared again from her life, and she had accepted his kind of lifestyle. Linda's affair with Eric had never surfaced when she talked to Sipho. Joyce new that the affair between Eric and her friend was still on, but she never tried to talk Linda out of it again. The visitations between Linda and Sipho were the same as when Linda was in Vereeniging. Linda was almost a year now in Helen Joseph and she hadn't seen Sipho or talked to him over the phone.

One evening Linda got a call from Joyce. "Hi Linda, how are you, my friend? How is Helen Joseph treating you?"

"Oh, Joyce my friend I haven't heard from you for a very long time. How are you doing?"

"I am fine thanks Linda can I ask you a personal question?"

"Surely you can. You know you are my friend, and you can ask me anything."

"Are you and Sipho still talking?"

"Yes. Why are you asking me that? Is there something wrong?"

"When did you last talk to him? Is he aware that you are now working in Helen Joseph?"

"Yes, he is aware that I am working here. We had talked about it. I haven't talked or seen Sipho for quite some time because I have been busy with weekend calls."

"Has he tried to contact you by phone?"

"Yes, I guess."

"Did you return his calls?"

"As I have said to you Joyce, I have been busy, I didn't get time to do so. What's wrong? Did you see Sipho?"

"Yes, I met him in Sandton yesterday."

"Did you guys talk?"

"Yes, we did. In fact, we had a coffee together."

"Oh, what is he saying?"

"So, you don't know that your husband's company closed down four months ago and that he is out of work?"

"Oh, no, Joyce, I didn't know about that. Who told you that Sipho is my husband? Did he tell you that?"

"Linda my friend, I knew even before we completed that you were married to Sipho and that you were pregnant at some stage, and you pinned that pregnancy to him."

"Is it Sipho who told you all these lies?"

"Unfortunately, no, your boyfriend that made you pregnant talked about your unfortunate scene of drunkenness and how he slept with you and dumped you at your place in the middle of the night."

"Who is that boyfriend because Eric can never do that? Can I come back to you I need to call Sipho now," said Linda as she dropped Joyce's call. She was very angry with what Joyce had said and she blamed it on Sipho for creating lies that are unfounded.

"Sipho it's Linda here. Where are you?"

"Hi, how are you? I am in my flat. Why?"

"I am on my way coming there."

"It's late now Linda. How are you going to get here? There is no public transport at this time."

"You don't worry about that, that will be my problem," said Linda knowing that she was going to drive her three month old BMW 320. When she bought the car, she did not discuss it with Sipho which is why he did not know about it.

Linda got into her car and drove to Sipho's place. She knocked and the door was not locked.

Chapter 35

"Hi. How come you didn't tell me that you have lost your job? Why do I have to hear from other people that my husband is no longer working? And why are you spreading lies about my pregnancy?" she was on her feet when she was asking all these questions to Sipho.

"Why don't you take a chair before you and I talk," said Sipho as he pulled a chair for Linda to sit. "Good evening Mrs. Mokoena. How are you doing? Can I offer you a cup of coffee?"

"Don't try to patronize me please Sipho. I am not your fool. Answer my questions," said Linda angrily.

"Good evening, Mrs. Mokoena once more. Why don't you sit down so that we can talk like adults?"

"Good evening," responded Linda as she was sitting down. She realized that Sipho was not in a fighting mood and that she was wrong not to be polite to him after she hasn't talked to him for months. "I am sorry that I never had a chance to respond to your calls, I was too busy at the hospital," she said

"Can you please repeat all the questions you asked me," said Sipho with a low tone voice trying to calm Linda down.

"Let me rephrase my questions. Why did you not tell me in time that your company was closing down?"

"Is that the only question you asked before?"

"Forget about the others I was not myself when I asked them."

"If you read all the messages, I sent you last year and the beginning of this year you would know that I informed you about everything step by step as it was happening. I told you that the company was liquidated, and they seized all the assets, and they couldn't pay us our salaries for the last month of operation. Linda, I know you are too busy with your life that is why I will not bother you at all. I spoke to Joyce because we met in Sandton and we started talking, she wanted to know how my work was and I had to tell her."

"I am very sorry Sipho. Like I have said my work kept me busy."

"It kept you so busy that you could not even respond to your cell phone messages not even have a chance to call me back, or most probably you were selective to the calls that you wanted to respond to? You must say thanks to Joyce. I was about to leave for another province to find a job for myself."

"Please don't go. There is no other province that will be able to employ you either than this one. Stay and look for a job here."

"Where am I going to stay Linda? I have exhausted all my savings I am penniless now. How am I going to pay for the rent? I can't even go and stay with my friends none of them is working."

"Come and stay with me. We can stay together at my flat."

"I don't want to be a nuisance in your life Linda. I want you to live your life the way you want to. Let me find a way of living my life without you."

"Is that what you have planned to do? Are we no longer married?"

"I am not so sure about that any longer. I want to allow you to be who you want to be and what you want to be? I would like to set you free so that you can fly high like a bird and feel the freedom that you want," said Sipho as a solitary tear trickled down his cheek.

"I am very sorry for everything I have done. You cannot go and live with somebody else when I have space for the two of us in my flat. When are you supposed to move out from here?" asked Linda

"I am owing the Landlord this month rental already. I spoke to him about my situation, he understood and gave me this month to stay without payment."

"Let's pack all the small things and go. We will fetch the rest later."

"We can't travel with bags at night they will mug us, besides there is no public transport this time."

"I am driving my own car."

They packed all the clothes, took all the kitchen stuff and some linen. Locked the door and headed for the car.

"Is this your car? That's a beautiful one."

"Thanks," said Linda as she pulled the car off.

It was almost a month that Sipho had moved in with Linda. They had collected everything from Sipho's flat. Some of the furniture was kept in the storage that Linda was paying for. For that month Sipho would wake up in the morning and prepare breakfast for Linda and then go to the shop to buy a newspaper and check the job vacancy section for jobs. He would use the landline to make calls to different companies. He submitted his resume to some of the companies that showed interest, but nothing was forthcoming.

In the evenings he would prepare the dinner before Linda came back home. Sipho was the kind of guy that would be indoors the whole day. He liked reading and listening to music. At no stage did Linda find him out of the house when she was back from work. One afternoon Linda got a call from Eric. "Good afternoon my love, how are you doing?"

"Good afternoon to you, my love. I am doing well thanks. How are you, sweetheart?"

"I am very well thanks for asking. Are you at work now? Are you still in Vereeniging baby?"

"No, I have moved from there now. I am doing my community service in Helen Joseph hospital. Do you know where that is?"

"No, my love, where is it? You will have to direct me when I come back."

"When are you back in town?" asked Linda with a smile.

"In two weeks, time my love. I will come and see you immediately after I land. I miss you a lot."

"I miss you too my love. You must tell me when you land. Where are you now?"

"Remember I told you I am out of the country," lied Eric again.

"Oh, I remember now. You are not sure exactly when you will be back?"

"As I have said to you baby that it will be two weeks from now but I cannot give you the exact date. Have you found a place to stay or are you still staying in the hospital premises?"

"I've got my own flat not far from the hospital. That is why I am asking you when will you be coming so that you can find me there." Forgetting that she stays with Sipho.

"Bye now. I will call you again next week time willing."

"Goodbye my love, please do call next week when you find time. I love you." She dropped the phone. She stood there and thought how is she going to see to it that Sipho is not at home when Eric arrives. She wouldn't like Eric to see or find Sipho in her flat. "I must find a way of chasing Sipho out of the flat during the day," whispered Linda to herself.

After her conversation with Eric, Linda drove home and found Sipho lying on the couch with headphones listening to music. The flat was clean, and the evening meals were prepared. She slammed the door as she was closing it. Sipho jumped out of the couch to check what was going on. She walked past Sipho without greeting him and straight to the bedroom. Sipho knew there and then that there was something wrong. Instead of following her to the bedroom he remained in the lounge and continued listening to his music. Linda walked out of the bedroom and went to Sipho. She pulled the headphones out of Sipho's head and threw them on top of him. "We need to talk," she said.

Sipho woke up, sat straight on the couch and looked at her. He was taken aback by what she did, but he decided to keep quiet.

"When do you think, you will start working? You sit here at home the whole day doing nothing besides listening to your music and lying on that couch."

"But you know Linda I am buying a newspaper every day. I have sent my resume to several companies. I am waiting for a call from any one of them," responded Sipho.

"It is not going to help you lying on your back and waiting for the companies to call you. You are the one who is looking for job, not the companies. Other men wake up in the morning go out and search for work."

"What do you want me to do?" asked Sipho

"From tomorrow onwards you will wake up early, wash and go to town to look for work. I don't want to come back from work and find you sitting here. I am not going to feed an old man like you. My money is for me to do things that are important. Every time I come back from work you are here. I can't even move in my house because of you. You must find a job. You cannot be my burden for the rest of your life. If you chose the right course at school, you would not be out of work by now." Sipho stood there and looked at Linda as she was talking.

"Can I get money for the bus for tomorrow then, so that I can go to town to look for work?"

"Sipho, men who don't have transport money walk to town. Where do you think am I going to get the money to feed you and transport you? Do I look like your bank to you? You must walk to town tomorrow like all other men do."

"That's fine. Can I get another key for the flat so that I don't have to wait outside when you are still at work in the afternoon?"

"What do you mean? What key do you want? You will be leaving in the morning before me and be back in the evening not earlier than me. I don't have money to cut another key for you. Oh, the other thing, you will have to take food here from home for your lunch. Only use the leftovers that are in the fridge. If you do come back early which I don't expect you will, wait for me outside until I come back."

"But Linda that is not fair. I cut you keys when you were staying with me. I have never let you stay and wait outside, why don't you leave the key under the doormat or above the door so that I find it there at least?"

"Sipho, I call the shots here. It is either my way or nothing. You are not going to tell me how I should run my house. If you are not happy with what I say, you have a choice," said Linda with a raised voice and looking Sipho straight into his eyes.

Sipho realized that he has made Linda angry he withdrew there and then. Took his music and went outside for a walk.

Chapter 36

Exercising in the mornings was one of Thandi's hobbies. In East London, she was a member of the Athletic club and when she came to Cape Town, she joined one of the gyms. Now the plot was far from town, and it was going to be expensive for her to wake up every morning and drive to the gym in town. She decided to clean the perimeter of the plot's fence. She would wake up every morning from Monday to Friday and jog around the perimeter except on the weekends when her husband was at home. When Freddy bought her a puppy she started jogging with the dog.

Freddy liked his morning breakfast. Thandi would prepare the breakfast herself and she never wanted Martha to do any cooking for her husband. Freddy was used to having a full meal before starting his day every time he was at home. Thandi would wake up for her jog and come back to prepare Freddy's breakfast while he was still in bed. The only time she would not prepare breakfast was when Freddy was out of town. Thandi would spend the rest of her day after Freddy's departure working in the garden planting flowers and vegetables. Going to town for shopping and doing some errands was not in her. The only time she would do that was when her husband was around, and they would go together. She had certain days in a week where she would not cook an evening meal. They would go out to a restaurant for a meal. Thandi would select the restaurants because she was very particular about her husband's diet.

The other thing that Thandi would do twice a week was to soak Freddy's feet in warm water with bathe salts, wash and massage them. She did this because of Freddy's weight, he would always come back home complaining about his feet and tiredness. Unfortunately, by the time Freddy arrived at home from work it would be an awkward time for Thandi to organize a masseur. That is why she had to do this herself.

Freddy had a very heavy schedule at work. It was difficult for him to find time to sit down and have a proper nutritious meal. He would always tell her PA what to buy for him. In most cases, it was fast food which the wife was discouraging for somebody of his weight. Freddy would snack time and again with fatty food that was in his fridge. Instead of him losing weight he was gaining. He had no time to attend the gym or wake up with his wife for a morning jog. The only time Freddy would take a walk was when the two of them were on holiday during December vacation time. After his father's death, Freddy had tripled the profitability of the company in two years. The workload was starting to take its toll on him. Thandi noticed that because he was starting to be irritable when he came back home late or early hours of the morning. Thandi suggested to him that she should assist in running the company by taking some of the responsibilities. Freddy refused and said his mother never worked after his father bought the company and there was no way that his wife would work.

"Seeing that you don't want my help at work, how about us having a baby then?"

"That decision is yours. I told you that I don't want a child now I am too busy to concentrate on that."

"I am the one who will carry the baby and you can continue with your work without any disturbance."

"If you want a baby then that is your call," said Freddy

This left Thandi a bit confused. His father wanted grandchildren for the sake of the business. For some strange reasons, his son does not want to talk about children. She decided all by herself that she was going to stop taking contraceptives so that she could conceive.

Freddy would spend long hours in the office with his accountant, lawyer and operations director. They were planning to expand the market of the company to overseas clients. They were targeting the Asian countries the market that his father had already started. This then exposed him to more stressful work.

To keep herself busy Thandi started helping Sarah to renovate the salon and add on more new machines. She would visit the salon now and then. "Sarah, you need to employ somebody who is going to do your books. You are too busy to do that. And you knock off late every day. It is not practical for you to say you will do them after hours."

"Yes, I thought about that Thandi. I discussed this with my children one of my girls is doing bookkeeping with Damelin College. She is completing it next year. If we are going to get somebody it will be for just one year. She wants to come and join me in the business," responded Sarah.

"After the diploma with Damelin why don't you send her to the University to do a degree in accounting? At least you can afford both at school now. If you have any financial problems, you know you can always come and talk to me."

"You know Thandi that is what she wanted from the onset, it's just that then I could not afford to take her to the university. I think she will be very happy if I can tell her that."

"In the meantime, you can get a person to help you with your books until your daughter qualifies."

"I will tell her to apply to the local universities."

"No Sarah, tell her to apply to all and then she is the one who is going to choose where to go if she is accepted into all. How did she pass her matric?"

"If I remember, very well she got very good symbols at grade 12, that is why she wanted to go to university."

"What did she want to do at university?"

"She once said to me she wants to be a CA which I don't even know what that is."

"Tell, her to come and see me over the weekend. She must bring her matric results with her."

"I will do that," responded Sarah.

"Sarah let me go home to prepare dinner for my husband. I will talk to you later," said Thandi.

On her way to the car her cell phone rang. She picked up the phone and a voice on the other side said, "Is this Mrs. Phillips."

"Yes sir, it is."

"Mrs. Phillips, you are talking to your husband's doctor at the hospital. Is it possible for you to come to the hospital now?"

"Yes doctor, I am on my way. What is the problem doctor?" she asked

"There is nothing wrong so far. Mr. Phillips is here, and he is fine I would like to talk to you about him ma'am. You will find me in casualty Mrs. Phillips"

Thandi drove straight to the hospital. Parked her car and rushed to casualty. She found the doctor busy talking to her husband. Thandi went to Freddy and hugged him with a kiss. Freddy was motionless and listening to the doctor. He just responded to Thandi's greeting with a low voice.

"What happened darling?" asked Thandi "Is he alright doc?" There was no response from Freddy's side. The doctor grabbed Thandi and asked to speak to her privately.

"Your husband is fine Mrs. Phillips. We just ran some few tests. He collapsed at work, and they called the ambulance. Your husband is diabetic Mrs. Phillips, and his blood pressure is also very high. He will recover very soon. He is just disoriented now because it was his first attack."

"Did you tell him about the diabetes and high blood pressure?"

"Not yet, I was waiting for you. He hasn't fully recovered yet."

"What are we going to do now?" asked Thandi.

"We will admit him for overnight observation and discharge him tomorrow. He needs to take a rest. He is over working himself. He must watch his diet and do a lot of exercising for his weight. Your husband is still too young to have all these complications."

"Can we put him in a private ward please? I would like to stay with him"

"I have arranged for that Mrs. Phillips"

"I would like to make a quick call to my house. Which ward is it?"

"It's the top floor ward no 501A."

Thandi went outside to give Daniel and Martha a call.

Later Freddy recovered fully, and he noticed that Thandi was next to him.

"Where are we? What happened with me? Why are you here?"

"You are at the hospital. You collapsed at work, and they called an ambulance. You have been here since this afternoon. The time now is 18h20 and you came here at about 15h00."

"Who told you that I am here?"

"It is the family physician."

"Did he tell you what the problem is?"

Knowing her husband and to avoid any conflict Thandi said "No, all what he told me is that they are still waiting for the laboratory results which they ran on you."

"Are the results not back yet?"

"No, the doctor will get them tomorrow. Can you still remember what happened?" asked Thandi to change the direction of the conversation.

"All I can still remember is that I was in the boardroom giving a presentation to my executive management staff about the company future plans."

"And then what happened?"

"I can't recall. The next thing I find myself here."

"Did you take anything prior to that?"

"Like what?"

"Did you drink or eat anything before that?"

Freddy was quiet for a while. He knows that his wife does not approve of him eating fast food. He had to find a way not to tell her the truth. "No, I was about to eat after the presentation."

"So, you went on the whole day without eating anything? I told your PA that she must always see to it that you eat. That is why I wanted to cook a lunch for you whenever you are around. Did you eat at all today?"

"As I have said to you that I was still going to have my Lunch. Can we get out of this place? I am not going to sleep here. You know how much I hate hospitals."

"The doctor still wants to observe you overnight."

"If there are any complications at home you will have to call him, I will not spend my night here that's all."

"I will be here with you my love you will not be alone," said Thandi trying to persuade her husband.

"I am sure you are not listening to me. I don't want to be here," said Freddy with a hasher voice.

"Can I go and have a word with the doctor then?" said Thandi because she could see that her husband was becoming agitated.

Thandi went out to look for the doctor. "Doctor he wants to go home now. Will there be any problem if you discharge him? I promise you; I will personally look after him at home."

"No Mrs. Phillips, there will be not problems. I just wanted to keep him here and see if nothing was going to develop. If he wants to go home, I can discharge him now if that is in order with you," said the doctor

"I will appreciate that doctor. You don't have to organize an ambulance we will use my car."

"There is some medication I have ordered already, and I would like you take with you. I gave the sister-in-charge a prescription for your husband's treatment. I hope all goes well. Don't hesitate to call me if there are any new developments with him."

"Thank you doctor I will do so. Can I get a porter and a wheelchair to wheel Mr. Phillips to the car please?"

"The nurses are already organizing that for you ma'am."

Thandi went back to the ward. She found Freddy dressed up already and waiting. "You can't walk to the car. They are bringing a wheelchair for you," said Thandi.

"I am not going to be wheeled to the car I will walk I am not an old man," replied Freddy.

When they arrived at home Freddy call his PA to bring his laptop. He wanted to prepare for the meeting with the staff about the distribution center he was planning to open in Johannesburg. He went to their bedroom and lay on the bed while he was waiting for his PA to bring his laptop.

Based on what the doctor said. Thandi started to prepare some light healthy meals for Freddy. She prepared Greek salad with chicken strips and serve this with apples, pineapple and papaya. Thandi brought the food to her husband in the bedroom. Freddy looked at the food and asked Thandi if that is all she had prepared.

"Yes, my love this is what the doctor recommended."

"If this is what the doctor recommended, then go and give that food to him. I am not going to eat food without red meat. I am the one who is working in this house not that doctor of yours. Take this food and get out of my bedroom. I am not going to eat that," screamed Freddy at Thandi.

At that moment the doorbell rang. Martha opened the door, and it was Freddy's PA.

"Good evening. Mr. Phillips had asked me to bring this laptop," said the PA

"Thank you, lady, I will tell Mr. Phillips, and I will take it to him," said Thandi. "Martha took the laptop from the lady."

Thandi took the laptop to Freddy. "Where is the person who brought this laptop?" he asked.

"It's your PA and she is gone."

"Tell Martha to call her back."

Martha went outside to call her. Lucky enough she was still in her car. The lady came back and stood by the door.

"Martha! Show her where Mr. Phillips is," said Thandi with little embarrassment.

"Can you do me a favor and take money from my jacket and buy me the special of 500g spareribs, four rolls and French fries. Please do hurry because I am starving. Don't forget 500ml of carbonated drink please," instructed Freddy

Thandi called her father and told him about what had happened. She started from when Freddy was admitted to when the girl came back with food from local restaurant.

"I am scared Daddy. Freddy is diabetic and hypertensive. He doesn't want to listen to me and stick to the doctor's orders," said Thandi with tears in her eyes. "His father died of the same things."

"My baby, you know that I don't like to interfere in your family affairs. This is between you and him. Try to talk to him and show him the disadvantages of eating unhealthily when one is diabetic. You will have to be very diplomatic when you talk to him about his illness. Diabetes to man is a very sensitive issue because it goes beyond just being diabetes and affects his manhood," said Lesly

"I know all about that daddy, and I think it is something that is going to affect both of us. We must address it together but not him alone. I will be directly affected if it becomes serious. I am still too young daddy to have my husband being diabetic and hypertensive."

"Can't you guys go and see a counselor?"

"Freddy does not believe in counselors," said Thandi "Ok daddy let me not bother you about my marital problems. How is mummy doing?" she changed the topic to take her father attention away from her problems.

"Your mom is doing just fine."

"Bye daddy. It was nice talking to you. Pass my regards to everybody at home. I love you daddy."

"I love you too my angel, say hi to Freddy."

"Will do so."

Chapter 37

It was a Friday afternoon; Freddy was in a meeting with all his executive management team. The topic was about opening a distribution outlet for their products in Johannesburg. He was working on the feasibility of the project alone except the financial part which he gave it to the finance director Sam to tackle. This was going to be the first time that him and the Sam meet to discuss the profitability of the project.

Freddy stood up and presented about how the operation was going to start, the structure required, human resources to be employed, how the marketing was going to be implemented and the distribution using the company's own trucks. When he was done, he invited questions and there were none. He gave the platform to Sam his finance director.

Sam's presentation was in line with what Freddy had presented in terms of the size of the structure required, human resources for all other operations except the trucking and marketing cost. The difference was the high cost of distribution trucks and the viability of the operation in the long term. Sam was suggesting that they rent the trucks from the owners with drivers, to cut down on human resource that will be permanently employed by the company. Secondly, he indicated that the project would work only at the beginning and at the long run the cost of transporting the steel to Johannesburg might prove to be too expensive unless the company can be sold to an independent person who will buy the steel but not the company. This would increase their selling price and push them out of the market. "With that Mr. Phillips I don't think this will be a viable proposition in the long run," said Sam.

After the presentation Freddy was very angry and he stood up and said "I should think I am the owner of this company not you Sam. If that is what you used to do to my father, I am not him. I call the shots here now. What I said goes whether viable or not. Am I making myself clear?" To avoid any further discussion Sam nodded his head in agreement. "You must just go and sharpen your pencil and give me different figures tomorrow morning," continued Freddy.

"I will do so sir. You will get them first thing tomorrow morning," said Sam

"Gentlemen, can we all go for a meal now? Everything will be on me tonight."

They all agreed to go except for Sam who cited workload and some commitments at home.

When they got to the restaurant, they ordered their meals. "The doctor said I have a high blood pressure, and somebody told me the red wine does brings one's blood pressure down. So, gentlemen I will be taking my first glass of wine today. You guys you can order whatever beverage you like. There is no limit to what a person can order. Let us eat and drink to our new project in Johannesburg," said Freddy.

After three hours of wining and dining, Freddy was starting to feel the effects of the two bottles of expensive wine that he consumed alone. His voice became loud and noisy. He started boasting about his wealth to everybody. This annoyed his friends and they started leaving the restaurant one by one without thinking about how Freddy was going to get home. By this time, he was very drunk and drunk for the very first time.

When everybody was gone Freddy was left alone in the bar with the bar attendant. He knew who Freddy was and he had a lot of respect for him. The bar attendant woke him up and asked if he needed some help to drive home.

"No, I can drive myself," said Freddy. He walked staggering to his car and started the car and drove off. On the road the car was swaying to all directions. He jumped a red traffic light. The next thing he heard was a police siren behind him. He slowly pulled his car aside and stopped. He lowered his window with difficulty.

"Good evening, sir," said the officer.

"Oh, it's you Mr. Phillips? Are you aware that you jumped a red traffic light sir?"

With a sluggish voice Freddy asked, "where was that officer? I have been driving very slowly and carefully."

"Mr. Phillips can you come out of your car please sir?" asked the officer as he signaled to his partner to come and help him. "He is very drunk. We have to drive him home otherwise he is going to kill himself."

"Yes, you right. We cannot afford to lose such an important man. These are the people who are giving our brothers and sister work. This man is feeding the community," responded the second officer.

"I will drive his car then you can follow me."

Freddy got out of his car and sat on the passenger seat. The officer drove him up to the gate of the house and they allowed him to drive the car all by himself through the gate inside his yard. He stopped his car in front of his garage and switched the engine off. He got out of the car.

"Thandi where are you?" he shouted her name. "Open up the door I am back. Thandi come and open the door for me," he continued shouting. He moved toward the door and started banging the door and calling Thandi's name.

The noise woke up Daniel. He went outside and moved toward the door with the key. "I will open the door for you sir," said Daniel with a surprise.

"No, you go back to your room. I've got a wife. She will open the door for me."

Thandi was not sleeping when the car arrived, she was busy reading a book and waiting for his arrival. She was watching her husband through the window. What caught her attention was the blue light at the gate that reflected on her window. It stopped at the gate with lights on for a while before it drove off and her husband car drove in the yard. She was curious to know what were the cops doing with him. When she looked at the time of his arrival it was 02h45. She put on her gown and went downstairs to unlock the door. When Thandi opened the door, she was completely flabbergasted to see Freddy drunk. She stood at the door and looked at her husband with amazement. She had never seen him drunk before. She didn't even know that Freddy drinks. Tears rolled down her cheeks as she was looking at her husband who could hardly move his legs. She stretched her arms to hold him and assist him into the house. "What are you looking at? Is this the first time you see me? Let me get into my house. Is it not you who told me that the doctor said I am diabetic and hypertensive? The only easy way to get this thing away is red wine my love. I drank wine today to get rid of this sickness that your doctor said I have."

"But Freddy-," said Thandi as she was stretching her arms to hold him.

"Shh!!! Shut up and get out of my way. I don't need your help I can walk all by myself."

He walked up the stairs taking one step a minute holding on the guard railing. Thandi was behind him to support him in case he misses a step and fall. He ultimately reached the top and went straight into the bedroom. He threw himself on top of the bed with arms and legs wide apart. He slept in such a manner that it was difficult for Thandi to have a space in the same bed.

Thandi took off his shoes and she could not turn him around to take the jacket off because of Freddy's weight. She rushed back to the door to lock it. When she came back Freddy was snoring. She slept downstairs in the visitor's room.

"Lord is this the beginning of something to come or is it just a spur of a moment thing?" she whispered to herself before she went to bed. She said a short prayer and went to bed.

Chapter 38

It was early in the morning and Linda was preparing for work when her cell phone rang. She picked it up and answered it, "morning, its Linda here."

"Good morning my friend. You are talking to Joyce. How are you?"

"Woo Joyce. How are you, my friend? It's long time."

"I am fine thanks, and how are you doing?" responded Joyce

"I am well my friend, thanks for asking. Is the community service keeping you busy?"

"Yes, it does, the hospital is very busy and the calls are heavy. What about you?"

"Yes, my friend the calls are the ones that are killing me. Vereeniging was better than this. There must be a reason for this call," said Linda

"What do you mean? Can't I call my friend when I am thinking of her?" asked Joyce

"I didn't say that. You know you can call me at any time."

"Linda, I am getting married next year in June. I will inform you of the date very soon."

"Wow, those are great news Joyce. I am happy for you, my friend. Who is the lucky guy?"

"I am marrying my boyfriend the very same one from university times."

"Oh, that's fantastic."

"Secondly, I am seven months pregnant."

"Wow that's wonderful Joyce. Have you checked if it's a boy or a girl?"

"The scan shows a girl."

"Great."

"My fiancé has been promoted to Cape Town. He is going to manage the branch in Cape Town."

"Is he going to leave you behind?"

"No, we will be leaving next year after I completed my com-serve."

"Work wise, where are you going to work?"

"I have applied to two hospitals for a post of registrar in O&G. I want to specialize in Obstetrics and Gynecology with either Cape Town or Stellenbosch university."

"Did they agree to give you the post?" asked Linda.

"Yes, both hospitals have agreed to take me. I must just make up my mind and decide which one I would like to take."

"You are very lucky my friend. You must know things are different down there."

"I know. Where is Sipho?"

"I knew you would always talk about him. I think you and I should have swapped men."

"Linda in case you have not noticed, you have an extra ordinary wonderful husband, if you don't know it by now, you will never know. All I can say is you are throwing a good lover away. My fear is that somebody somewhere will see that and snatch him away from you. You are playing with Sipho as if he is a toy. That man wasted all what he had to make you who you are today. If it was not for Sipho you wouldn't be a doctor today," echoed Joyce.

"I am sorry my friend. What you see in him I don't see. What he is to you unfortunately he is not that to me. I have no feelings for him at all. There are better guys than him, guys who can give me everything that I want. I used Sipho to get me to where I am today because he allowed it. I will not feel pity for people who cannot use their brains. Any woman could have done that to Sipho."

"I totally disagree with you on that one. Not all girls are behind material things like you, my friend. All I am saying to you is if you knew that you are not interested in him, you shouldn't have played a fool of him and lied to him by saying he was responsible for your pregnancy. You forced him to a dummy marriage that was of your convenience because you were afraid to be a mockery to your friends. Poor Sipho played along not knowing that you were all along fooling him. I partly understand him because he was blinded by his love for you. Ok my friend. I didn't call to talk about your marital affairs."

"Hey, I forgot to tell you that I bought new wheels for myself," said Linda to change a topic

"Oh, what is it?"

"It's a big B."

"You love BMWs neh?"

"You've said it all. Please don't forget me when you get to Cape Town."

"No, I won't my friend. What are you planning to do after com-serve?"

"You know how much I love Paeds. I have talked to the head of Pediatrics at Johannesburg General (JG) Hospital about a possible post of registrar and she has agreed. I will not even go and work I will go and specialize immediately after com-serve."

"The same with me."

"What about the baby?" asked Linda.

"My mom is coming down with us. She will look after the baby."

"Bye now girl, I am almost getting late for work."

"Bye my friend. Pass my regards to Sipho."

Linda dropped the phone without responding. She just hated the fact that Joyce loves Sipho more than Eric. She always talked about Sipho to her but never talked about Eric.

Linda completed her community service and got a registrar position with Pediatric department at JG Hospital. She moved out of the flat and bought a small house not far from the hospital.

Chapter 39

Sipho was doing casual work here and there. He was still looking for a permanent job. One morning he decided that he was going to try East Rand around Wadeville. The only challenge he was faced with was the lack of transport money. Wadeville was further than the other places that he used to visit. The previous night he explained to Linda about his intentions and expressed his challenges. "The return trip train ticket is about R20, and the bus is R15. Can you give me money for the train ticket because the bus leaves early, I will miss it?" asked Sipho.

"I don't think that is my problem, how you find a job is your own problem. I don't care how you get there you must sort that one out without involving me. I have been feeding you all along you have been looking for work but all in vain, and you want me to give you transport money that I don't have? Be serious Sipho," said Linda with annoyance.

"The place is far otherwise I would walk but it's going to take me the whole day. I think it is the only place that is my last hope to find work," pleaded Sipho

"I don't care Sipho. If by the end of this year you don't have a job you must know you are not going to be in this house any longer. I am not going to feed an old man like you forever," said Linda as she was going to the bedroom and banged the bedroom door behind her. The door opened again, and she threw blankets at Sipho and said "From today onwards you are going to sleep on that couch until you can pay for this bedroom linen. I don't think I need an illiterate like you next to me any longer." She closed the door and went to bed.

In the morning Sipho woke up very early and made up his sleeping place, washed himself using the outside water tap and went to the train station with the hope of meeting somebody he knows who can help him with the train fare. It was a chilly May morning. Not far from the entrance to the station were three guys standing around the fire warming themselves. He decided to join them to warm himself too. "Hi guys," he greeted them. "It's quite chilly this morning," he said.

"Yah my bra, it's very cold," responded one. "It looks like we are heading for a very cold winter this year," he continued.

"Hey Dude, you are saying its cold and yet you are not even wearing a jacket, what's wrong with you?" asked one from Sipho. "Are you not freezing? Come closer dude otherwise you will freeze to death."

"Yes, it is cold. I did not realize that it was cold when I left home. It is only when I was on my way and far from home that I notice that it is very cold," said Sipho knowing that his jacket was inside the bedroom where Linda was sleeping, and he didn't want to wake her up.

"Dude are you going to work like that?" asked one.

"I don't think I have a choice, to make things worse I only realized now that I left my train ticket in the jacket that I was carrying for work yesterday. I think I will have to go back and not go to work today and lose today pay."

"No, bra you can't take that chance. I span si-skaars (scarce) nowadays. If you lose your job today it will take you years before you find another one. I will bail you out today if you will pay me back one day. "Where are you going and how much do you need for today?" asked the first man.

Thinking about the day and the fact that he doesn't have a cent for the day's meal, Sipho looked at the guy and said "I am on my way to Wadeville my bra and a train ticket is R20 return. One R50 my bra I will be grand. If you give me today, I will square you up (give back) before the end of the week," said Sipho with a persuasive voice, committing to pay back the money yet not knowing how.

"Sharp my bra. I will give you R 100 so that you buy for yourself some tshisanyama (barbecue) during the day. I don't want you to starve. Is that ok?" asked the man as he was taking out R100 and gave it to Sipho.

"We are shooting the same direction all of us my bra, and the train is already coming. Let's kill the fire and go," said the third man.

When Sipho got off from the station in Wadeville he met two of his friends Thabo and Seth standing at the shop next to the station talking. "Hey, look who is here," said Thabo. "I haven't seen you for a very long time Dude. Where have you been?"

"Hi guys!! It's lovely to see you. Are you well?" said Sipho as he was shaking their hands and hugging them. "It's been a very long time," he continued

"What brings you here Dude?" asked Seth

"Work is work my bra," responded Sipho "And you guys what's up?"

"Same thing Dude since that time we have been looking but nothing my brother," responded Thabo with a smile.

"Where are you guys going now? I might as well join you," asked Sipho.

"We have heard that there is a steel company from Cape Town that is coming here. They are going to open up a branch for their distribution and are going to employ people," explained Seth.

"Where did you get that from and when are they starting?" asked Sipho

"A friend of mine who is working next to the place where they are cleaning the warehouse, they will be operating in. He is not sure when are they coming up. We want to be around the area every day in case they need people," said Thabo.

"Guys things are bad. Jobs are hard to come by. If I get one now, I will stay on it I don't care what type of job it is. It is hard to find yourself without a salary and a cent in your pocket when you were used to have something. I can't take it," said Sipho.

"I thought you are better off because you are married to a doctor. Is Linda not qualified yet?" asked Thabo.

"Yes, Thabo is right. You should be better off Sipho. Doctors are getting a lot of money. Her salary should be able to take care of both of you meanwhile you are trying to find work. Themba's wife is helping him a lot. He is not struggling as much as us the bachelors," commented Seth

"To add more to that, Linda is where she is today because of your sacrifice toward her education. You used up all your investments to take her through her last years of her degree. She was literally living on your income," said Thabo.

"I remember when you told us that you were saving for you to start a business. When you met Linda, you were no long talking about saving for business but about getting Linda to fulfill her medical career," echoed Seth

"Okay you guys, you must know I did what I did for Linda so that she can get her education. I was not investing on her to take care of me so that I should stay at home," replied Sipho.

"We are not saying you mustn't work. All what we are saying is that you guys are married now and what was yours then was hers and so must it be now. If you were able to take everything of yours for her education, I personally think she should be able to take care of you now that you are out of job," said Thabo.

"She is taking care of me," said Sipho to cover up.

"No, that is not true Sipho. The Sipho I know never looked like this. You look worse off than you were when you were single. You have never looked like this Sipho. You are one guy who likes himself. I am sorry I didn't want to say this but now I am forced to say it. It is cold and you are wearing clothes like this, come on dude don't make us fools bra," continued Thabo.

"I might as well add this Sipho. Where is the guy that we all know who was always nicely dressed? Where is the lively Sipho that we know off? Your face is not shaved, and it looks like you have not done so for some time now. You have lost weight. What is happening with you?" interjected Seth.

"Everything is fine guys. It's just this thing of being out of job and you find yourself penniless. My cell phone is not working, and I am practically broke," said Sipho and he was almost into tears. He did not want to reveal to them his domestic and marital problems.

"That's exactly what we are saying. Why is Linda not bailing you out? Why are you penniless such that you cannot even afford to buy airtime for yourself? You know what Sipho, both Seth and I are not married, and we all lost our jobs at the same time as you. We have been up and down looking for work like you do but we are still intact. Something is wrong somewhere somehow with you. Are you sure you are enjoying your married life?" asked Thabo with concern and he was looking directly into Sipho's eyes.

Sipho felt a huge lump on his throat, it felt like it was choking him. He temporarily lost words to respond to what Thabo and Seth were saying to him. He knew that his friends could see through the mask he was wearing, the mask of misery, depression and frustration. He was not a good liar, nor could he pretend. Life to him was either right or wrong. Here he is now caught in a situation where he can't defend himself. He knew that all what they were saying to him was true. He is entangled in the bond of love that does not take him anywhere. The bond that damages his manhood, dents his pride and belittles him to nothing. A small voice said to him, "How did I get myself into this mess? How do I come out of it?" These were the two questions he had no answer for. With his friends questioning his integrity and doubting the decisions that he had taken, he felt that he had to defend himself even if he had to tell them a lie. He realized that he had to withhold his tears and put up a man's face and be brave.

"I am happily married. The life between me and Linda is fine. I am one person who cannot take the fact that I am not working. That is the only thing that is stressing me right now. Linda has been good to me, and she is fully supportive of all my endeavors," said Sipho with a changed voice.

"I find it very difficult to believe that one, you must know that I know you for being an honest person, I will have to accept it," said Thabo.

"At least it was good for you to plow all your resource toward Linda's education. She is your wife today and you are reaping the benefits of that. It is important for her to back you up. You must then stop worrying about being unemployed because this is wasting you a lot. You won't even have energy for the other things," said Seth joking and laughing at Sipho. They all laughed.

After queuing for the whole day and with no work prospects the three decided to go for a drink in one of the small food shops in the area.

They talked about the past and shared jokes until late. At the station Seth and Thabo's train arrived first and Sipho's train delayed arriving. By the time Sipho arrived at home it was 21h00. He found the house gate locked and there was no access for him. He moved around the perimeter and realized that there was somebody in the house and he could not call Linda loud and shout as it was late already, and he did not want to disturb the neighborhood. He went to the nearby garage and put up there for the night.

Chapter 40

The opening of the Johannesburg distribution branch brought a lot of excitement to Freddy. It was the beginning of expansion of his operation beyond Cape Town. He took his entire executive management to Johannesburg on the day of the launch. After the launch they were all going to fly back to the head office in Cape Town. Freddy called his PA to organize a huge celebration function for the entire company for that evening. "Spend whatever it takes to make this one a success. Tell the Production Manager to inform the chairman of the shop stewards that there will be no night shift tonight, but everybody must be there for the celebration."

"Do I organize a band for music sir?" asked the PA

"Yes. The function must be under a marquee that will accommodate all of us."

"Should it be inside or outside the premises?"

"It will be difficult for you to find anything outside now. Use the grounds behind the factory they are big enough to accommodate all of us."

"Mr. Phillips. Do I invite your wife sir?"

"No this is just for the workers only. It's not a formal function in fact it is just a get together celebration."

At the Cape Town airport Freddy requested the team to join him at the factory for the celebration. They all acceded to the request. The team drove to the factory after they had landed.

The celebration function started at 19h00. Freddy stood up to explain the reason for the gathering and he said "Today I would like to extend my sincere gratitude to all the Community Steel workers for our great achievement on expanding our company beyond the borders of Cape Town. It has been a dream of this company to extend our wings to the horizon. Nothing will stop us to fulfill this dream. The Johannesburg operation is the start of the things to come. I am standing here as the proud owner of this company fully supported by the executive management and you as the workers of this company."

"We love you Mr. Phillips," said one worker from the crowd.

"I would also like to tell you that I am planning to go beyond the borders of South Africa. My next trip will be to Asia where I would like to continue with what my father started, sell our products there. If it means that I must form partnership with one of the giant companies in steel industry there, I will do so. That will surely create more job opportunities for our country and our people in the Cape."

"Go for it, Mr. Phillips we are behind you all the way," shouted another worker.

"Tonight, I want all of us to enjoy this occasion. There will be no work after this. When we are done with the celebration everybody will go home. There is enough of everything for everyone. Enjoy yourselves. There are glasses with champagne on your tables, shall we all pick up our glasses and toast to this achievement?"

They all picked up their champagne glasses. "To Community Steel!!" screamed Freddy lifting his glass high.

They all followed "To Community Steel. Bottoms up!!!!"

The function continued with Freddy drinking a lot of red wine. When his PA realized that he had a lot to drink and he would not be able to drive home and it was getting late, she called Daniel to come pick him up. Daniel arrived at the factory at 23h30. Freddy's PA tried to convince him to get to Daniel's car and go home. He initially rejected the idea of being driven home and he felt that it was still too early for him to leave the function. Ultimately the PA won, and he went home with Daniel at about 00h20.

Daniel helped his boss to get out of the car. He walked him inside the house. As soon as Freddy got into the house, he shouted loud, "Thandi where are you? I am back. Why did you send Daniel to pick me up and not you?"

Thandi got out of the bedroom and stood on the balcony upstairs. She looked at her husband and went down the stairs to meet him. "Thanks Daniel. You can leave him now," said Thandi. She put Freddy's left arm around her neck and held him around the waist and climbed the stairs with him.

"I am your husband Thandi you ought to take care of me. I work very hard to keep the fire burning in this house," said Freddy with a sluggish voice. "Do you hear that Thandi?" asked Freddy with a louder voice.

Thandi kept quiet and just looked at him. When they reached the top of the balcony Freddy pulled himself away from Thandi. He looked at her and said "Did you hear what I said to you or not. Are you deaf why are you not responding to me?"

"What do you want me to say?" asked Thandi

"Is that all you can say to me after I told you what I do for you in this house?" said Freddy

"Can we go and sleep now it is late?"

"You are telling me to go to bed? Don't you know that nobody tells me what to do? You don't have respect woman," said Freddy as he slapped Thandi on her face. This came as a surprise to Thandi as she was not expecting it. Then a second one was followed by a kick in her stomach. She fell and rolled down the stairs uncontrollably. Thandi's scream caught Daniel's attention. He ran back to the house to check what was happening. He found Thandi lying at the bottom of the stairs with her face down sobbing.

"Thanks God she is still alive," he said. He quickly ran out to call Martha who was on the way responding to Thandi's scream.

"No woman has ever talked to me like that, not even my mother," said Freddy. He turned around and went to his bedroom. "I am giving you everything and you still want to control me. I am the man in this house not you. Your job here is to give me babies and that is what you are failing to do. Don't you know that I am the richest black man in this town? Daniel, Daniel!!" he called

"Yes sir," responded Daniel.

"Bring her up here," he said pointing to his bed.

Daniel ignored him and talked to Martha. "Quickly bring a blanket and we have to take her to the hospital," said Daniel.

"Ma'am!! Ma'am!! Is she still alive Daniel? Oh no my Lord. This boy is like his father. He is going to kill this poor child," said Martha.

"I am quickly going to take the car out of the garage. Please hold her until I come back." Daniel ran out of the door.

"Ma'am, ma'am talk to me please," pleaded Martha as she was talking to Thandi. She tried to turn Thandi around. As she was turning her, she noticed blood on her lower part of the body. It was a lot of blood. "Oh, Thandi I hope you didn't lose the baby." She quickly dragged her away from the blood stain that was on the tile. She put Thandi down and ran to the visitor's bedroom to fetch a pillow and a small blanket to support and cover Thandi. Just after covering her and as she was putting Thandi on the pillow Daniel arrived.

"Can she stand?" asked Daniel

"I should think so. She is awake and I think she can move. Can you go and open the car door meanwhile I am bringing her," said Martha trying to send Daniel away from seeing the blood. She didn't want Daniel to know that she was pregnant because this was their secret with Thandi as women. Thandi didn't want to tell Freddy before the end of the first trimester. The only person who knew about the pregnancy was Martha. Thandi was just over three months pregnant.

After cleaning Martha picked Thandi up and she was in great pain. She asked Martha to be very steady with her. She stood up with great difficulty. With the help of Martha, they walked slowly toward the car. Daniel drove very fast to the hospital. The hospital paged her doctor who arrived without wasting time. Thandi was admitted. After some thorough examinations the doctor discovered that she bled profusely and had lost her pregnancy. Freddy's kick that landed on her belly must have done some damage to her womb. The doctor indicated that her chances of conceiving a baby in future were very slim. Thandi complained about her left arm that had pains. The X-Ray revealed a fracture of the radius. The doctor had called the police when he saw how badly Thandi looked. He wanted to open a case of abuse but when the police came, he changed the story because Thandi refused to lay a charge against her husband for the fear of damaging his reputation. She told the doctor not to tell anyone about the incident and that Freddy should never know that she lost a pregnancy and that there is a possibility of her not be able to conceive again.

Freddy woke up very late the following morning. He looked around the bedroom for Thandi and she was nowhere. He woke up and put on his gown and went downstairs. He went to the kitchen because there was a noise coming from there.

"Morning Martha," he greeted

"Good morning, sir," said Martha with the slight bend of her knees as a sign of respect.

"Have you seen my wife?"

Martha was quiet for a while. "Yes, no sir, can I go and call Daniel I think he might know where she is," said Martha shivering not knowing what to say exactly. She knew very well that Daniel is the only person that Freddy listens to.

"Where is Daniel?"

"He is outside washing the cars sir," said Martha as she was going out to call Daniel.

"No stay here, I will go to him," said Freddy with a bit of suspicion.

Freddy walked outside and found Daniel busy cleaning one of the cars inside. "Good morning Daniel," he said.

"Good morning, sir," replied Daniel.

"Are you well this morning?" he asked with caution as he could realize that there was something wrong. Thandi had never been away from home so early in the morning. Martha's doubtfulness about Thandi's whereabout made him more suspicious. It was important for him to be very diplomatic with Daniel as it seems he was the one with information. "Daniel, do you have any idea where my wife could be this morning?" he asked Daniel respectfully. Daniel is the one who brought him up. They know each other very well. He was also aware that Daniel was a very straight forward person who did not take any nonsense.

Daniel looked at him and looked down. "What was wrong with you last night? Why do you allow liquor to make a beast out of you? Do you know that you nearly killed that girl? What's wrong with you Freddy?" asked Daniel with a concerned face.

Daniel brought Freddy up and taught him quite a lot of things. Daniel is fully aware of the respect they have of each other though Freddy is now his boss. As an elder he can still reprimand him if he put his foot on the wrong direction. When it comes to domestic affairs Freddy respects Daniel a lot.

"What did I do?" he asked

"Don't you know what you have done?"

"I know I had a lot of red wine at work. How I got home I can't tell. What happened last night?"

"Do you use drugs Freddy?"

"No, you know I don't," he responded

"What kind of liquor did you take yesterday that made you not to remember what you did?"

"I have just told you sir that I took a lot of red wine."

"Thandi is at the hospital. She's been admitted there from yesterday evening."

"Oh my God! What happened?"

"I think it will be proper for you to get into that car and drive to hospital as soon as possible and find out from her."

He rushed back to the house and called his PA to organize a bouquet of flowers. "Call the hospital for Thandi's ward and arranged for the flowers to be delivered to her," he said to his PA. He washed and drove to the hospital.

Thandi had ordered the doctor not to allow anybody in her ward, not even her husband. She was kept in a secluded single ward. She was not in a mood to talk to Freddy after the incident.

"My name is Freddy Phillips, and I am looking for my wife Thandi Phillips," he said at the reception desk.

"Mr. Phillips I will have to call your wife's doctor. He said we should call him if there is anybody looking for Mrs. Phillips," explained the lady at the reception desk.

"Okay."

The doctor came and greeted Freddy. "Good morning, Mr. Phillips. How do you do sir?"

"I am well doctor and how are you?"

"I am very well thanks. How can I help you sir?"

"I am here to see my wife."

"Can you come with me to my office Mr. Phillips please?"

"I am very sorry doctor. I am not here to sit in your office I want to see my wife."

"I would like to talk to you Mr. Phillips."

"Doctor I don't have time for trivial talks I want to see my wife, can't you hear that?"

"If that is the case Mr. Phillips, your wife is my patient and I have given instructions that nobody should see her because she is still in a very critical condition. She can't be disturbed."

"Damn you doctor, that is my wife you are talking about," he said with a loud voice.

"I am sorry Mr. Phillips. If you don't leave now sir, I will be forced to call the security and remove you from the hospital premises."

"If that woman dies in there, I am telling you I will sue you and this hospital," said Freddy as he was on his way out of the hospital.

Thandi could hear her husband voice from her ward. She wanted to wake up and go to the reception, but she had no strength. She didn't want to ring a bell for a nurse. She ended up closing her ears with her hands to shut off the noise from her husband.

Chapter 41

When Sipho and his friends arrived at the Community Steel Warehouse the following day, there was a queue of other work seekers already. They joined the queue. One of the guys said to them "If you guys want to be employed, they issue out coupons at that window and people with coupons will be the ones called out for employment." Sipho and his friends rushed to the window. Seth and Thabo got there first as Sipho was still tying the lace of his shoe. By the time he got there, there was someone else before him. He got a second number behind his friends. He said to the man in front of him:

"This is encouraging. Are you always coming here?" asked Sipho

"This is my third day," the man responded.

"This is my third week," said Sipho not telling the man the truth.

At the gate a man came out of the factory and said to all of them "All those with coupons I hope you do have your identification books with you. It must be a green barcoded SA identification book."

"Wow at last a person is going to get a job," said Sipho to the person in front of him.

"I should think Linda will be happy when she hears that I managed to get a job at last," he whispered.

"To those of you who have coupons, we will take a certain number today and then another number tomorrow. If your number is not called today, please do keep your coupon for tomorrow and for days to come. Everybody with a coupon will be employed as long you have green SA ID. No coupon no job," said the clerk.

As the queue was getting shorter and shorter toward Sipho, he was getting more excited. His friends were also elated about the job prospects. The queue got very short, and it was his friends and the man in front him turn. The clerk took Seth and Thabo. After writing their names he lifted his eyes and said "That's it for the day guys. We will continue tomorrow with the list. We have to process these that we have taken, so that by tomorrow they can start working."

"Can't you just take the two of us sir please," begged Sipho. "I am coming from afar. Please be merciful just the two of us."

"If I take the two of you then the man behind you will also plead for himself and the other and the other. So, I will stop here to avoid that. I will continue tomorrow. It is not like you are not going to be employed, not today but tomorrow. At least tomorrow you will be in the first two, you will not have to wait the whole day like today. You can see your coupon number is placing at position two. You will have to be here early because when we call your number you will have to be here. Once we jump you, your turn will be after we have completed all the numbers. Once that happens, I cannot guarantee you any employment," said the clerk.

"Sipho, can you wait for us please?" asked Seth.

"Yes, I will."

On their way to the station Thabo and Seth were thrilled about the new job. They tried to console Sipho, and they were telling him that he also will be employed the following day. Sipho got the last train before his friends and not long the train for the other two arrived. By the time Sipho disembarked it was 22h30. He had to walk home alone because there was nobody else who had disembarked at the station, in fact the train itself was almost empty.

He got off the station and started walking home. The streetlights were not working unlike the previous night, and it was very dark. One could not see further than a few meters away. The path was paved. He decided to walk faster. As he was turning in one of the corners, he felt something heavy landing on his left shoulder. He went straight to the ground and luckily, he balanced with his hands and did not hit the ground with his face. When he tried to wake up another heavy object hit him on head, somebody kicked him on the belly, another shoe on his face. He crouched in to protect his face with both his hands. Another heavy blow landed on his ribs.

He tried to scream but the voice could not come out. The three guys continued to assault him as he was on the ground. The next thing one of them saw a police patrol car coming. They all ran away. Lucky enough as they were running away one of the police spotted them, but they disappeared in the bush nearby. The police got out of the car, and they used their torches to search for what the guys were attacking. They found Sipho fallen in a shallow ditch bleeding, swollen and unconscious.

They searched for his identification, but they could not find anything on him. They drove him to the hospital. Sipho could hardly talk. After the police explained what they saw, they left him in the care of the hospital staff. His face was swollen beyond recognition, some of his ribs were fractured and he had a cut that was bleeding heavily on the head. He had lost blood and he needed some few stitches on the right side of his head.

Sipho was admitted into the ICU. His face was bandaged and only one eye could see hazily. He was supported by the machines to assist his breathing. He regained his consciousness after two days but still could not talk, nor see properly or recognized where he was.

He kept his eyes closed because he did not know where he was. The next thing he heard was a familiar voice not too far from him saying "I am in a hurry doctor. The Paeds department has a meeting starting in two seconds from now. I am rushing there," said the voice.

Sipho could recognize the voice and trying to think who the owner was. Unfortunately, he could not see properly and could not move his arms and fingers as they were swollen. Then he later remembered that it was Linda's voice.

"Where am I?" he thought to himself. "I heard Linda's voice. How did I get here? Where is my coupon for the job? How am I going to get to work?" he tried to move his body. The pains reminded him where he was. A solitary tear came out of the only eye that could see. He could feel pains all over his body.

After a week he was taken out of ICU to a male medical ward. The swelling from his eyes, face and fingers had subsided though his voice was still not back. The bandages had been removed and his eye could see but he could not walk yet. He wrote his name on a paper and handed it over to the nurses.

He called one of the nursing sister and requested a pen and a paper. He wrote on the paper: Do you know Doctor Linda Sibeko? He showed the paper to the nurse. After reading the message the nurse nodded her head signaling that she does know her.

Do you know where she is working? he continued writing. "Yes Sipho, I do, do you know her?" she asked.

Yes. Can you tell her that Sipho wants to see her please? "Okay."

The sister went to Paeds department to look for Doctor Sibeko. At the reception desk she asked for Doctor Sibeko, and she was shown where she was.

"Doctor Sibeko."

"Yes sister."

"I am from the male medical ward can I talk to you in private please?" they moved outside the room. "There is a gentleman in the male ward by the name of Sipho. He is asking to see you."

"Sipho? What is he doing here?" asked Linda.

"What happened here Doctor is that this man was brought in about a week back by the police at night. He was attacked and beaten up by thugs. He came in with swollen face, fractured ribs and he was unconscious. They took everything he had, and we could not identify him because he could hardly talk. He was kept in ICU on ventilation for few days. Last week he was moved to male medical ward. He still can't talk. He wrote his message on the paper as I was talking to him."

"What is his bed number," asked Linda as if she doesn't know him.

"Bed 21A."

"Thank you, sister. I will come after my ward rounds," said Linda. She hadn't looked for Sipho for the past week since Sipho disappeared. She had never bothered to report him missing to the police. She decided to go to the ward and talk to Sipho immediately the nurse was gone. She walked into the ward and saw Sipho on the bed. She went to him and closed the screen to isolate him from the rest so that they could have privacy. With a low voice she whispered into Sipho's ears and said "You make one mistake of telling these people that you are my husband I will personally see to it that you remain in this hospital for the rest of your life. Don't ever call me again or talk to people about me. I am a medical doctor in this hospital, and I will not have you to come here and tarnish my status. Am I making myself clear?"

Sipho nodded to show that he heard her.

She turned around and went out of the ward. Sipho turned and face the wall and tears began to roll down from his eyes. "God what have I done to this woman? Why does she hate me so much?" he whispered to himself.

Chapter 42

Thandi was discharged from the hospital. She called Daniel to pick her up and drove her home. The first thing when she got at home was to call her father just to check how the family was.

"Good afternoon, Daddy."

"Oh! Goodness God. Thank you. Hi my baby! How are you? I am so happy to hear your voice."

"Why Daddy?"

"Daniel told me what happened, and I couldn't come and see you because he told me that nobody is allowed to visit you. I also wanted to respect that. How are you doing now baby?"

"What did Daniel tell you that made you not to come and see me," asked Thandi

"He said you fell from the stairs, and you were slightly unconscious," explained Lesley.

"Yes, I did I slipped on the last step and lost my balance. I fell uncontrollably. I also broke my left arm."

"That sounds very funny. Are you sure that this had nothing to do with that husband of yours?" asked Lesley suspiciously.

"Yes daddy. Freddy is great. I will be fine. How is mom doing and my two little brothers?" asked Thandi to change the topic.

"Everybody is doing well. Your mom and your brothers have gone to visit your grandmother she is not feeling well. They are going to stay there for their school holidays."

"Are you now alone at home dad?"

"Yes, but your mom is coming back today. She has just gone to see her mom and drop off the kids."

"Ok. I've got to go now dad. Will talk to you later," she said.

"Thandi, you know that you are my child. If things don't work out with your marriage you know you can always come back home."

"I am fine dad, beside this is the life I chose for myself. I took vows with Freddy, and I will always respect them no matter what. I will not leave him daddy. I made a promise to his mother and his father. I appreciate what you are saying, and I love you as my father, but I have another person in my life that is very dear and important to me. And Freddy needs me more than anybody else."

"I am not trying to change your mind, all what I am saying you is that you do have a home if things are not working out. You know very well that I will always respect your decision. I have always taught you to learn from your own mistakes. Goodbye now. Love you."

"Bye daddy. Love you too," she dropped the call "Why is daddy talking like this, I hope Daniel did not tell him the truth," she whispered to herself. She dialed her husband's phone number and the cell phone was on voice mail. She decided that she was going to visit Sarah at the salon. Before she went out, she looked herself in the mirror. "How can you go out there like this Thandi when your face shows signs of being battered?" she asked herself.

This brought tears into her eyes. The words of her mother-in-law came back to her as she was standing in front of the mirror. She could hear her clearly saying to her "No matter what happens do not leave my son." She knew deep down in her that she was dealing with a wounded person. Somebody who has never been loved before and who does not know the value of relationship. He is a person who treats people like objects. Somebody who thinks material things are all that matters.

Her thoughts were disturbed by her phone. She picked it up and it was her husband "Hi baby. How are you doing?"

"Hi, my love, I am well and you? I saw your missed call. Where are you? Are you still at the hospital?"

"I am also well baby thanks. I called to tell you that I am out of hospital, and I am home now."

"I am sorry I was in a meeting. I should be at home in two hours' time. Can we go out for the dinner?"

"I don't think so but let's talk when you come back home. I am going to take a nap now. I am sure by the time you arrive I would be fine. Please do wake me up if I will still be sleeping."

"Will do so my sweetheart. Bye now. Love you," sounded Freddy apologetically.

"Bye baby. Love you too my darling."

She called Martha and asked her to give some fruit and her pain tablets. After eating the fruit, she drank the tablets and went to the bedroom and slept.

Freddy arrived with a huge bouquet of flowers and a box of chocolate.

He asked Martha if Thandi was still in bed.

"Yes, sir she still sleeping," responded Martha.

He walked up the stairs and opened the bedroom door very slowly and quietly so as not to make noise and disturb her. He tiptoed near to the bed put the flowers and the box of chocolates next to the bed and he tip toed back to the door. Just when he was about to get out of the room a voice said, "hi love, are you back?"

He turned around and went straight to her and gave her a kiss and held her onto him for some time without saying a word. He held her with both his hands on her face and looked straight in her eyes and said "I am very sorry I am sorry. I will never do this to you again I promise. I love you baby I really love you. You are all that I have please don't ever think of leaving me."

Thandi pushed her head toward his chest and hold him around his waist with her head on his chest and said to him "I love you too baby I love you, my darling. I will not leave you. I will always be by your side."

"Are you sure you don't want us to eat out?" he asked her.

"Baby I am not in a mood of going anywhere. Can I prepare something for us here at home if you don't mind?"

"Ok let me cancel Sam and Johnson. I have asked them to bring their wives with them so that you can meet them and their spouses."

"I know Sam and Johnson; you have told me a lot about them. I will meet them and their wives some other time."

"Okay, you stay in bed I will get Martha and the two of us will prepare something for us."

"Please don't go and burn my pots. I have never seen you cooking," she said with a smile

"I am the best cook you have ever seen. Wait and see what you are going to eat tonight," he responded with laughter and stood up and walked out of the bedroom leaving her alone to continue with her sleep or enjoy her flowers and chocolate.

As they were eating around the table Freddy told her about their trip to Johannesburg and the success of the distribution outlet in Wadeville. He also told her about his intended trip to Malaysia to expand the business. They talked about how Sam and Johnson have been committed to the business since his father's time. He also told her that for the trip to Malaysia he was intending to take the two guys with him. "They form a pillar of strength around me," he said.

Thandi was listening to the conversation half-heartedly. The pain that she was feeling from inside of losing her child was beginning to take its toll. What made it worse was the fact that she could not share the pain with somebody she loved and who was the father of the child. She remembered her grandmother's words when she told her how she dealt with her pain when she lost a child that was born before her mother. She could still hear her grandmother's words reverberating in her ears saying "My child. Men cannot comprehend the pain that women go through when they have lost a pregnancy. You should never waste your time trying to explain to them. You have to deal with the pain as a woman." It was worse with her because Freddy didn't even know that she was pregnant.

As they were talking Freddy could see that there was something bothering her, but he was afraid to ask less he peels off a healing wound. Freddy was not sure if he should continue with the conversation even though he could see inside the closed book or to keep quiet and take the risk of quietness.

"The food was delicious. I didn't know that you can cook. Do you have some work to do?" asked Thandi.

"Thanks, my love. Martha did the bulk of cooking I was helping her here and there. Yes, baby I had to finish my presentation. We have a meeting with government people tomorrow."

"I am going back to bed. Leave the dishes Martha will take care of them," she said as she stood up to go to bed.

"I won't be long because I have already started the presentation on my way here."

He stood up to give his wife a kiss and said to her "Good night my love. I will join you as soon as I finish my presentation."

"Good night sweetheart. Please don't forget to switch the alarm on when you are coming to bed," she said

As Thandi got into bed and about to sleep, her phone rang. She picked it up and looked at it. She saw that it was Sarah.

"Hi Sarah. How are you doing?"

"I am doing well Thandi thanks and how are you doing?" asked Sarah with a low voice.

"I am doing fine thanks for asking," she responded with difficulty.

"Thandi everything that is this house and at the saloon is still yours. You can come back home at any time you want too. You are not forced to stay there if you don't feel like, or it is too much for you."

"What are you talking about Sarah. This is my home now. I am married to Freddy, and I will not go anywhere. How told you about what had happen?"

"It is not for me to tell you who told me. My concern is your life my dear. Your grandmother left you with a lot of wealth and you don't need that marriage to keep you alive. You can come back and take over everything. I will rather have you back here than seen you dead."

"Sarah I am a married woman now. Freddy is my husband. The wealth that you are talking about will not give me the joy of being Freddy's wife. I will not leave my husband for anything. I took a vow with him. Death do us part."

"But Thandi-"

"There is no but about it Sarah. I will be fine. Thanks for your concern. You keep well ok. Pass my greetings to your daughter. Good night," interjected Thandi

"Good night Thandi. I love you."

"I love you too Sarah." Thandi dropped the phone.

"I wonder who told her about the incident," whispered Thandi.

Chapter 43

The loss and the mourning of her baby brought more misery to Thandi. She was always indoors. She lost weight and was in tears most of the time. What was more painful to her was the fact that she was not going to be able to conceive again. The contact between her and Freddy was not as usual. She allowed Freddy to spend more time at work than at home. She didn't know what to do with her time. One day still in her bed Martha walked in her bedroom and said "Ma'am I think it is high time that you get out of that bed and move around. You are sitting here mourning the death of your child. Do you know how many children are abandoned by their parents from birth in the hospital and need mothers to take care of them? Maybe you should consider adopting one."

"Are there kids like that at the hospital really?" asked Thandi.

"Yes, ma'am there are. I can go with you to the hospital if you would like to see them."

"Yes of course, I would like to see them. When can we go there? I have never been to a public hospital."

"Can we go this afternoon?" asked Martha.

"Yes, Martha I don't have any commitments for the day."

After Thandi had introduced herself and her purpose to the nurse at the front desk in the Pediatric ward, the nurse decided to call the sister–in-charge. The sister-in-charge introduced herself and asked who Thandi was. "Are you Mrs. Phillips the wife to the famous Mr. Phillips?" asked the sister.

"Yes sister. Is there something wrong?"

"No ma'am, there is nothing wrong. It's just that we never get visits from rich people like you in our facilities. Can you please wait here I will be back soon," said the sister? She came back with a lady in white coat. "Doctor this is Mrs. Phillips the wife to the owner of Community Steel, she is here to visit the pediatric ward and has a special interest in our work with the abandoned children. Mrs. Phillips this is Dr. Hause the head of Pediatrics in the hospital."

"Good afternoon, Mrs. Phillips. How do you do?" asked the doctor.

"Good afternoon doctor. I am well thanks and how are you?" responded Thandi.

"I am good Mrs. Phillips. How can we help you?" asked the doctor. After Thandi explained about her visit and what prompted the visit, the doctor sympathized with her and decided to take her around the whole department.

Thandi's heart was touched when she saw the neonates at the nursery and when they got to the children's ward she was almost in tears. After the tour Dr. Hause invited Thandi to her office for a cup of coffee. "How are you coping with the loss Mrs. Phillips?"

"It is not easy Dr. Hause, but I am trying my best."

"Was it your first pregnancy?"

"Yes, it was doctor."

"Once again I am very sorry."

"As I have said to you before, that this is the first time I am visiting a public hospital and I am amazed at the amount of work being done here. You know us with our medical aid we visit private hospitals only and we never get to know the challenges faced by our people in the public hospitals. I am very impressed with what you guys are doing with the little that you have. I would like to play a part in giving back to the community by joining you in this project of taking care of the sick and abandoned children. I am going to donate to your department an amount of one and half million rand toward the renovation of your pediatric wards. I hope this will go a long way to helping you achieve your goals as a department."

"Wow, Mrs. Phillips that is a great and generous offer, you really are a God sent, it is as if you knew how much we have been struggling to make ends meet. We are very grateful for the offer, and I know the hospital Superintendent will be delighted to hear this, I can't wait to tell him the exciting news."

"Whatever is left you can buy linen for the ward. If there is any shortage you must inform me, please. I really would like to see this place looking as beautiful as those little angels that I saw today. I would like to spoil them. What do I write on this check," she asked as she was taking out a check book out of her bag?

"You can address the check to the hospital and in brackets you write pediatrics. Once again thank you very much for the donation," said the doctor.

"You are most welcome doctor. I hope one day I will visit the hospital as one of your patients."

"You mean coming to give birth? How I wish I could be here on that day."

"Why are you saying that doctor? Are you planning to leave the hospital?" asked Thandi

"I am due for pension Mrs. Phillips so I can leave at any time. I hope there will be another doctor by then."

"Thank you for your time, Dr. Hause. I hope to see you again," said Thandi as she was getting out of the door.

"It's my pleasure Mrs. Phillips. Thank you for everything and thank you for the visit."

"Where is Martha now?"

"Here am I ma'am," reply Martha

"Thank you for bringing me here. This has opened my eyes, I really enjoyed being here, and I am definitely going to come again"

Chapter 44

Freddy had the Midas touch. Everything business wise was going well for him. The trip to Malaysia was a success. He came back from Malaysia with his team very excited. The Malaysians agreed to buy the steel for 5 million over the period of 18 months as the start. The steel was going to be shipped in batches to Malaysia. Freddy and his crew were given the assignment of working out a schedule of how much steel could be produced in six months and the lead time to Malaysia once shipped. Once that was all worked out the Malaysian team was going to fly to South Africa to conclude the deal.

They landed in Cape Town from Johannesburg at 22h30. He requested the team to go to the factory to work on the proposal so that it can be emailed the following day. He called the factory manager, raw material supervisor, workers union representative and his PA to the factory. The whole crew worked on the proposal with telephone calls made to CEOs of the different suppliers at night. During the working session the PA ordered a lot of food for the crew.

At 05h30 the other crew members left except for Freddy, Johnson, Sam and the PA. They stayed behind to fine tune the costing of production and prepared the document for submission. Everything was done and dusted by 07h15.

"Good morning guys. I will see you if at all at about 14h00 this afternoon, said Sam and Johnson to their boss and the PA.

"Thanks Sam and Johnson, thanks for your sacrifice. Pass my apologies to your wives for keeping you here the whole night after you were not at home for almost a week. Tell them once this deal is signed, I will send you guys to Mauritius for a paid holiday. I appreciate everything that this team had done for Community Steel. You don't have to be here for the 14h30 meeting. I will take care of it. You can take the day off today," said Freddy.

He sent his PA home, and he closed the curtains of his office and locked his door. He told the lady at the company switch board not to wake him up for any call either than a call from overseas. He took a nap on his reclining chair. He didn't want to go home because he was expecting a response from the Malaysian people on the proposal. He was hardly three hours in his sleep when his land line rang. It was the lady from the switchboard. "I am sorry sir for waking you up. You have an urgent call from Malaysia. The gentleman wants to talk to you now."

"Ok put him through."

"Good morning, it's Freddy Phillips on the line. How can I help you?"

"Mr. Phillips, you talking to Mr. Chai the owner of Chai Steel. We met last week. Good morning to you sir. I believe it is in the morning in your country by now. We are in the afternoon already in ours. I hope you and your crew had a pleasant flight back home. Mr. Phillips thank you for the proposal it looks very good."

The conversation between him and Mr. Chai went on for almost 15 minutes. He was doing a lot of scribbling during their conversation.

"Thank you, Mr. Chai. We will meet in Johannesburg next week on Thursday." He dropped the phone. He was very excited about the deal but still had some reservation.

"It is only when these guys are here in the country next week will I know that this deal is through," he whispered to himself. "I will not tell anybody about it until I sign on the dotted line." He packed his briefcase called Daniel to come and pick him up. Got home and freshen up for the next meeting which was at 14h30.

Thandi was not around she had gone to town.

It was Wednesday afternoon when Mr. Chai called Freddy to tell him that they had arrived in Johannesburg safely. "I have emailed you the contract just now. I want you to have a look at it, so that we can discuss it tomorrow, if there are any matters you are not comfortable with."

"Thank you, Mr. Chai. I can see the contract. Let me have a look at it I will come back to you soon. Where about are you in Johannesburg?"

"We are at the Michelangelo Hotel in Sandton. What time are we going to meet on Thursday?" asked Chai.

"Let me meet you guys at the hotel at 11h00 if that will be in order with you."

"That's fine with me. I will schedule the other meetings from there on wards. We are going to be here for a while, we will be going back on Tuesday next week. We have some other business to take care of."

Freddy summoned Sam and Johnson to his office. He asked his PA to print three hard copies of the contract. The three closed themselves in Freddy's office and scrutinized the contract. After some very minor changes here and there they emailed the contract back to Mr. Chai who responded back to them immediately with an acceptable response. "Guys this calls for celebration. This is one of the biggest contracts that we have worked on successfully."

"I fully agree with you Mr. Phillips. This is a breakthrough for our company. It is going to open doors for us for future overseas businesses if we handle it well," echoed Johnson.

"Let's break the news to the work force," said Freddy.

"Don't you think we can do that when you come back with the signed contract on Friday morning?" asked Sam.

"I should think Sam is right sir. Do that on Friday morning when you come back from Johannesburg," said Johnson

"Fine guys I will do so but the three of us let us go and celebrate for our hard work. The company is going to pay for all tonight expenses," said Freddy "We are not going to spend the whole night. You have a plane to catch tomorrow morning," said Sam to Freddy.

"Yes, I know that. Everything is in order. I will try and go to bed early tonight"

"Why don't we go now if that is the case?" asked Johnson.

"Yes, let's go," said Sam.

"Where are we going?" he asked

"To the Waterfront, I am also starving. I feel like eating some seafood tonight," said Freddy.

"If that's the case then the Waterfront will be the best place now," added Johnson.

"I will drive with one of you guys to the Waterfront then I will call Daniel to pick me up from there. He will drop me at the airport tomorrow so that I don't have to leave my car at the airport." said Freddy.

"Let's all use one car. Sam and I don't live far from each other. I can drop him and pick him up tomorrow morning if that's fine with you Sam?" said Johnson.

"It's ok with me," responded Sam.

They all drove in Johnson's car to the Waterfront. Freddy called Daniel to pick him at about 22h30 from the Waterfront. He also called Thandi to tell her that he was going to be late. They spent five hours at the restaurant eating and drinking. They were all in a happy mood. They got so drunk that they did not have time to remind Freddy about the time to go home. At 22h45 Daniel got out of the car to go and look for his boss. He found him in the restaurant completely drunk. He carried him to the car and then organized a cab for Sam and Johnson because they were not in a state where they would be able to drive themselves. He then asked the restaurant owner to forward their bill to the company and he promised that it would be paid. The owner did not have a problem because he knew Freddy in person and knew Daniel as Freddy's driver.

Daniel carried Freddy inside the house and left him by the door because he instructed Daniel to do so. Daniel got out of the house and proceeded to his room. Thandi was standing at the inside balcony next to their bedroom. Freddy walked up to the stairs railing and called Thandi to come and help him up the stairs. He called for her several times before Thandi responded from the balcony and asked him why he was calling her. "You asking me why am I calling you? How the hell do you think am I going to get to my bedroom?" asked Freddy.

"Can't you go up the stairs all by yourself?" she asked him politely.

"Are you crazy woman? Don't you know that it is your duty to see to it that I get to my bedroom safe? You know I can't climb these steps without your help, or you want me to call Daniel to come and help me?" Thandi went down the stairs to help him up. They got into the bedroom and Freddy asked Thandi to help him taking off his clothes. "I am doing all this for you. You ought to be happy and not give me the stinking attitude you are giving me now. There are a lot of women out there who would like to be Mrs. Phillips and take care of me."

"Do you think all that you are doing is important to me? Is that what you think?" asked Thandi with fury and raised voice. "If you think there are better women out there, why don't you go to them then?"

Freddy turned around with a blow that landed on Thandi's face. The blow sent Thandi on the floor, when she tried to get up, he followed the blow with a kick. The kick was so hard that she rolled on the floor. She did not make any noise. She absorbed all that without screaming. She did not want Daniel and Martha to hear the commotion. It's only Freddy's voice that was raised.

Outside Daniel and Martha were standing outside their rooms listening to the commotion.

"Do you think we should call the police?" asked Martha

"I don't know Martha I honestly don't know. If Freddy goes to jail, we will lose our jobs. He is currently paying our salaries," said Daniel

"Then you have to go and stop him Daniel. That boy is going to kill that poor child. She is such a sweet girl," said Martha.

"Get out of my bedroom you barren ….. You are sitting here, and you can't even give me children. Get out of my house. I will get a woman who can give me children. You are an ungrateful woman. I work hard to give you the life that you are enjoying, and you come and tell me that nonsense. Tomorrow morning, I am going to Johannesburg to sign multimillion rand deal for this family, and you come and treat me with disrespect," shouted Freddy.

Thandi stood up and walked out of the room. She closed the bedroom door behind her. She went down the stairs to the visitor's bedroom and cleaned herself, said a short prayer and went to bed. Before she slept, she called Freddy's PA to check the time for Freddy's flight in the following morning. The PA told her that it was a 07h30 flight to Johannesburg. She called Daniel on his cell phone to inform him about the flight and to take his boss to the airport.

The following morning, she woke up early and went to the main bedroom. She found Freddy sleeping and she tip toed to the dressing room and took out Freddy's clothes for the trip. She prepared the breakfast for her husband as it was a norm for him to have his breakfast before any morning trip. After this she went back to the visitor's bedroom and slept.

Freddy woke up late that morning. He rushed to the bathroom and quickly ate his breakfast and called Daniel to take him to the airport. He did not have time to give his wife a goodbye kiss as usual because Thandi was sleeping when Freddy left.

Freddy was late by the time he got at the airport. Daniel dropped him at the drop-off zone. He rushed to the check-in point. Because of the weight and him rushing, he started to perspire heavily. His breathing started to be heavy and regular. Just some few meters to the check-in-point Freddy collapsed and fell on the floor. The security quickly called the Paramedics, and they took him to the airport emergency room, and they tried to resuscitate him. An ambulance arrived and took him to the hospital. Freddy died on the way to the hospital because when he got there the doctor declared him DOA.

It was 09h15 when Thandi was woken up from sleep by the knock at the door. It was Martha knocking.

"Who is that?" she asked.

"It is me ma'am," responded Martha

"Come in Martha."

Martha opened the door and stood by the door.

"Ma'am there are two policemen outside and they want to talk to you. They are refusing to tell me why they want to talk to you."

Thandi quickly put on her gown and rushed to the mirror to check if she can receive them. No, she looked very bad one of her eyes was puffed up badly.

"Martha bring them in and let them stand by my door I will talk to them," she commanded

The two constables walked in, and Martha ordered them to stand next to the door because Mrs. Phillips is not well, and she can't come out of the room.

"Mrs. Phillips we are the police is it you in there?" asked the constable

"Yes, constable it's me," she responded

"Mrs. Phillips we would like to talk to you," said the constable

"I am very sorry constable you will have to talk to me standing there I am not in a position to talk to you in person."

"Ma'am there has been an accident; your husband Mr. Phillips is late. He died this morning on the way to the hospital. He collapsed at the airport before checking-in."

There was silence for a while. "Mrs. Phillips! Are you still there?" asked one of the police.

Martha opened the door and closed it again she went to her boss and wrapped her arms around her. Thandi did not know whether to cry or not. She was confused because she did not expect this. Losing a husband is very painful to every wife irrespective of what the husband was to his wife. Especially if it is an unexpected death.

"Yes, constable she is fine. I will be with her thank you," said Martha Thandi locked herself in her bedroom and ordered Martha and Daniel to allow no one into the yard.

She wanted to be alone for the day so that she can go through the mourning and digest what has just happened to her.

The pain she was filling brought mixed emotion in her. Losing a husband was extremely painful. The thoughts of the end of the abuse were bringing a relief in her. The body needed a rest, but the mind refused to give her that rest because it was working overtime. She was lying on her back on the bed completely oblivious of the surrounding noise and the time.

In that quietness of her bedroom, she heard Freddy's voice saying, "tomorrow morning I am going to Johannesburg to sign multimillion rand deal for this family, and you come and treat me with disrespect."

She looked around thinking she was hearing Freddy. She kept quiet again. Then another voice of her father-in-law, "you are now the only Mrs. Phillips alive. You are a member of the Phillips family. Community Steel is part of this family. I have worked hard to build that company Thandi. Please whatever happens, do not allow your husband to sell it to anybody. It must remain within the family for the years to come."

She got on her feet and started pacing the room. "Freddy is gone. He will not come back again. Do I lie in this room and lose the company too? I am the only Phillips that is now alive. I promised my father-in-law not to lose that company. Thandi wake up girl and smell the coffee. The time for mourning is coming but now save what you are about to lose."

It was in the afternoon when she called her husband's PA and told her to get Sam or Johnson to call her. Johnson returned the call immediately. "Good morning, Johnson. It's Mrs. Phillips here. I hope you guys have heard what happened by now?"

"Yes, ma'am we have. We have also informed everybody in the factory already," responded Johnson. "Sam was just about to call you."

"Did somebody call the Malaysian guys to let them know about what has happened?" she asked

"Yes ma'am, I had sent them an email immediately when we got the news. Mr. Chai has acknowledged receipt of email and has sent their condolences. They have postponed the signing of the contract depending on our availability," said Johnson.

"Thank you. I will call him later. Can you forward me his number and the email address please? I will try to arrange for the funeral soon. Unfortunately, we cannot keep them for long because the business must go on." After the call Thandi called her father.

"Freddy has passed on Daddy," she said with tears in her eyes.

"I heard it from the news this morning. When I called, Martha answered your phone and said you gave them strict instruction not to be disturbed. I was waiting for your call. How are you coping? Do you need me to come over?"

"Yes, daddy yes. I will appreciate if you and mom you can be here."

"Your mom will not make it because of the children. I will be there first thing in the morning. When are you intending to bury him?"

"We will talk about that tomorrow, though I was thinking to do that as soon as possible because of the business."

"Ok let's talk tomorrow then."

Chapter 45

The funeral was scheduled for Saturday. The factory was closed. The funeral was held at the Cathedral. Sam had organized that all managers from work should come driving in black Mercedes Benz cars with their spouses wearing all black dresses, black hats and men wearing black suites and white shirts.

On top of the black attire that Thandi was wearing, she had a big black hat with a thick black veil that covered her face and dark sunglasses. This was to conceal the part of the blue eye that the make-up could not cover or mask. During the whole funeral proceeding she never lifted her head up. After the church service the convoy of black Mercedes Benz cars with the limousine in front and other cars for the employees made a procession behind a black hearse to the graveyard.

The sun was shining through trees, the flowers were in full bloom and the grass was green. It was all quiet at the cemetery, only the chirping of birds could be heard amid tranquility. Suddenly a black hearse followed by a limousine, a convoy of ten black Mercedes Benz cars and a group of people on foot broke the silence as they slowly moved into the graveyard while negotiating the winding road in the cemetery toward an empty tomb that was well decorated with red and white flowers.

Everyone inside the cars was wearing black suit and white shirt. Women were wearing black dresses and very modest black hats befitting the somber occasion.

Those who were in cars all alighted except for one occupant in the limo behind the hearse. Everybody walked behind the coffin carriers in a procession toward the open tomb. Men were behind the coffin carrier and followed by women and children.

Thandi was sitting alone at the back of the Limo as she had requested to be alone with just the driver.

She was sitting there with one of her eyes puffed up, heart pounding heavily and her mind going through the days, weeks, months and years of the rough ordeal she had in her marriage. She was looking outside the window but could see nothing; all that she could see and hear was the movie that was playing in her mind of her husband shouting, screaming at her and the abusive words that were now the daily bread whenever Freddy was drunk. The car had stopped for her to get out, but she could hardly notice that she was miles and miles away.

The door of the limo swung open, and the driver was standing waiting for the occupant to alight. The driver bent down and said something to the person inside the limo.

"Ma'am all the other mourners are by the graveside. Are you coming?" asked Daniel with the backdoor of the car wide open.

"Oh yes, I am Daniel. Are we at the graveside already?"

"Yes ma'am."

Thandi came out of the limo wearing black dress and a black hat with a thick black veil that covered her face. Her father was not standing far from the car. When Thandi came out he went to meet her halfway. She walked slowly toward the grave in her father's arm.

Though her face was concealed to the public she was still looking down as she made her way to the graveside, she remained like that during the entire proceedings. She was going through a heavy pain of losing her husband.

As the song "Time to say goodbye" was playing at the background and the coffin descending, Thandi went down on her knees and cry out loud as she removed the veil from her face and threw it on top of the descending coffin.

She lifted her head for the first time in public and looked up in the sky, took a heavy breath as tears were streaming down her cheeks. She looked at the coffin and said loudly, "what a painful journey of love. I will always love you Freddy. It is only God who knows why you left me so early in our lifetime. You've cut our married life too short and abruptly.

You leave me with empty life. Goodbye my love." She then threw herself on the ground and prostate with sobbing in the soft sound of music.

Daniel quickly stretched his hands to lift his boss's wife up, but Thandi's father Lesley told Daniel to leave her alone. He asked all other mourners to go back to their cars to give his daughter a chance to be alone at the grave side for few minutes. Only Daniel was allowed to keep an eye on her at a distance.

Her father knew everything about the way Freddy had abused his child over the years. He called her almost every day and begged her to come back home and divorce Freddy. Thandi would refuse to leave her husband and would tell her father that God hates divorce. She would say to him "Daddy if this is God's will that I should go through this then let it be so, I am praying for Freddy every day of my life. Besides this is a life I choose. Let me go through this with him."

When most people were gone, Thandi called her father aside, "could you please ask Johnson the operation director and Sam the financial director of Community Steel to remain behind I would like the two of us to talk to them."

"Is this now about the business?" asked Lesley

"Yes daddy. I would like them to come and present to me in your presence about the status of the company before you fly back to East London if you don't mind. There isn't that much that you will say, I will be doing most of the talking and questioning but for legal issues I am expecting you to take a leading role I will also ask for the HR director to be present."

"Would you like to talk to them at the same time or on different days?"

"Different days would be better, but I am thinking about you going back."

"I will be around for the rest of the week, I just have some business to do with one of our clients in Paarl then the rest of my time is to help you to recover, and then leave on Saturday with the morning flight. So, two different days would be the better option."

After Lesley and Thandi spoke to Johnson and Sam about the presentation, they both said they will be available on the agreed dates. Sam further suggested that his presentation be done at the company's boardroom as it will require a projector.

"What are you going to do with the company? Are you going to sell it or run it?" asked Lesley.

"I won't sell it daddy; I promised my father-in-law that I will look after it. I am going to get out of this house and go to work as from tomorrow. The Malaysians have extended their stay for another week to accommodate my schedule. We need to conclude the contract and start the production. I cannot afford to lose this contract. It will give the company a lot of exposure to overseas market."

"What do you mean when you said you are going to work tomorrow? Don't you want to stay at home and grieve for you husband at least for a week?" asked Lesley

"Daddy, Freddy is gone, and I have buried him. That company is my life now. I need to get up and start managing it. Nobody is going to do that for me. I have promised my father-in-law that the company will remain within the family. Right now, it needs me. The time for mourning is gone. It's business time now my daddy."

"Well, I can accompany you to the meeting if you don't mind," said Lesley

"Thanks for the offer Dad but I will go there with Sam and Johnson. These guys are going to be part of the company from now onwards. They were a cornerstone of this company during my father-in-law and my husband time. I am intending to use them also."

"Ok, if you say so. What are your plans about the company?" asked Lesley.

I am planning to break the company into two, instead of owning 100% shares. I will hold 70% and offer the other 30% to the two guys and the workers. The 15% will be for the workers, 5% to junior management and 10% for the two guys at 5% each if they are interested."

"Why are you offering the two guys shares in the company, if I may ask?"

"I want a long-lasting commitment from both daddy. Besides, Freddy told me that they have been with his father and acted as advisers for the company since from the beginning. They have been loyal to the company and executive directors since then. They have been a pillar to his father and to him. Don't you think it is time for them to be rewarded for their loyalty dad?"

"Ok, I think that is fair enough. Why 20% to the workers and junior management then?" asked Lesley.

"If the workers and junior management are part of the company, I should think that will motivate them to work hard and be dedicated to the company because they will be working for what is partly theirs. The issue of us and them scenario between the workers and owners in Community Steel will not exist. Everybody will see and view the company as for us all," responded Thandi

"And how are you going to sell the shares to them and the workers? Community Steel is a huge company, and the share price should be in millions"

"This is one of the things we will talk about on Friday after I have sold the idea to them, and they showed interest. Sam will tell us how much is the company worth and then we will work out the share price. I will give them at a discounted price," continued Thandi

"I am also interested in owning shares in Community Steels. Can you sell some to me also?"

"Yes, dad I will give you 10% of my 70% if those shares will be registered under my younger brethren's names. Will that be fine with you?"

"That is more than generous. I wasn't thinking of me I was think more of your brothers. It means I will have to sit in the board meeting on their behalf until they are old enough to do so."

Johnson presented the position of the company from the operations point of view to Thandi, Lesley, Sam and the chairperson of the Shop-steward on a Sunday afternoon. Everything was in order except the finalization of the deal that her husband was going to conclude with the Malaysian company. That was still pending, and the Malaysians were still interested. After she and Lesley had exhausted all questions Thandi thanked Johnson and the rest. She told Johnson that she would like to see him and the two other guys Friday morning to discuss some other issues. "I am also going to arrange a meeting with the Malaysians for Tuesday morning, and I would like you, Sam and the shop-steward to accompany me to the meeting."

"Sam, can you call the Malaysian and set up a meeting for this week. I wouldn't like to delay their order. Call them and tell them that we would like to see them on Tuesday morning at 09h30 in the same hotel. If that will be fine with them," said Thandi.

"They said they are ready for us at any time Mrs. Phillips. I spoke to them yesterday," continued Sam.

"Can you all call me Thandi please and stop this thing of Mrs. Phillips. Well, that's fine them. We will leave with the 06h00 flight on Tuesday morning. Sam get the PA to book the flight for the four of us," instructed Thandi.

The following day Sam gave his presentation to the same group. His was longer and more detailed. There were a lot of questions from everybody. Sam handled them all well and to the satisfaction of everybody. The company was in a healthy situation and very profitable.

"Do we have enough raw materials for the Malaysian order?" asked Thandi to Johnson.

"Yes, we do Thandi, everything has been ordered from the suppliers they are just waiting for us to finalize the procurement process, which Mr. Phillips was going to sign when he came back with the signed the contract."

"After signing on Tuesday, are we going to have enough raw materials to start? How are we going to see to it that we meet the deadlines?" asked Thandi

"The work force is prepared to work overtime Mrs. Phillips. We have already discussed this in our meeting last week," responded the shop-steward.

The signing of the contract went well, and the Malaysians were happy with Thandi and like her attitude toward business.

Chapter 46

It was a Friday morning in Thandi's house. She had called Sam, Johnson, her father and the chairman of shop stewards.

"Seeing that everybody is here, I want to discuss with you about the future of this company. I am planning to restructure the company and divide it into shares. I have decided to offer some company shares to Johnson, Sam and the workers. Depending if you guys are interested in the offer, we can talk about it on individual basis."

"How much are you offering the workers Mrs. Phillips, sorry Thandi? At what price?" asked the shop-steward.

"I want you to answer my first question of interest," responded Thandi

"Oh. Yes, we are. It will be very stupid for the workforce not to take the opportunity to be part of this company. Without consulting them I am sure no one will say no to this offer," responded the shop-steward.

"Well point taken. Let me hear from Sam and Johnson before we can talk about the allocation and price of shares."

They both showed an interest with enthusiasm.

"Well seeing that you all keen to my idea, let's start talk about the distribution of the percentages. I want to give 15% to the workforce and 5% to junior management and only to those workers and junior management who have worked 5 years and more with the company, 5% to Johnson and 5% to Sam for their loyalty of 15 years of unbroken service to the company. The shares to all of you guys will be sold at 20% discount. My father is buying 10% of my shares for my siblings also at 20% discount. If you all agree to my proposal then the shareholders of this company will be: 60% to the Phillips family, 20% to company employees, 10% to Khumalo family, 5% to Johnson and 5% to Sam. The

Phillips family will always have the right of first refusal to any one of you who will want to sell shares at market value," said Thandi.

"I think that is fair enough. I never thought that one day workers will be part of this company. That is quite encouraging Mrs. Phillips and it's a very bold step on your side. On behalf of the workforce, I would like to thank you for your generosity. Have you thought about how is the workforce going to pay for the shares? I am sure they must be in millions," asked the shop-steward.

"That's a very good question. Sam and I we will work out your pension contribution and see how we can utilize that for those who will be interested. I want you to go and sell this to the entire workforce and let us meet again on Monday in two weeks' time. To you Sam and Johnson, I will meet you individually to discuss the details. Thank you," concluded Thandi.

Do you want me to prepare a contract for this Mrs. Phillips?" asked Johnson with a smile.

"No Johnson, since you and my father are also involved into this, I will get an outside law firm to prepare a contract for us."

Thandi asked that Johnson to remain behind. "Can you organize a meeting for 18h00 with all other executives, senior managers for all divisions and supervisors. Arrange for catering with a braai for all those who will be present. All shift supervisors must be present. No brandy for catering only wine."

"Yes Thandi. How much should we put aside for catering for the meeting?" asked Johnson.

"Sort that one with Sam. You guys you know your people. Oh, don't forget to invite all the shop stewards. Thank you."

"I will do so," said Johnson.

"Can you tell my husband's PA that I will start working on Monday and she must clean my husband's office but leave the desk and everything on it please. She must leave all the pictures my husband's photos hanging and any other thing that will require my attention should be on top of the desk."

"What about her?"

"Who?" asked Thandi

"The PA."

"She will remain as my PA because she knows a lot. I don't want to get somebody new. I don't have time to train," continued Thandi as she was on the way to the car.

"Do you think she is going to cope with this work that is so demanding? She has never worked before. She had been always a housewife," commented the PA to Johnson after receiving a phone call from Johnson.

"I should think she will. This is a woman with a master's in Business Economics and she managed her grandmother's salon. That is the biggest and busiest salon in Cape Town. She also looks strong and sounds intelligent to me. She might just be the right person for the job, who knows? Her work ethics sounds excellent for the few days I have engaged with her. The Malaysians were highly impressed with her," responded Johnson.

Chapter 47

Linda and Eric were involved in a heavy romance in Linda's bedroom. And both were naked in bed. After love making still out of breath Eric got off and turned Linda around and said to her "Miss Sibeko we have been in this relationship for a while now. What will stop you from saying yes if I were to propose?"

She jumped and sat on her bums and looked Eric in his eyes. "Are you serious?"

"Yes I am. I think it is high time we take this relationship to another level," he continued.

Linda kept quiet for a while. She thought to herself "What the hell am I going to do with Sipho. This is the opportunity I have been waiting for. I cannot let Eric get away because of that fool. We have signed at the magistrate court. I will have to get rid of him first before I marry Eric."

"You will have to show me the seriousness of your statement first. I cannot say yes or no when you have not proposed yet," said Linda

Eric jumped out of the bed and reached for the pocket of his jacket. He took out a purple velvet box and opened it. He knelt on Linda's side of the bed and held Linda's left hand and said to her "Linda Sibeko will you be Eric Jones' wife?"

She looked at him and smiled and she bent forward and gave him a kiss and said, "Yes Mr. Jones I will be your wife."

Eric stood up and kissed her and they went back to bed.

"Linda, can I ask you a big favor? I am hoping you are not going to reject this. I know it might be too late to ask for it, but I know it can be done."

"What is it, Eric?" asked Linda anxiously

"You know how much I love you. I am very sorry that I did not ask you to marry me long ago. I would like to spend the rest of my life with you. You and me husband and wife forever," he said trying to soften Linda's heart and buy her sympathy.

"What is it that you would want me to do Eric? I promise, if it is within my reach, I will do it for you," said Linda and she was desperate to hear Eric's request.

"I would like you to be Dr. Jones not Dr. Sibeko if that will be fine with you," said Eric with a very begging voice and both his hands in front of his chest like a person saying a prayer.

This touched Linda's heart and she felt that if she could deny Eric such a simple request, she will be betraying the love that this man had showed her. "Okay let me talk to the University and HPCSA and check if that can be changed. I don't think there will be any problems."

"What is HPCSA?" he asked

"HPCSA stands for Health Professional Council of South Africa. It's the body where all health professionals are registered."

"Oh, I can see. Are they the ones who can change this?"

"Yes, because they must issue me with new certificate. They will need our marriage certificate first."

"So why don't we go to court next week and sign there?"

"Are we not going to do a white wedding Eric?" she asked him

"Yes, baby we are but we need to do the surname change soon."

Linda was stuck because legally she was still married to Sipho. How was she going to get rid of him and stay with this man that she loves?

"Eric there is something I have to tell you before we move forward with this whole thing," she said with concern

"What is that baby?" he asked

"I want you to listen attentively ok."

"Yes, I am all yours."

"Before my parents died, they forced me into a marriage with somebody I never met before, and I didn't love at all. Though it was a customary marriage, you know in our country that is treated as a legal marriage."

"What happened to the guy then?" he asked,

"He is still alive, and he is around."

"Are you still married to him?" asked Eric with concern.

"Yes, we are."

"Do you love the guy?"

"No, I have never. We don't even sleep together at all."

"What do you want to do then?"

"Let me deal with it. As long as you promise me that you will be able to help me to deal with this my way."

"Well baby anything you want me to do I will do it. Even if you want me to get rid of him, I will do so."

"No, no I don't want to do that. I will sort this one out my own way. Is that ok with you?"

"That's fine with me baby as long as he is not going to hurt you."

"Do you know any lawyer that I can talk to?"

"A lawyer, what a hell do you want a lawyer for baby?" asked Eric with a frowned face.

"I want somebody who is going to work out a divorce document and serve it to Sipho using his old address. The document will be served in his absence to the address, and I will talk to the owner of the flats. I will collect the document and don't hand over to him. On the day of the court, he will not pitch-up and I will get a free divorce."

"Why do you have to go through all that baby? Why don't you just divorce the junky and get rid of him?"

"No baby, if he can get good advice and a good lawyer the guy can clean me up. He has nothing for himself, and I would not like to share my car, my house and all that I have with him."

"Ok love I will get my lawyer to call you," said Eric with a smile.

Linda met with the lawyer and explained to the lawyer her case about her marriage to Sipho. She told the lawyer that Sipho was still hospitalized, and she would be very glad if the whole process can be expedited within a week.

The papers were delivered to Sipho former address that appeared on their marriage contract. The Caretaker of the flats received and signed them as requested by Linda. Linda collected the papers on behalf of Sipho. Linda took the papers and never showed them to Sipho. The day of the court was scheduled for the Friday Sipho was discharged from the hospital. He didn't know about the divorce nor the court appearance.

Only Linda was present in court on that Friday. The court granted her a free divorce in Sipho's absence.

Chapter 48

Sipho was discharged from the hospital after two weeks and he had fully recovered. It was a Friday afternoon when he left the hospital. He went to the Pediatric department to look for Linda so that he can get the key for the house. He was told that Linda was off for the day. He decided to go straight to the house. Linda was at home. He saw her car parked outside on the driveway. She was not alone at home because there was a second car parked behind hers. He approached the house and knocked at the front door. He knocked several times without any response. He tried to open the door and it was locked. He decided to check the back door. When he tried to open the back door, he found it unlocked. He opened the door and moved in quietly. On the table in the lounge there were two wine glasses three empty bottles and one-half full bottle of red wine.

He heard some murmuring coming out of the bedroom. Instead of calling Linda's name he decided to walk toward the bedroom and check if she was there. As he was approaching the door, he heard some sounds coming out of the bedroom. The bedroom door was not completely closed. He gently pushed the door open very quietly. There was Linda busy making love in bed with somebody else. He turned around and left the door ajar. He went to the lounge very devastated. He sat down with his head hanging and thought to himself "How can Linda do this to me? I wonder how long has this been going on. Who is this guy that she is sleeping with?"

He was disturbed in his thoughts by a loud voice, "Wow, Sipho how did you get in here? The door was locked. What do you want here? When did they discharge you?" asked Linda as she was standing in front of Sipho naked.

Sipho was stunned. He just looked at Linda with amazement. He tried to find words, but they had evaded him.

"I am talking to you. How did you get in here?" asked Linda furiously.

"Who is that Linda?" a voice from the bedroom asked. "How the hell did he sneak in here?" His voice was coming closer to the lounge. "Who the hell are you?" asked Eric with a gun in his hand. "What do you want in here?"

"Ok, sweetheart let me handle this please. This is the man that I told you about who was my husband. What he wants here I don't know because I have divorced him long ago. Sipho this is my new husband, his name is Eric, so you better get out of my house and leave us now," said Linda with a harsh voice and pointing at the door.

Sipho looked at Linda with amazement.

"Yes, why do you look surprised?" asked Linda. "Honey make him get out of here a.s.a.p. please."

Eric cocked his gun and said, "my friend you have heard what the lady is saying. Get lost my bra now or else," said Eric with a gun at Sipho's forehead.

He gave Sipho a kick in his chest and he fell on his back on the couch. He put his foot on Sipho throat to choke him with his foot. Sipho tried to wiggle so to remove Eric foot on his throat.

"Ah, ah, you dare move that foot away from your throat you are a death man," he said with the gun pointing at Sipho's face.

Sipho stopped wiggling and look at Eric. "Get off the couch and on the floor. Turn around and face the floor."

Sipho obliged without hesitation to avoid any further ill treatment. Eric gave him a kick on his ribs and said, "get up and leave now before I changed my mind and put a bullet through your skull."

"Linda, can I get at least my clothes please," said Sipho with a begging voice.

"What clothes are you talking about? Everything that is here it says Linda. Sweetheart get this thing out of here please; he is making my blood to boil."

"You heard what the lady said. Out of here now. You are not welcomed here you parasite."

He stood up with great pains because Eric's kick disturbed some healing wounds from inside. He was groaning as he was trying to stand up. He walked with all four toward the table to support himself to stand up.

Linda went close to him and gave him a push with leg on the side. That send Sipho back on the floor on his side. She turned around and said to Eric, "Eric this thing must go. It looks like it's going to die in here. I don't want a corpse in my house."

Eric grabbed Sipho by the shirt on his shoulder, opened the door and dragged him out of the door.

"If I open this door and found you still in this yard, you must know I will not hesitate to shoot you. Do you hear me?" said Eric pointing Sipho with a gun and showing him the gate.

"But, but-," said Sipho with a stammering voice

"Hey!! There is no but here. Get out of here now," said Eric with a loud angry voice.

Sipho stood up with a vehement anger in him of this man pointing a gun at him. He slowly moved toward the gate. He looked at the car Eric was driving, and he realized that for anybody to buy a big, beautiful Mercedes Benz like the one he was looking at, that person should be moneyed.

"What was I thinking? A poor technician like me marrying a doctor, my friends are going to laugh at me," he talked to himself.

He got out of the yard and went into the street. He meandered aimlessly not knowing where to go and what to do. He was deep in thoughts. He was thinking about the money that he paid to the university for Linda's fees. His child that Linda carried. Part of him was blaming himself for being too much close to Linda and temper with her life. At the same time, he was blaming Linda for not being honest with him. As he was walking aimlessly, he found himself next to N1 South. He decided then to hitch- hike and get as far as possible from Linda and the province. In his mind the only solution was suicide but not close by. He planned to kill himself far from the province and Linda as possible. A truck driver stopped and picked him up.

"Hi where are you going sir, hitch- hiking without some luggage at this time of the day?"

"I don't know, can you tell me where you are going with your truck?" asked Sipho.

Chapter 49

The contract with the Malaysian company was signed and the production was running well. Everything for Community Steel was under strict controlled management. Thandi was enjoying the full support of both her managers and the work force. The profitability of the company had increase under the new management. Thandi was chairing all management meetings and her father was the chairperson of the board. She would travel to Johannesburg time and again for business meetings and visit the distribution operation which was running well and was breaking even with small profits. The small profits were not bothering her that much because she trusted that the business was showing a potential of growth with good marketing strategies.

One morning after her normal morning runs with her dog around the yard, she was busy making some juice for her in the kitchen when Martha moved in. "I can see that you have everything under control now ma'am. Your body is back in the normal shape that I am used to. You look well again. How is the company doing?" said Martha.

"Yes Martha, the company is running very well and everybody at work seems to be happy. That is why I am trying my best to get my body back to shape, so that I am also mentally fit for my work," she responded.

"I should think there is only one thing that is now missing in madam's life."

"And what would that be Martha?"

"Now that he is no longer there, ma'am needs to find somebody that will keep you happy and you need a man in your life."

"A man, Martha! Are you serious?" asked Linda with a laughter.

"Yes ma'am. You need a person to keep you company. You are always alone in this house and this is a very big house for you to be alone with that dog of yours. In the cold nights ma'am needs somebody to keep her warm. I want to hear noise of children running around here, and that can only happen when there is a man in your life," continued Martha

"Do you know how difficult it is to find the right man Martha?"

"Yes, I know it is, especially for a person like you who is always indoors. You need to go out so that you can meet people. Man will not come to you, but you must go out there and socialize then you will meet somebody. Relationships are not built inside the house but out there were people are."

"Martha, you should know me better by now, I am not the type of person who will go out to parties or functions. You know I am a loner and I like my house and Bobby."

"So, are you intending to die alone in this house?" asked Martha.

"No, it's not that. I am sure I will meet Mr. Right one day. God will give me a man that is suitable for me. I don't want to go through what I have gone through in life. You are the person who should know better."

"Yes ma'am. You should not just take any man now. I would not want to see what you have gone through happening again. Strange enough your mother-in-law went through the same thing."

"What do you mean when you say my mother-in-law went through the same thing Martha?" asked Thandi as if she had no clue what Martha was talking about.

"Did Daniel not tell you what happened?"

"No. You know that Daniel does not talk that much about other people affairs. What happened?" asked Thandi inquisitively

"Mr. Phillips was very abusive to the Madam. He used to call her names in front of the boy. She lost two babies before Freddy was born."

"What do you mean by losing two babies? Were those babies born already?"

"She miscarried both. I don't know whether it was through abuse or stress. I know for sure that one of them she bled profusely after Mr. Phillips beat her one morning. That is why I was so afraid the day you bled."

"Did he ever beat her in front of Freddy?"

"Yes, several times. He broke her leg at some stage. Madam was admitted twice to hospital because of the beatings."

"Did Freddy witness all that?"

"Yes, he did. He was extremely disrespectful to his mother. His father would never call him to order for using vulgar language to his mother in front of him."

Thandi could not hold her tears by now. She realized that her husband was the victim of circumstances. She now could understand what her father-in-law meant when he said to her, "there are things that I have done to his mother in front of him. I pray that he will never do those things to you my child." This also brought back her mother-in-law words she spoke to her at the hospital "Thandi I have gone through a lot in my marriage with Freddy's father. I hope and wish that you will not experience the same. I am praying that my son will treat you as a lady and be a man enough not to abuse you."

"What kind of a father would expose his son into such a gruesome behavior?" she verbalized that loudly.

"Mr. Phillips is the one who had made Freddy the way he was. The only person who would speak sense to Freddy was Daniel. They were in good terms. Daniel is the person who can tell you all about him."

"Martha I am going to be late I have to go now. Have you ironed my skirt?"

"Yes, ma'am I have, it's on top of your bed."

After dressing up Thandi called Daniel. "I will be coming back late today will you drive me to work, and I will call you when you have to pick me up."

"Yes, ma'am I will do so," responded Daniel

On their way to the office Thandi received a call. It was the lawyer that represented the workforce in their negotiations for the shares.

"Thandi here, good morning."

"Good morning Thandi. You are talking to Zola. How are you doing?"

"I am well thanks and how are you?"

"Very well thanks for asking. Why are you so scarce?"

"I should ask you that. After the negotiations you just disappeared."

"I have been trying to get hold of you using your land line and every time I called you were out of town."

"I am sorry for that. What's up?"

"What are you doing tonight?"

"I will be meeting with my management team for some operation matters. Why?"

"There is something at Baxter theater tonight. I was thinking I will pick you up for that show."

"No, I won't make it. I am very sorry. I cannot postpone tonight's meeting," said Thandi.

"When will you be available for a cup of coffee?"

"Iyoo, it is difficult to say because I am very busy, and I sometimes knock off very late."

"Can you just give me a day at last, next week or next month? I will take whatever you give me," said Zola with a persuasive voice.

"Okay I don't have my diary with me here I will give you a call when I get to my office after I have checked my diary."

"Thank you very much. You have a fabulous day."

She dropped the call and rolled her eyes upwards. Daniel was watching her from the mirror. "What's wrong ma'am?" he asked.

"It is these guys who keep on calling me for an appointment. They think because I am a widow, I am suddenly available. What makes me sick is the fact that some of them are not after me per se, but they are looking at the business."

"Don't you think it is high time for you to see somebody? It has been long since Freddy died, and you have been all alone."

"I know Daniel, but I don't want to rush things. There are times that I would feel lonely. I want a man who will come to me for who I am not for what I am."

"Then it means you will have to go to functions regularly."

"Not necessarily. My Mr. Right will find me wherever I am Daniel."

"If you say so then I will give up. Whatever you do ma'am, please don't choose somebody that will take you back where you are coming from. I have seen a lot of domestic violence I won't like to see that anymore."

"Strange enough Daniel, I was talking to Martha about the same thing this morning. She is also concerned about my loneliness and at the same time she does not want me to get somebody who is going to abuse me like Freddy did."

"All of us are ma'am."

"What do you mean by all of you? Who is all of you?"

"I am talking about Martha, Sarah your parents and myself."

"How did my parents and Sarah know about my abuse?" she asked

"Martha and Sarah are friends for a very long time. In fact, Sarah wanted you to come back and take over the salon rather than staying in an abusive relationship, but Martha told her that you will never agree to that. I told your father about all your abuse. I have witness them all. I wanted him to come and fetch you, but he refused and said you will never agree to that. Your father knows how much you valued your marriage. Your parents brought you up very well ma'am."

"How did you witness them?" asked Thandi.

"Every time that boy would scream loud, I knew what was going to follow. His father was the same to his mother. He just followed into his father footsteps with everything."

"Martha told me that you were very close to my husband. Why didn't you talk to him about it?"

"We spoke about a lot of things when he was still young. I should think his father's influence was too much into him. I could not talk to him when he started abusing you because he was paying my salary"

"So, what you are telling me Daniel is that if I can start doing wrong things you will keep quiet?"

"No, I won't. With you ma'am things are different. I know your father very well and we are open to each other. You are also an open book to me. You don't shun away from my advice, and you are not stubborn like your husband was."

"Ok, thanks Daniel. I will call you when I am ready to be picked up," said Thandi as she got out of the car in front of the company. "Tell Martha I will get something to eat from Woolworths after work she mustn't cook for me."

Thandi greeted the PA and continued to her office. She opened the door wide, and she was struck by a bouquet of flowers on her table. She called her PA and asked her about the flowers. "They were delivered this morning," said the PA.

"Where have they come from?" she asked as she was checking for a note. There was a note, and it was written: 'Enjoy your day you beautiful woman.'

"Take these flowers and throw them in the trash box. Why is the person such a coward? No name. Is the person expecting me to guess the name?"

"Possibly the person might have seen you or talked to you at some stage boss," said the PA.

There and then she remembered her conversation with Zola. She opened her diary and found a date for him, and she called him to give the date "Hi, Zola, it's Thandi. I will be able to see you next week on Tuesday. I have an open day till 17h45."

"Thank you Thandi I appreciate that. Let us meet at the Waterfront 12h30, if that is in order with you?"

"That's fine with me but let's make it 14h00 if that will be fine with you. Whereabouts at the Waterfront?"

"14h00 is fine with me. Is Quay 4 Tavern alright for you?"

"Yes, I am cool with it," said Thandi.

"Do you like them?" asked Zola

"What?"

"The flowers."

"Oh, you send them?"

"Yes."

"Why is the note without a name?"

"I just wanted you to guess and see if you would know where they are coming from."

"Okay, thanks any way."

"Hey, I asked you if like them."

"They are beautiful."

"That's not my question Thandi., said Zola with a soft voice.

Thandi realized that if she is not going to respond to the question the man is not going to drop the phone. She said, "yes Zola, I like them."

"I am glad if you do. Goodbye will see you next week."

"Goodbye." She dropped the phone.

"Wow, Boss you have an admirer. Who is this hunk that sends you such beautiful flowers? Is he dating you? Do I know him Boss?" asked her PA.

"Yes, you have seen the guy. He is the one that represented the workforce on the day of the shares meeting. I am not dating him," responded Thandi.

"Oh, I remember him. Is that the man with a chocolate suit? He is a very handsome guy Boss, and it's a big fish why don't you catch it?"

"I am not interested in big fishes. I don't have time for boyfriends now."

"You have agreed to meet him. Why?"

"He has been pestering me. I want to get him off my back."

"Wow, that's the problem with you girls who are beautiful in all respects," she said showing with her hands from the face to the curves of the body. "Here we are, available to any man but we are struggling to get flowers like these or to be dated like you guys. You are rejecting his flowers? this shows you are not interested in him. Can I at least then take the flowers if you will not have them?"

"They are all yours," said Thandi.

It was 21h30 when Thandi was done with the meeting. She called Daniel to pick her up. He did not take long to arrive. Thandi was feeling very tired. She got home and washed said a short prayer and went to bed and slept. During her sleep she had a dream. She dreamed as if she was sitting next to her swimming pool with a strange man. The next thing both were swimming and playing in the pool. The man carried her in his arms as they were swimming. The dream continued with her and the stranger in a beautiful green park playing together. The man was chasing her among the trees in the park and she was laughing and in a jovial mood. What was strange was that the man was not Freddy or the guy she spoke with during the day. The man in her dreams was tall and very handsome. She woke up and went to the bathroom. She looked herself in the mirror and realized that she was sweating. "Who was that?" she asked herself. "I have never seen that person before, and his face was not clear. Why did I wake up?" she was angry with herself. She decided to go back to sleep in case she catches the same dream again.

Chapter 50

Sipho had been sleeping since he boarded the truck. The truck driver didn't bother to wake him up as he could see that the man was tired and emotionally drained. It was in Colesberg when the truck driver stopped the truck for a diesel refill. Sipho woke up for the first time. "Where are we, my friend?" he asked.

"This is Colesberg my friend," responded the driver

"Where the hell is Colesberg? In which province is that?"

"We are in Northern Cape now my friend. You did not tell me where you are going," said the driver as he was getting off to do some spot checks on the truck.

"I told you that I don't have any specific destination. I will get off where my spirit is telling me to get off from your truck," said Sipho as he looked around in the truck for something that he didn't know.

As he was looking his eyes came across the rope behind the driver's seat. He pulled it to check its length. He decided that it was long enough for whatever he wanted it for. He left it there and told himself that he was going to take it when he was going to disembark.

"My friend I need to arrive in Cape Town tomorrow morning. I drove the whole night now I need to take a rest and sleep enough for the long drive to Cape Town. I don't know what will you be doing while I will be sleeping. If you want to continue with your journey, you are free to do so."

"I will sit and wait for you because I don't have money to go anywhere," responded Sipho

"Are you not hungry then?" asked the driver.

"I am but I don't have money to buy food."

"Let me just finish with the truck, we will go inside and have a breakfast then I will go and sleep while you will be moving around. Is that ok with you?" said the driver.

"Can't you buy food, and we go and eat in the truck instead of eating inside there?" asked Sipho.

"Sure, we can do whatever you want. I will get a takeaway then."

"Tell them to put your takeaway in a plastic bag please," said Sipho.

He wanted to use the plastic as his luggage bag.

"You didn't tell me why you are going where you don't know. You are on the journey without a single piece of luggage with you."

"It's a long story my friend. If I can tell you, it will take the whole journey," responded Sipho.

"Yes, I do have the whole journey to listen to it. Are you going to tell me? Let's get our food then talk," asked the driver.

After eating Sipho continued with the conversation.

"We were still talking before our meals. My story that I want to tell you involves a woman," said Sipho.

"Well, if that's the case, spare me the details. I know where you are coming from brother. I have been there myself. Women can send a man to hell in a Mustang at 250km an hour. I am a truck driver today because of a woman. I wanted to be a lawyer. Those dreams faded away the day my father sent me to go and look for a job. This was for a pregnancy that was not mine."

"What do you mean when you say for pregnancy that was not yours? How do you know that the pregnancy was not yours? Didn't you sleep with the girl?" asked Sipho curiously.

"The girl had a boyfriend before me. A month or so after they broke up, she got involved with me. Within a month in our relationship, she told me that she was pregnant, and I am the father of the child. When I was still thinking about the pregnancy, she told my sister who told my mother, and it went to my father. My father took me out of school to work for that child. He didn't want to hear a thing."

"How did you know that the child was not yours then?" asked Sipho

"It was only after she gave birth that I knew that the child was not mine. I calculated the period of her pregnancy after birth. I realized that there was no way that child could be mine. She was already two months pregnant when our affair started. It was too late I had already started to support her and the baby. My father didn't want to hear a thing about the kid not being mine."

"Where are they now? Are you still supporting them?" asked Sipho

"She qualified as a nurse and left Cape Town for Rustenburg. That was the last time I heard of her. She never asked anything from me again."

"What about the child?"

"The girl was not my child. My friend let me sleep otherwise I will get late in Cape Town. As for you, I don't what your destination is," said the driver without hearing Sipho's side of the story.

The driver woke up at 21h00. He asked Sipho to bring him some water to wash his face. After an hour of so checking the load, they were on the road again. The driver stopped the truck again to use the bathroom.

Sipho woke up and asked, "Where are we now?"

"We are in Worcester now and we are left with about two to three hours to Cape Town depending how busy Du Toitskloof is. Don't you want to use the bathroom?" he asked Sipho.

"No, not now."

When the driver got off and closed the door, Sipho took out the rope that he saw and put it in the plastic bag and hide it behind him. On their way to Cape Town Sipho saw a board that was indicating an off ramp to Stellenbosch. "Can you drop me off here," he said to the driver.

"These are farms and small holdings it's still far to Cape Town," said the driver.

"Yes, this is where I want to get off," he insisted.

"Look at the time, it's still too early and dark outside." said the driver as he pulled the truck on the side of the road under the bridge.

Sipho opened his door and thanked the driver for his hospitality. "May God bless you, my friend. I wish I could say till we meet again but that will not happen."

"Hey, you never know it is possible. This is a small world," said the driver.

"I am definitely sure that it will not happen, this is the first and the last time you see me. Today by mid-day I will be either in Heaven or in hell," said Sipho as he closed the door.

"Hey, hey, wait. What do you mean? What are you going to do? What is in that plastic in your hand?" He opened his door to chase Sipho. Sipho disappeared in the dark of the night. He came back to the truck to check what was missing. He realized that the rope at the back of his seat wasn't there. "Wow that poor bloke is going to hang himself. Something must have happened to him in Johannesburg. Why hang himself so far away?"

Chapter 51

"Hi, my friend, how are you doing? I hope you haven't forgotten that my wedding is next month. Have you guys bought the tickets yet?" asked Joyce.

"I haven't forgotten my friend. I bought the tickets last month. I can't miss my best friend's wedding; besides how can I miss a trip to Cape Town. How is your fiancé?" responded Linda.

"Very well my friend he is doing fine. Thanks for asking."

"How is the baby doing? I am sure she is a big girl by now," said Linda.

"She is doing well my friend and she looks like her father. There is no resemblance of me in her. I was just an incubator."

"Well, I hope she is as beautiful as her father."

"Are you bringing Sipho with you to the wedding next month Linda?"

"I knew that was coming. That is why I said to you we should have exchanged boyfriends. I know how much you love Sipho. I don't know why you didn't marry him instead."

"Don't be ridiculous Linda. Sipho is just a very good friend. Besides you ought to be happy to have a husband like him. If all man were like him, women would enjoy their married lives."

"Let me tell you about this Sipho of yours that you idolize so much."

"What has he done?"

"I was at work when I was called at the reception desk that I had a visitor. When I got there, it was the sheriff of the court. He handed me an envelope and he asked me to sign for it, which I did."

"And what was it my friend?"

"Divorce papers."

"You must be joking."

"Do I sound like I am to you?"

"And?" asked Joyce

"I decided that I was not going to sign them because I wanted to discuss the content and find out what the problem was," continued Linda.

"And?"

"After work I went home, and I found him in bed sleeping. Fortunately, he woke up when he heard the noise."

"I am listening, girl."

"I confronted him about the divorced papers. I asked him why he has never said a thing to me about his unhappiness."

"And what did he say?"

"You know your boyfriend; he doesn't say much. He was quiet at first until I started pestering him."

"What did he say?"

"He said our marriage was a mistake right from the beginning. He thinks I don't have time for him. I am always at work. He is also not happy that I was specializing. He also accused me of killing his baby because I don't love him enough."

"That's unlike him. The last time I spoke to him, he was so happy about your marriage. In fact, Sipho loved you from long ago. And then, did you sign the papers?"

"No, I told him I am not going to sign them. I told him that I am a doctor today because of him. I told him that if he was not there, I would be somebody's maid somewhere. I told him that he sacrificed a lot for me to be where I am, and I told him that I am not going to leave him when he supposed to reap the benefits of his sacrifice."

"And what did he say?"

"Nothing, he just kept quiet even when I told him that for me to specialize is going to make our life easy. I will have more time for him and our children if I am a specialist."

"Did he agree with you?" asked Joyce

"No, guess what? The next thing I came back from work the house was empty. He took everything I bought, and he was gone."

"And what did you do girl? Did you report him to the police?"

"No Joyce. Sipho is my husband how could I do that?"

"What did you do then?"

"I engaged a lawyer. The court granted Sipho a free divorce because I wasn't there on the court day. He was given a permission to take whatever is his in the house."

"Did he then take what was his?"

"No, my friend, you know what was in Sipho's room. I stored all his in the garage. That he did not take instead he took everything we have just bought."

"And where is he now?" asked Joyce

"Somebody told me he is staying somewhere in the East Rand with some college girl."

"So, are you without somebody now?"

"I had dumped Eric because I wanted to concentrate on Sipho. Now that this has happened, I had to beg him to take me back."

"Did he agree?"

"Eric is not vindictive. He is a gentleman. He understood and we are now back again in full force. In fact, I will be coming down with him."

"I am glad for you, my friend. I did not expect this from Sipho. It is true when they say, "still water runs deep."

"That's you boyfriend you loved. I never expected that from him too," echoed Linda.

"So, I will assume that he paid himself all that you owed him. I know your taste in material things is not cheap."

"You say that again my friend. I bought that furniture from Bokos. I am still paying for all of it even now. I had to settle for something cheaper now to keep myself going."

"Okay my friend. I will see you next month," said Joyce.

"Before you go my friend, how is obstetrics and Gynecology? Are you enjoying it?"

"Yes, a lot. And you, how is Paeds treating you?"

"You know me with kids. I am enjoying it a lot. I thought Sipho and I will have a lot of kids because he also loves children, but I guess I was wrong. Bye for now."

"Bye my friend."

Linda felt relieved now that she had given the wrong impression of Sipho. It will be easy for her to tell and invite Joyce to her wedding with Eric. She knew how Joyce felt about Sipho. She was also afraid that Sipho should never meet Joyce and give her a full story of how he was treated before she painted a different picture about Sipho. Now that she has told Joyce her side of the story, it is going to be very difficult for Sipho to convince Joyce otherwise.

Chapter 52

The dream threw Thandi sleep into abyss and kept Thandi awake. She tried to remember the picture of the man she dreamed about but all in vain. She looked at her watch and the time was 05h40 then she decided to wake up and go for her normal morning running. She put on her jogging gear and called her dog, and they went out around the yard. She was in a good mood for running and she ran more runs than normal. The dream she had, revived something in her that energized her. It brought a sense of hope of something that she doesn't know of. She didn't feel the pain from the runs as the dream was over and over in her mind during the jogging period. Her adrenaline was high.

She ultimately stopped to stretch herself. It was then that she realized that she was sweating like a horse after the race. When she was busy stretching, her dog started barking at the edge of the fence looking toward the forest nearby. The dog's persistent barking and running up and down between her and the fence forced her to pay attention to what it was barking at. She moved closer to the fence and looked at the direction where the dog was looking and barking. She could not see a thing. She stood for a while looking and there was nothing. She turned around to go to the house, as she was turning, she caught something with the corner of an eye dropping from the tree. When she turned around, she saw a rope from the tree and something hanging but obscured by the tree branches. She quickly moved closer to the fence and saw person legs hanging and kicking in the air.

"Daniel!!! Daniel!!!, quickly come quickly. Run Daniel run please," she screamed as she was running toward the main gate to the bush. Daniel got out of his apartment running thinking that his boss was in trouble.

"Ma'am!!! Ma'am where are you?" he called. Daniel saw her boss running toward the main gate. He followed without asking where she was going. The dog outran her to the scene and started barking at the hanging man. She got at the scene and lifted the man to minimize the rope tension around his neck. She waited for Daniel to arrive to assist her. Daniel arrived and helped his boss to lift the man up.

"Is he still alive Daniel?"

"Yes, ma'am he is still kicking his legs. How are we going to get him off the rope?"

"Let me quickly run and get a knife. Is he well supported on you?"

"Yes, ma'am and be fast because he is very heavy. His weight is killing me."

Thandi ran to the house and came back driving so that they can take the man to hospital if needs be.

When they had taken the man off the rope, he was still comatose. "Daniel you will have to come with me to the hospital. Let's get your license and you will be driving; I want to call my physician and see if we cannot meet him at the hospital."

The physician was waiting for them at the hospital. They took the man to casualty as per doctor's instructions. "Mrs. Phillips, one of you must open up a file for the man meanwhile I am attending to him and waiting for the doctor to come," said the nurse.

"Daniel, you stay with him and the nurse I am going to open a file for him. Oh, Daniel we don't even know the man's name. Can you check in his pocket if his ID is not with him?"

Sipho's ID was not in his pocket. Daniel found a hospital discharged paper in Sipho's pocket. The paper had Sipho's name and surname. There was also an address that only reflected the street name without house number and the area where the street was. Thandi took the paper and checked the man's name. After she read the name and the surname, she realized that it was somebody that she had never seen nor heard of his name before. The street name was also unfamiliar. "Can you open a file for Mr. Sipho Mokoena please? Here are his particulars," said Thandi to the clerk.

"What is his address ma'am and ID number please? Here in this paper, it's only street name without house number and ID number," said the clerk.

Thandi was bit lost, and she did not know what to say, she decided that she was going to use her own address and told the clerk that she doesn't know his ID number.

"His next of kin ma'am in case of emergency."

"Thandi Phillips."

"Contact number?"

She gave hers. All her responds were spontaneous. "I don't know this man. Why am I giving my information for him? What if his family is here? I think I should have reported this to the police, and they were supposed to handle this," she whispered to herself.

"Ma'am we don't have this man on our records. Does he have a medical aid?" asked the clerk.

"No, I don't think so. I will pay everything for him," responded Thandi

"Today the payment will be R1000 and if he is going to be admitted we will need a payment of R20 000 up front."

"Let me find out from the doctor if he is going to admit him. I will come back to you," said the nurse that was standing next to Thandi.

The doctor came to casualty and met Thandi.

"Mrs. Phillips I will have to admit this man and run some few tests and also get him to see a psychiatrist when he is back to normality," said the doctor.

"How long is this going to be?" she asked.

"It is very difficult to tell at this stage, but it will not be less than a week. He is a very lucky man. If you were just a minute late, he would have died," said the doctor.

"Ok then doctor let me leave him in your capable hands. You have my number you can give me a call to update me. If there is any emergency and I am out of town I will leave Daniel numbers so that the hospital can contact him."

"I will do so Mrs. Phillips," said the doctor.

"Oh, another thing doctor, can you organize a private ward for him please? I don't want him to be in a general ward. I don't know what led him to this and I wouldn't like him to be subjected to questions from other people."

Thandi paid a cash check of R50 000 to cover all medical cost that will be required to attend to Sipho. They drove home with Daniel. "Have you heard or know of any Mokoena family Daniel?" she asked

"No ma'am not at all. This is the first time," replied Daniel "I think you can prepare for work I will go to the police to find out if there is any man reported missing and if they know the surname."

"Thanks Daniel. I will appreciate if you can do that for me. Please do call and inform me about the outcome. If I am in a meeting leave a message with my PA, then I will call you back. When you talk to her, don't relate the story, just tell her that you called, and you want me to call you back. Daniel, nobody must know about this besides you and me. If the police know nothing about this man, we will have to keep him until he is fully recovered. Ok?"

Daniel agreed.

At the police station there was no case of a missing man reported and the Mokoena surname was also not known to the police.

"So, it means this man is not from around here. Where has he come from? Why come commit suicide here next to us? He was very lucky that the madam saw him otherwise he would have died," murmured Daniel.

"Is that Mrs. Phillips?" asked the voice

"Yes, it is Dr. Andrews."

"Mr. Mokoena's brain is intact there is no damage. He should be able to gain conscious soon. All the other tests are negative. I have booked a psychologist for him that is what the psychiatrist recommended."

"Thank you doctor. Please do keep me posted on everything."

"I will do so Mrs. Phillips."

Chapter 53

It was four days later when Thandi was called by the doctor. "Mrs. Phillips the report from the Psychologist is available and Mr. Mokoena will be discharged tomorrow from the hospital."

"Thank you doctor, I will tell Daniel to pick him up from the hospital."

"Did you guys manage to trace his family?" asked the doctor.

"No doctor. Nobody knows about his family, and nobody has reported a missing person. The police don't seem to know the man either."

"We have to do something Mrs. Phillips so that this man does not attempt to kill himself again."

"I will keep him at my place for the time being while we are waiting to hear from his family. Daniel will keep him busy. You shouldn't worry yourself about that doctor. Thank you for everything. Is he still going to see the psychiatrist?" asked Thandi.

"No, there is no need at this stage. The psychiatrist is happy with the report from the psychologist," responded the doctor.

"Thanks once more Doctor Andrews."

"You welcome Mrs. Phillips. If there are any problems with him in the future feel free to call me. He is stable now. I don't think he will have complications or do anything out of line."

"Did you have a one on one with him?"

"Yes, we did talk. He is a very intelligent man, and he did not want to reveal much about himself. He did not want to talk about what led him to commit suicide. He also does not know why he opted for suicide instead of dealing with the problems that he had."

"Did he tell you where he is from?"

"He said up in the north. Exactly where, he said he would like to say where now but later."

"What time should Daniel be there tomorrow? I will not be able to come because I am in Johannesburg, and I will be back late tomorrow."

"Tell, Daniel to be here at 12h30. I have told him about you and that you have paid for his medical bills. Any way Daniel was here earlier on, and they talked this morning. He left after talking to him. This was before I knew that he was going to be discharged."

"Oh, then that will make things easier if he knows Daniel and they have talked. I will tell him to pick the man up tomorrow then."

"His name is Sipho Mrs. Phillips I should think you will have to address him like that so that he does not feel as a stranger."

"Oh, yes I know doc. I am sorry. I will do so doctor I promise. Thank you once again. Bye now."

After dropping the phone Thandi called Daniel. "Hi Dan, will you please pick up Sipho tomorrow from the hospital?"

"Yes ma'am. What time should I be there? I was with him yesterday evening and this morning. He has recovered a lot. What are we going to do with him ma'am? He doesn't seem to have a place to stay."

"Let's talk about the other things tomorrow. Tell Martha to prepare the visitor's room for Sipho. I will talk to him when I get back. Don't forget to pick me up at 19h30 tomorrow please," said Thandi.

"I won't forget ma'am."

Daniel picked up Sipho the following day and drove him to the house. "Where are you taking me too?" asked Sipho.

"My boss has instructed me to take you where we are staying," replied Daniel

"Is your boss the lady that you said helped me?" asked Sipho

"Yes, she is the one."

"Where is she now? Is she at home?"

"No, she is up in Johannesburg."

"Where is her husband? Does he know about my coming?"

"Her husband died, and she is currently not married."

"So, she is one of those rich arrogant ladies who have money and don't care about the other people."

"Why are you saying that? My boss is a very decent person. She is full of love, that is why she took care of you and paid all your medical cost. You can't just club everybody under one umbrella."

"I am sorry if I have said something wrong. I am where I am today because of a woman."

"Not all women are the same my friend. What happened? Do you mind telling me about it? I am older than you I might be able to help you. Is it the woman that made you to take the decision of terminating your life?"

"Yes, this is what happened." Sipho started his story from the beginning because he felt comfortable with Daniel from the very first time they met at the hospital when Daniel visited him.

"Sipho, let me get you clearly. What you saying to me is that you paid for this lady's university studies and she qualified as a medical doctor. You had to sacrifice your happiness so that she can be a doctor today?"

"Yes Daniel."

"I understand where you are coming from now. I don't know what I would have done if I was in your shoes."

"Can you understand why I am so bitter toward educated women?"

"Didn't you think of doing something to her?"

"No, that never crossed my mind."

"Why so?" asked Daniel

"When I was young my father told me that I should never raise my hand to a woman. It doesn't matter what she has done to me. If I am in a situation where she has heavily offended me, I should walk away or take a drive for a while to regain my sanity. Beating her will not solve any problems or change anything. You can't change an adult person to be what you want him or her to be by using violence. You either accept him or her and learn to compromise or if it's unbearable and intolerable to live with the person, take what is yours and leave. Why do something to him or her? You haven't created this person but God. He is the only who can change him or her. If you are prepared to bear and tolerate him or her, just give the knees their food and wait for God's answer. Bear one thing in mind, I was married to this person so there was no way I could raise my hand or my voice to her. You know what the other thing my dad said. He said people out there will treat your spouse the way you treat her or him. He said I must always treat my partner with respect and dignity. Linda will never find a man that will treat her the way I did."

"Your father taught you very well. So, you have kept that since then?"

"Yes, I have Daniel and it has works for me."

"Why then take your life."

"I never expected her to organize a man to kill me after all that I have done for her. If she didn't want me, she should have just divorced me and let me go."

"But still Sipho I don't understand why take your life?"

"It's one of those decisions that was based on emotions."

"Do you regret why you have done that?"

"Yes, I do. It was an injudicious decision. I will never do it again."

"I am glad if you have learned something out of this. There is one thing I want you to know from today onwards. Nobody is indispensable more especially when it comes to love. If you move on in life you will learn to love again. Life is too precious and enjoyable to lose it over one person who has disappointed you. One thing I have learn with love is that love can find love again. You can't just burn a good and interesting book because of one bitter and frustrating chapter. If you don't like that chapter in your book, just tear it off or skip it and continue to enjoy the rest of the book," said Daniel as they were disembarking from the car.

"That is well said. I should have known that Linda was just a wrong chapter in my life. There is surely still a lot of good life for me out there. Thank you, Daniel, for that," said Sipho as he was following him.

Thandi arrived in the evening and saw that Sipho was sitting in the lounge. She went to her bedroom to freshen up. She came back to the lounge.

Daniel joined Sipho at the lounge after handing over her boss bag to Martha.

"Good evening Sipho," greeted Thandi.

Immediately Thandi entered the lounge Sipho stood up to greet her.

She went to Sipho and stretched both her hands to greet him with one knee slightly bent.

Sipho bowed his head in respect with both hands shaking Thandi's hands.

"My name is Thandi Phillips I am pleased to meet you sir," said Thandi with her eyes looking on the floor.

"Good evening, ma'am. My name is Sipho Mokoena. How do you do?"

"Very well sir thank you and you?" replied Thandi.

"I am well ma'am thank you very much," said Sipho with a slight gentle smile

"Can you stop calling me ma'am and call me by my name please Sipho. Daniel, can you call Martha to come and join us here."

"Martha and Dan, I would like to talk to Sipho in your presence. Sipho I am sure Daniel has already told you how we got to know you and how you ended up in this house. I am not going back to that now. I just want to tell you that you are welcome to stay here until you decide to go back to your family wherever it is. Feel free to ask anything from Martha or Daniel. Is that okay with you?"

"Yes ma'am."

"My name is Thandi! Please address me as such. Tomorrow is Saturday, Daniel will take you to town to get something to wear for yourself."

"Thank you, Thandi. Do you want me to relay my story to you?"

"It is not necessary now. The most important thing is to get you back to what you were which I don't know. The doctor said to me you are a very intelligent man and I want to believe that. When you are settled, and still with us, you will be able to tell me everything."

"To keep Sipho busy can he work with me for the time being?" asked Daniel.

"Yes, Daniel I think that will be a very good thing," replied Thandi "What do you think Sipho?" she asked.

"Yes, I will do that and the other thing I don't have a family. I will be glad if I can be offered a job."

"Let's say for the time being you will be working with Daniel until we can determine what to do. I should think it's late now. Let us all go to sleep we will continue with this discussion some other time," said Thandi.

"That's fine with me," said Sipho.

"Ok, good night, everybody," said Thandi.

Chapter 54

Working in a factory environment of men had made Thandi strong. She was not the housewife that Freddy had turned her into. She had taken decisions that some of them the management were not in agreement with and implemented them to success. She had negotiated deals on behalf of the company. She had transformed herself from the soft lady who managed a salon to the hard lady who was now managing a team of men only. This night she was standing in front of the mirror naked and realized that the feminine side in her was still alive, somehow Sipho's presence reminded her of that. As she was looking at her body, a series of question came to her mind. She looked at her breasts and softly talked to the mirror "Lord, will these breasts ever nurse a child? Will my womb ever carry a baby again? Will I like most women ever bring life into this world? Will these hands ever carry a baby that is my own? Will I ever be in the maternity ward like most women? Will I ever love a man again in my life Lord? How about my head on a man's breast and brushing his beard?"

All these questions brought tears in her eyes. She realized that her success in the corporate world does not bring the fulfillment of her womanhood. She felt that she was not complete with all the questions not answered. For the first time since Freddy's death, she thought of what her future would be like without a man in her life.

It was at this time that she realized that she was not created to be a career woman. Her maternal feelings were weighing heavier than her corporate success. She knew that being a wife and a mother was more important to her than being the CEO of a very successful operation. This reminded her of her grandmother's words when she said to her, "something I realized later in life my child is that, when elderly women meet in a group and talk about life, most of their conversation is about their married life, their husbands, their children and grandchildren."

With all the thoughts and the pain that she was feeling she lay on the bed naked and fell asleep. She dreams as if she was pregnant and in labor pains at a hospital. She was taken to the labor ward. She could hear nurses in her dream screaming at her to push and she was pushing very hard with sweat all over her body. Then the next thing there was a sound of a crying baby. "It's a boy and you are not done yet there is still another one." That was the voice of a sister. "Push ma'am push the baby is coming out," the voice was loud again. She was pushing again and with no time the second baby was born. "Another boy," the voice said. She woke up and the pillow was wet with tears and sweat from her body. She went to the bathroom and cried. "Lord why are you doing this to me why? You know I will never conceive again." She talked to herself as she was looking at the mirror with tears streaming down her cheeks. After a while she wiped the tears and went back to bed and slept.

Chapter 55

Joyce's wedding went very well, and she had settled in Cape Town. Her family was happy in Cape Town. She was working in one of the hospitals in the O&G department as a registrar. She picked her cell phone and called Linda to check on her. "Hi Linda. You are talking to Joyce. How is life my friend?" asked Joyce.

"Hi friend, life is great in Jozi and how is Cape treating you?" asked Linda.

"Cape Town is treating us well thanks. How is Eric?" asked Joyce

"Eric is fine, and we are planning to have a child," responded Linda with excitement. This was the first time Joyce asked her about Eric not Sipho.

"Oh, wow that's great, when are you planning to have this baby?"

"We have been trying and I can't seem to fall pregnant yet," said Linda

"But you did fall pregnant with Sipho at some stage is it not so?"

"Yes, I did," responded Linda with hesitation.

"Why are you struggling now?"

"I don't know my friend."

"Did you guys seek some medical help?" asked Joyce

"We did, and everything is normal with both of us."

"Why don't you then do artificial insemination?"

"We did that, and it did not work out."

"In vitro?" asked Joyce

"We did only two cycles and Eric refused to do more because he cited cost and stress?"

"I am very sorry my friend, but you shouldn't give up."

"No, I haven't given up," said Linda.

"How is Eric taking it?"

"It is very difficult to tell because most of the time he is in and out of town."

"My friend did you ever take time to understand what is it that Eric is doing exactly? He is your husband now and I think you need to understand the type of business he is in."

"I am still busy with my studies. I told myself once I am through with my studies, I will have to sit down with him and understand his line of business. I don't want a situation whereby he falls sick, and I don't have a clue of what he does."

"That is exactly why you should know. If he was employed, it was going to be a different story. We are talking about your husband's business here. Anything that would happen to him might require you having to run the business yourself. From the look of things, it looks like a very profitable business. The cars he drives are not cheap," said Joyce

"All I know is that the night club is one that is making more money than all other businesses."

"You haven't heard of Sipho since?"

"No, the last time is when I told you that they said he is staying with some college girl in East Rand. I don't know whether he is still alive. You loved Sipho neh! I don't think he will ever be out of your mind. It surprises me that a smart learned lady like you would be concerned about a stupid and a crook like Sipho."

"I want to be honest with you my friend Sipho had never demonstrated the character you told me about. That is why it was not easy for me to take what you told me. You are my friend, and I don't have any reason not to believe you," Joyce said that to flatter her friend because she knew exactly how treacherous her friend could be.

"I know. I have no doubt in my mind that you do believe me. I was just talking."

"Okay my friend let me leave you now. Goodbye," said Joyce.

"Goodbye my friend. Don't be scarce, you must keep on calling."

"I should think you need to do the same you too."

Chapter 56

It was a Friday morning and Thandi was late for work. She was rushing for a meeting, and she asked Daniel to drop her at work and pick her up later. Daniel dropped Thandi and came back to pick up Sipho and they drove to town.

Sipho was getting used to Daniel. He started opening more to him. He realized that he was also starting to get to know Thandi though the conversation between the two of them was hardly there. They were avoiding each other. Everything that Thandi wanted to say or know about Sipho she would ask Daniel about it. Sometimes she would ask Daniel to discuss it with Sipho. Thandi didn't want Sipho to work anywhere either than with Daniel. Sipho also developed a good relationship with Thandi's dog.

Daniel and Sipho were on their way from town in the car. It was a nice sunny afternoon. Sipho was driving and he said, "Daniel what kind of a person is this boss of yours?"

"What do you mean Sipho?"

"Part of her seems to be kind and there is this other part that looks like a no-nonsense taker."

"She is a very sweet woman. I don't want to tell you what happened to her life, and I have a feeling that one day the two of you will talk about it. I have never told her about your previous life," said Daniel realizing that the question from Sipho was a probing one and is based on interest.

"What Linda did to me made me to be very skeptical about educated women, it is something that I had even before she did what she did to me. I don't know why was I so stupid to fall into a trap that was so obvious. I am weary about educated and rich women."

"Sipho, can I tell you something. The day you told me about what Linda did to you I tried to analyze your situation. It is not Linda that was wrong but you. You failed to be man enough to take charge of the situation. You were too sweet to her that is why she took the advantage and played you for a fool."

"Do you mean I made her to do that to me?"

"Yes, that is exactly what I meant. There is a very strong, principled man in you. Your kindness must not be your weakness when it comes to women. No woman wants a man who is going to be a door mat. Women want a strong, bold and a masculine man who can stand up on his word. I am not saying you have to be abusive and stubborn out of the blue."

"Was I too timid to Linda?"

"From what you have told me, you were. I bet even the child that Linda carried was not yours. I doubt very much that a person of your character could have raped Linda. You are too gentle to do such things. You have sound principle to be an abusive man to any woman. Linda took an advantage of your quietness and humbleness."

"Can it be possible that the pregnancy was not mine? You know what, Linda's friend Joyce warned me about Linda. I never wanted to listen to her thinking that she was jealous of our relationship."

"Let me tell you something about Thandi because I can see that you are interested in her, that is why you have started this conversation."

"Oow! No, no, Daniel how do you know that?"

"I have watched you how you look at her. You must know I was also a young man like you at some stage in my life. You are not going to pretend as if you are not. If you want Thandi you will have to be bold and be a man enough, stop this nonsense of education and richness about women. Love between two people transcends material possession and education. When a man loves a woman there are certain things that the woman expects from that love. Education and richness, I am definite they are not on top of the list. Your failure as man to satisfy her basic needs will not be met by the material things that you can provide or your high education. If you love her, treat her right and meet all her basic needs, that will make you a man that she will never disrespect. Be a man and tell Thandi how you feel about her, before another brave young man grabs her right under your nose. Thandi is a woman, and you are a man. If you don't grab this chance now, I am afraid it might be too late for you" said Daniel emphatically.

Daniel liked Sipho because he is a principled young man. His wish was that his boss could have a good, kind, and strong principled man like Sipho. To him Sipho was the kind of a man that can give Thandi the best love and care that his boss is longing and wish for.

"But Daniel Thandi looks like a no-nonsense taker," said Sipho jokingly

"Yes, she is but at the same time she is a woman that needs love from a young disciple man. Thandi has gone through a lot Sipho and all that has made her the strong woman that you see today. There is also another element in her. She is a woman like all other women she has needs, I have no doubt in my mind that she would like to be loved, cuddled and cared for by a loving man.

I should think she has mourned enough for her husband. She should be ready by now to continue with her life." Daniel didn't want to tell Sipho how tender Thandi's heart had become since Sipho's arrival. Her dress code has change to that of a young lady that is in love. The tomboy attire of a factory manager was gone. His fear was that the tenderness might be exploited by another man if Sipho does not react quick.

"It looks like you know her very well. I am very vulnerable right now in terms of love. I really do feel lonely and need a partner in my life. I need a woman that I will love and a woman that will show me some respect. That is why I said to you I need to find a job so that I can go out there and look for the woman that I can take care off."

"You are right Sipho, without a job you will not be able to take care of any woman now."

"Why is Thandi not allowing me to go and look for a job in town? I am well now, and I will never do that stupid thing I have done ever again. Or else why is she not employing me?"

"I think Thandi has experienced a lot of death in a very short space of time. I can sense that she cares about you too. Possible that is why she is protective over you," said Daniel as they were arriving at home.

Martha came to them and said to Daniel "Thandi called and said you must come and pick her up because she is done with her work for the day."

"Sipho, can you take everything out of that car I will use Thandi's car to fetch her from work." said Daniel.

"Is there anything else you want me to do because I want to take a swim it is very hot?" asked Sipho.

"No, I am fine you can swim."

When Daniel arrived at Thandi's workplace she was already waiting at the reception. She got into the car and Daniel drove her home.

"How is our man, Daniel? Is he coping? Do you think he is well now?" asked Thandi.

"Yes ma'am, he is one hundred percent well. We had a long chat just now from our way back from town," responded Daniel.

"Oh, what were you guys talking about?"

"Just man stuff ma'am, man stuff."

"So that man stuff is not for my ears?" asked Thandi

"Yes, of course it's not for your ears ma'am. That is why I am saying it's man stuff. The only thing I can tell you ma'am is that Sipho has been hurt in his life and the man has a very good heart."

"Hurt by who Daniel? Is that the reason why he wanted to take his life?"

"Who else can hurt a man to the point of suicidal? It's a woman of course, a woman nobody else. You see ma'am, when a man gives his life to a woman, he gives it all, it is very difficult for him to turn back. Any disappointment from the lady would surely ruin that man's life. Men are not good in handling rejection not at all."

"Is that the case with Sipho?"

"No, I didn't say it's the case with Sipho. I am just making an example."

"But Daniel for him to come all the way from Jozi with nothing and come to commit suicide here, it must have been something very serious."

"I don't know ma'am. I am not going to talk about other people's affairs. Tell me. Freddy is gone long ago, and you are still without a partner. What is happening?"

"Unfortunately, Daniel partners don't grow out of trees, and I just cannot take any man that comes to me. You know I have been through a lot; I don't want to fall in the same pit in my life."

"What are you looking for if I may ask?"

"Daniel you are the last person who can ask me that question."

"No, it's because I want to know," said Dan with a smile.

"I want a man who is going to love me for who I am not for what I have. I want to be happy Daniel. I want the love and happiness I never had. Surely and surely, I don't want a man who is going to abuse me again."

"Thandi there are things that God is not going to bring to you in a platter. He wants us to open our eyes sometimes and look at some of the things that are in front of us."

"What does that mean Daniel?"

"Ma'am I have never been as explicit as I am to you more than now."

"You are talking in riddles Daniel; I don't understand what you are saying."

"Time will tell ma'am, if you say you don't understand me now, you will later. When the ball is in your court you must play it, otherwise somebody else will come and play it for you and that won't be nice. Don't lose what you have in your hand," said Daniel as they arrived at the house.

"What are you talking about Dan?" asked Thandi with a laughter.

"You know what I am talking about ma'am. You pretend as if you don't. You are not a child any longer."

"But Daniel I am a woman I am not supposed to initiate anything."

"Says who ma'am. Do you want another woman to come here and take what is meant for you? If you don't, it is going to happen. He's got everything that any woman wants from a man. This is a kind of a man that I think is more than suitable for you. In fact, to me he is a God send to you. Don't shilly shally about the opportunity that God has presented to you."

"What if-?"

"What if what ma'am? You must know one thing ma'am, you can't win a lotto if you don't take a risk of playing it," responded Daniel as he closed the car and moved toward the direction of his apartment.

Bobby, Thandi's dog would normally come to her once he hears her voice but today Bobby was nowhere to be seen.

"Martha where is Bobby today?"

"Bobby was with Sipho the last time I saw him ma'am," replied Martha.

Thandi got through the front door of the house. As she was climbing the stairs she was in a full view of the back of the house where the swimming pool was. She looked at the swimming pool direction and there was Sipho standing. He had his back to the house and wearing tight swimming trunks only. His muscular body fully exhibited. She stood at the stairs for a while admiring Sipho's physique. She has never seen muscles like that in her life. As she was standing there looking at Sipho, she felt something moving from the bottom of her body radiating through her whole body to her head. She went up the staircases very slowly with her eyes zoomed at Sipho. The eyes sent a signal to the brain that released all her feminine hormones. Her body reminded her of her womanhood. His body quickly reminded her of the dream she had. The body was exactly like the one she was looking at. "Lord could this be a man that was in my dreams?" she whispered.

She quickly went into her bedroom and put everything she was carrying down, took out a Visa card from her bag and went outside. She called Daniel, "Daniel come here. I want you to take Martha and go and collect Sarah and you guys you can go anywhere for a weekend. Here take my card and use it in any way you guys you want to, go entertain yourselves. Don't ask me any questions just go now. You can take anyone of the cars you want."

"It's ok ma'am I will see to it that we all go now," said Daniel with a smile. He could understand what was going through his Madam's mind because he also saw Sipho playing with the dog at the pool side.

As Thandi was turning her back on Daniel going back to the house, Daniel called her. "Ma'am, remember what I said to you. You need to strike now. Even if it means you must start. Just do it"

Thandi locked the front door and went upstairs to her bedroom. She took out all her bathing costumes and look for the most revealing and sexy one. She came out of the house wearing a bathing suit that exposed her beautiful figure and a beach towel on her shoulder.

"Hi Mr. Mokoena, how are you this afternoon? Do you mind if I join you?" she said to Sipho's amazement.

Sipho was shocked because he did not hear her arriving and Bobby did not show any signs of her presence. He was now lying on his back on one of the pool reclining chairs. He turned around to greet her. His eyes popped out when he saw Thandi wearing a two-piece swimming costume. He inspected her from the top to the bottom and bottom to the top. He couldn't believe what was standing before him. His heart started to beat fast.

Realizing that whatever she wanted to do is working and Sipho was choked by what he was looking at. It made her feel good.

Still amaze with Thandi's appearance Sipho could not utter a word. He was lying there with his mouth half gaped and eyes glued on Thandi.

"Can I offer you a drink Mr. Mokoena?" she asked him as she moved toward the pool bar to take out some beverages from the bar fridge. Her back was on him, and she deliberately walked slowly and swinging her hips like a pendulum. She was fully aware that he must be looking at her back and at her bum.

As Thandi was walking away from him, Sipho was glued to Thandi with his eyes not blinking at all. He sat up straight waiting for her to offer him some beverage. She came behind the bar with two glasses of lemonade and soda. She sat next to him on the other reclining chair with Bobby in between.

Sipho accepted the drink and thanked Thandi for it.

As she was lying there looking at the sky, she remembered Daniel's words when he said to her "Thandi there are things that God is not going to bring to you in a platter. He wants us to open our eyes sometimes and look to some of the things that are in front of us and use our brain." There was a very shallow smile from her. "Lord could this be the man you brought to me. I will not let him go," she thought to herself looking up in the sky. She lifted her glass and said to Sipho, "cheers on your behalf."

Sipho lifted his to and said, "cheers to you too." Without knowing what he was doing.

He was spellbound by what was happening. He had never experienced such closeness of a lady like this let alone a beautiful one like Thandi. He held the soda glass in front of his mouth with his eyes looking nowhere and his mind somewhere, where nobody knows but him.

His problem was what next step must he take as a man. He could see clearly that it was an invitation from a lady.

When Thandi realized that Sipho looked lost, she stood up and took a dive into the pool. The water splashed out to both Sipho and Bobby and they were both wet. She came out of under water and turned around and looked at him because she deliberately splashed the water at him.

"Did you just splash me with water deliberately?" he asked with a smile.

"Did I? How come I did not see that?"

"You have made both Bobby and I wet."

"Oh, how come I did not hear Bobby complaining?"

"Bobby!! Did you hear that?" he asked Bobby.

Bobby made a squeaking sound as if he was agreeing with Sipho. "There you are did you hear that?"

"Well, I don't know what do you expect Mr. Mokoena when you are sitting next to the pool? You were not supposed to be lying there but be in the water. She laughed at him and said "I am not going to apologize for that, you can do whatever you want. You were supposed to be in the water not out there"

Sipho quickly remembered Daniel saying to him "Be a man and tell Thandi how you feel about her before another brave young man grabs her under your nose. Thandi is a woman, and you are a man. Education and richness mean nothing when it comes to love."

"I lost Linda to another man by being coward and nice guy. I am not going to lose this one," he whispered.

He dove into the water and swam under water to her. She went underneath the water to escape him. Sipho followed and chased her. He pulled her by the leg. She pulled her leg off from him and splashed him with water. He went underneath and swam toward her. She swam to the side of the pool, and he was behind. He swam to her, and he held her around the waste from behind. She turned around and looked Sipho straight into his eyes. Their eyes met. They looked at each other without a word.

"Be a man and be bold" he could hear Daniel saying that to him. Sipho knew that he must be a man and be the one to take further what she had started. He knew that he had to strike then. He pulled her toward him and gave her a passionate kiss. To his surprise she responded positively without questions. The squeaking sound from Bobby partially disturbed them. They both laughed at him but continued with kissing.

"Let's go inside," she whispered to his ear.

"Where is Daniel and Martha?"

"They are not around they are gone."

He got out of the pool with her in his arms. She supported herself with her arms around his neck. Thandi has never felt this before. She has never been carried by a man like this. She has seen this in movies, never thought one day she would be in somebody's arms.

He went up the stairs with her to the main bedroom. Sipho was on cloud nine. He has never been so close to a woman in his life not even Linda came so close to him with love. He carried Thandi to the main bedroom based on her instructions.

Only the giggling and the laughter coming from the bedroom that signified their happiness could be heard the whole house. None of them has ever experienced this childish behavior before. They were both absorbed to each other's romance without engaging in any sexual activity. Both were very principled individuals. They respected each other values.

They started chasing each other with pillows all over the house. Their laughter could be heard from afar. They were still in their swimming costumes when they sat in front of the TV in the main sitting room. The romance continued without engaging in sex. They spent the greater part of the night talking about their past experiences in their previous marriages.

The following day it was a Saturday and Thandi had planned to be at work. She called the PA and excused herself from coming to work. They woke up and prepares a picnic basket and shot straight to the Botanical gardens. From there they went to the Zoo. They enjoyed themselves the whole day. Thandi was like living the dream that she dreamed.

Chapter 57

Linda was on duty, and she fell sick while at work. She called Eric to come and pick her up but there was no response from his phone. She decided to drive herself home. When she was about to reach home, she realized that she cannot be alone at night when she was that sick. She decided to drive to Eric's place. His car was at home and there were two other cars. She parked her car behind one of the cars on the driveway. She knocked at the door and there was no response. She opened the door. There was loud music playing and some voices talking and laughing. She slowly navigated the house from one room to another checking and trying to find the origin of the noise. As she was moving closer to the noise, she realized that it was more than two people talking.

She opened the door to a room full of smoke. She moved in and there was Eric naked in bed with two naked girls on each side. On the floor was his friend with other two naked girls. They were all high smoking marijuana.

"Eric what is going on here?" screamed Linda.

He looked at her and asked who she was. Linda was very angry. She went to him and pulled him with his hand out off the bed onto the floor. This made Eric very angry too. He stood up and released a clap with his back hand on her. Linda returned it with the bag she was carrying, and she continued hitting him. Eric released a blow with a fist on her face and it landed her on the floor. He followed it with a kick.

"Get out of my house you damn…," said Eric angrily.

When Eric was about to kick her again, his friend jumped out of the mattress and pulled him away. He helped Linda on her feet and escorted her out of the room.

She drove home with the mouth that was bleeding and in tears. When she got home, she noticed that her mouth on one side had a cut that needed some few stitches. She called her friend who was working at OPD to come and stitch her from home.

"What's wrong with Eric? I have never seen him like that. Those girls must have lured him into drugs. I don't know him to be violent. Something is seriously wrong somewhere," she thought.

Linda felt that she could not share this with anybody, she had to keep it a secret.

After two days Eric drove to the hospital and was looking for Linda. He was told that Linda was off duty. He drove to her place. The car was parked on the driveway. Eric got off the car with a huge bouquet of flowers and a tray of different expensive chocolates. He knocked at the door and there was no response and he knocked again.

Whose is that?" asked Linda with a cheeky voice.

"Linda, can you come and open up the door for me please sweetheart?"

She stood up leisurely and went to the door. When she opened the door, she could not see Eric he was hiding behind the flowers.

"Wow, these are very beautiful flowers. Where did you buy them?" she asked as she was opening the door and went for the flowers. Eric moved in and closed the door behind him. He knelt before Linda and asked for forgiveness. He apologized profusely to her for what had happened, and he promised that it would never happen again. Linda felt pity for him, and she said, "I hope you will never embarrass me in front of your friends again. I have forgiven you."

"Can we go and eat out?" asked Eric.

"No, we will be wasting money. I can't eat properly with this mouth. Let's just stay indoors."

"Ok then. If that is what you want, I am fine with that."

"Eric in all what you were doing yesterday with those girls, are you using condom, or you just sleep with them without a condom?"

"Ow, Linda, what do you take me for? I cannot go out there without any protection. I know what I am doing I am not a fool," said Eric a bit agitated.

"Eric, I have the right to ask because you come back from wherever and sleep with me without a condom. You know why we are not using condom. I told you long ago that I want a baby."

"Ok I have heard you, my love. The main reason I am here is because I want to borrow your car for tomorrow. I have a consignment that is arriving tomorrow. My other cars will be in Durban," said Eric to change the topic.

"When do you want the car, and how am I going to get to work?"

"I will get one of my guys to drop you at work tomorrow morning. The car should be back in the afternoon."

The following morning Eric dropped two young men by Linda's place. They drove Linda to work and dropped her at about 07h20 and they drove off.

At about 15h45 Linda got a call from a private number on her cell phone and the person said, "Is that Doctor Linda?"

"Yes, it is. May I ask who am I talking too?"

"You don't need to know me. If you get a call from the police and they are asking you about Eric, tell them that you don't know that person. Never agree that he is your husband ok," he dropped the phone.

This got Linda worried. She started pacing up and down in the ward. It was 18h00 when her cell phone rang again. "Is that Doctor Linda Sibeko?"

"Yes sir it is. Who am I talking too?"

"Doctor you talking to Captain Mekwa from Potchefstroom police station."

"Yes captain, how can I help you?"

"Doctor Sibeko where is your car?"

"My car is outside at the parking bay captain."

"Are you sure doctor?"

"Yes, captain because I left it there this morning. Why are you asking me that question captain?"

"Doctor is your car a Blue BMW 380 with registration X 00 V V GP?"

"Yes, you right captain that is my car. How do you know my registration when you are in Potch?"

"Are your car keys with you?"

"They are in my bag in my locker."

"Can you check them for me please?"

Linda pretended as if she was walking to the change rooms. "Oh! My locker is open, and my bag is not in my locker. Somebody has broken into my locker."

"Doctor Sibeko, doctor Sibeko," called the captain. "Your car is here with us."

"How did it get there Captain?"

"Your car was driven by two men, one young man and one gentleman in his mid-forties. The young man claims that he was hired by this other man. Your car was stopped by the police, and they found cocaine at the street value of 1,2 million."

"What!! You must be joking captain."

"I am not doctor. These guys stole your car and used it to transport drugs."

"Who are they? How did they come in the hospital and be able to know my locker?"

"The young man's name is Joe, and the other man is Eric. In fact, this other man we have been looking for him for years. He once lived here, and he was involved in criminal activities and drug smuggling. He then left for Joburg."

"Is it possible to get my car back?"

"Not now doctor. Only once we are done with our investigations then the car will be transferred to Joburg police station where you can collect it. Your car is like now a stolen vehicle used to commit a crime," said the captain.

Linda was very devastated and disappointed at Eric. "How can he take my car to transport drugs? I wonder for how long has he been doing this?" she asked herself.

She decided to do some investigation on Eric. In her investigations Linda discovered that Eric was the owner of the night club, and he was using the club to masquerade his drug business. The club was the haven for drug dealings and night prostitution. Eric was not the Eric that she knew, he was a fake. He had no formal qualifications, but he was a well-known drug dealer.

What Linda found out on the day he beat her was his way of lifestyle. She also discovered that Eric wanted to use her because of her qualification and her status in the community. He wanted to accumulate wealth using her name and their marriage as a disguise.

"If this is who Eric is, where does that leave me?" she asked herself. "If he was living the kind of life he was living, am I safe from the virus?" All this made Linda anxious and nervous. She wasn't sure of her status after learning that Eric was sleeping around and doing drugs. She decided to do a HIV test.

Linda approached her lawyer to get some advice on what to do. Her lawyer advised her to stay away from all Eric's property even if they are married. The law will not exonerate her from all the drug dealings. She might go down with him. She will be safe if Eric is not going to mention her as his wife. He also advised her to get out of the province for a while until the case was settled.

Linda picked up her cell phone and called Joyce. "Hi Joyce. How are you doing?"

"I am fine thanks and how are you doing my friend?"

"I am well thanks. I didn't want to tell you this until it was through. I have applied for a job in one of the hospitals there last month and I was interviewed telephonically last week. Today they called me and said I got the job. I will be starting with them next month."

"Oh, Linda that's great. You can come and stay with us for a month or so meanwhile you will be looking for an accommodation for yourself," said Joyce with excitement.

"Thank you, my friend. I knew I could count on you."

"What is going to happen with Eric then? Is he going to leave the business and join you?"

"Those are the nitty gritty that we will talk about when I get there," responded Linda.

Chapter 58

Sipho and Thandi got married in a small church in front of very few selected people. Her parents, senior management team, her PA, Sarah, Martha and Daniel. Three months after the wedding Thandi called her father and told him that she is tired of working in the factory and she has a husband now who can take care of the company. She requested her father to sit down with Sipho for a week and go through the company policies and coach him on how to manage a big company.

Later, she called Sam and instructed Sam to teach Sipho everything that he needed to know about the company finances. She told Sam that Sipho would form part of the board and would attend all executive meetings.

Johnson trained Sipho in all operations related activities and procedures.

Thandi spent hours and hours drilling Sipho on corporate laws, how to manage Community Steel and the dos and don'ts of managing the company. She told him that she would like to stay at home and see if she can't fall pregnant again.

"I know the doctor said I might not conceive again but I trust that God will heal my womb and give me children once more," she whispered to herself.

Thandi, Sam, Johnson and Sipho flew to Johannesburg to visit the distribution warehouse. The visit to the warehouse was very short because they had some clients to see and introduce Sipho. Sipho did not get a chance to ask around for his friends.

Within six months Sipho was in full swing in managing Community Steel. Sam and Johnson were very supportive. Sipho was introduced to the workforce as the new CEO of the company. He also attended the board meetings as a person representing the family trust.

"Do you think is it necessary to change the family trust name to Mokoena?" asked Thandi.

"No, my love, you were married to the Phillips, I cannot dispute that. I really don't have any problems with their surname still used by you in all business-related matters," responded Sipho.

"The other thing, there are some few millions that are in my bank account from my grandmother's estate. I gave some money to the public hospital. Freddy did not want the money. He said it is mine and I should do whatever I want to do with it."

"What do you want to do with it then?" asked Sipho

"I don't know"

"Well, if you don't, let us leave it in the bank my love until you find something for it. Are there no charity organizations that you can donate to?"

"There are two NGOs for the disabled that I know of. I will visit them and see what I can do for them."

Thandi was three months pregnant. Her gynecologist doctor Joyce Mayo confirmed that she was carrying twins. She hadn't told her husband yet because she wasn't sure if the pregnancy was going to carry through. Both her and the doctor agreed from the first month to observe and monitor the pregnancy for full three months. In the fourth month she can tell Sipho. She explained to Sipho the reasons they cannot have sex the first three months of her pregnancy. Her explanation had nothing to do with her being pregnant. Sipho was fully engaged with the business, and he was doing a lot of traveling overseas and locally, so whatever Thandi requested was in order with him.

It was a Saturday morning and Sipho was still in bed when Thandi said to him, "my darling, I am four months pregnant"

"What, are you joking?"

"No, my love, I am not. You remember four months back, when I told you that my doctor said we can't have sex because of my gynecologic problems."

"Yes, I do because you sounded very serious."

"We suspected pregnancy then."

"Why did you not tell me then baby?"

"My womb was once damaged at some stage and my doctor then indicated that I might not conceive again. My doctor now said we should monitor the pregnancy before I can tell you about it."

"Oh, what happened to your womb?"

"It's a long story my darling. Do you know I actually dreamed about this day? I never thought that it will ever come to pass. God is great. I give Him all the glory."

"Wow baby. Did you dream about me or the pregnancy? How did you know that I was coming?"

"Both. I didn't know my love, but God knew that He was going to wipe my tears one day" she replied with a smile. "You are God sent. You must know that it is every married woman's desire to conceive and bear kids. I will always be grateful to God for bringing you into my life. I love you Sipho. You have brought joy in my life."

These words nearly brought tears to Sipho. It was the first time in his life hearing somebody saying them from the bottom of her heart. He held both Thandi's hands and looked her in her eyes and said, "you are the greatest gift that God has ever given to me. I will cherish and love you as long as I live. You have made me the man I am today Mrs. Mokoena." He gave Thandi a kiss.

When Thandi was about to give birth, her gynecologist introduced her to Dr. Linda Jones. "Mrs. Mokoena this is Doctor Linda Jones who happens to be my friend also. She is going to be your pediatrician. Doctor Jones this is Mrs. Thandi Mokoena. She does not like to be called Mrs. Mokoena but Thandi. This is the lady that donated one and half million Rands toward the renovation of your pediatric ward. As rich as she is, Thandi decided to use the public hospital for her pregnancy. She said to me she promised the people here that her second child will be born in this hospital."

"Hi Thandi, how are you doing? Wow! what a beautiful woman. This is surely unfair. Some women when they are pregnant, they are not as beautiful as this. Are you carrying twins?" asked Linda.

"Yes, doctor they are both boys."

"Ok, I will see you when you come to give birth. When are you due?"

"Next month doctor."

"Oh, that's soon."

Thandi gave birth to two health boys. Sipho was not in when his wife gave birth, he was out of the country on a business trip. Thandi called Sipho on his mobile number "Hi darling. You have two healthy boys, they are so handsome, and I should think they took after their father."

"Wow, that's great my love. You mean I am the father of two boys. God is great. There will be more boys in the house. I wonder how you going to deal with the three men in your house. Baby, I am proud of you. Was it a normal delivery?"

"Yes, baby it was."

"When are they going to discharge you?"

"On Wednesday morning. Why baby?"

"I want to fetch you and the boys from the hospital. What time?"

"They said, I should be done with everything at about 10h30. You shouldn't worry yourself Daniel will pick me up."

"Ok" said Sipho.

After talking to her parents and Sarah, Thandi called Daniel to inform him about the time and the day of her discharged from the hospital. On Wednesday at about 10h00 Dr. Jones entered Thandi's ward. "Good morning Thandi. How are you doing today? It's your last day today. Have you arranged for transport, or should I get the hospital transport for you?"

"Good morning, Dr. Jones. I am very well thanks. I have arranged for transport. Our driver is coming. My husband wanted to come and pick me up, but I told him not to worry himself."

"Wow, Thandi why did you stop him. I would have loved to see this lucky man, who has such a gorgeous and a loving wife like you. I hope he knows how much you love him. You haven't stop talking about him since you arrived here. It looks like he loves you a lot too. I would cherish a man that would love me like your husband loves you." said Linda.

"I am not going to lie to you doctor he loves me a lot. He is a very busy man. He is flying around because of our business. He is such a hard worker but still manages to be a very loving husband. Perfect gentleman indeed. As I said to you earlier on, he is God sent. You and Dr. Mayo can pay us a visit one day, that way you can get to meet him."

"Surely we will. By the way what is your business again?" asked Linda because she remembered what Joyce said about Thandi donating R1,5 million toward the renovation of the pediatric ward. She also talks about her husband being busy with the business.

"It's the company called Community Steels. My husband is the CEO of that operation. We also export steel overseas that is why he is time and again out of the country."

"I am hoping to meet him one day," said Linda as she turned her back and faced the wall and started writing.

"Good morning sweetheart," said a deep voice of a man standing at the door with a huge bouquet of flowers.

Thandi nearly jumped out of bed with excitement. "Good morning my love, what do you want here? I did not expect you. When did you come back?" she asked him as she was trying to sit up straight on the bed. Sipho rushed to her and helped her. He hugged her tight and gave her a very good passionate kiss. "These are for you, my love. Where are the kids?" he asked concentrating on Thandi. He could not see Linda as she was standing behind the door busy writing. He was standing such that Linda was behind him.

"The children are at the nursery. Baby this is Dr. Jones the pediatrician for the boys."

Linda had already turned around because she was shocked to hear the familiar voice. The voice reminded her of Sipho, but she knew it could not be him. She left Sipho in Johannesburg. When Sipho turned and looked at her, her eyes popped out and she became speechless.

"Oh, good morning, Dr. Jones," said Sipho with a question mark on his face. "Your face looks familiar. You look like somebody I know.

If it was not here in Cape Town and the fact that your body is slightly slimmer, your hair color and the scar on you face I would say you are someone I know from Johannesburg."

Linda was shivering like a reed, and she never kept contact with the man that was standing in front of her. She knew there and then that the face, the voice and the physical stature that it was Sipho. She immediately realized that he was not sure of her, and she decided not to reveal her identity.

"Come on my love people look alike. You don't know Dr. Jones at all."

"I am very sorry sir. I am sure you are mistaken I don't know you at all," said Linda trying to change the tone of her voice and avoiding looking Sipho in his eyes lest he recognized her even more.

"I am sorry for that doctor," he said. "Baby, dress up, let's get out of here."

"Thandi I am going to get the kids ready because they are in the same floor," said Linda as she was leaving the ward.

"I would like to see them," said Sipho.

"Yes sir, we will bring them here just now," said Linda trying to get out of Sipho's sight as quickly as possible. She instructed the nurses to prepare the kids and she went to her office. She locked the door behind her, sat on her chair and wept bitterly. "That's him that is my Sipho the man that Thandi has been talking about. That is the man who was once my husband. He has gained just enough to look that handsome. He is in expensive suits and shoes. Lord he looks so handsome and dignified. Could this be my Sipho who is now a businessman, the man Thandi cannot stop talking about? Is this the man Thandi says is the CEO of Community Steel? Thandi is a highly educated woman but the respect that she gives Sipho is just unbelievable. Could it be that she taught Sipho how to manage the business? Why didn't I see all this? Surely, they are multi-millionaires. Thandi is the woman that donated one and half million to this hospital, that is why she came to give birth here instead of the private hospital which I think she can afford it easily. Where did Sipho get all this money from? Or was Thandi's first husband the multi-millionaire?"

All these unanswered questions were accompanied by tears. She decided that she was not going to tell Joyce about this otherwise she would go crazy. She knew how much Joyce loved Sipho.

She stood up and looked through the window that was facing the car park. She saw the couple moving toward an AMG 63 ML that was standing at the car park hand-in-hand and talking. This brought more tears to Linda. As they were approaching the car two ladies got out of the car and took the twins and carried them. The car drove off.

Sipho and Thandi drove home with their kids. Thandi could not stop smiling. She was the happiest woman on earth because her dreams were getting fulfilled day by day.

At home Sipho discussed with Thandi about selling 60% of the warehouse in Wadeville. He was prepared to divide the other 40% and give 20% of each to Daniel and Martha for their long service in the family. Thandi agreed to the proposal.

"To whom are you going to sell the 60% to?" she asked.

"I am looking for an investor now. I will look for some bidders for the business. I will ask Sam to put it on the market."

Chapter 59

Eric was discharged from prison after he was acquitted of all the charges laid against him. There was a lack of enough evidence against him. When he came out of jail Linda was nowhere to be found. The night club was closed and some of his properties were vandalized and sold to different people. His money at the bank was not affected. Eric had to take a decision whether he would continue with his old lifestyle or take hundred eighty degrees turn and do something legal for a change. He wanted to move away from the harassment by the police and did not want to see the inside of a jail ever again. He knew that doing drugs was not healthy business for him, he was a grown-up man now and it was time he became a responsible member of society.

He called Linda on her cell phone several times. The number was not available. He went to look for Joyce. He could not find her.

On his way home he bought a newspaper for himself. He saw the advert for the warehouse bidding.

Sam had shortlisted two bidders. It was a local person and one from Swaziland. Sam, Johnson and Sipho went through the two bidder's applications. The South African bidder had more points, and it was also going to be strategic to deal with him. Mr. Jones was the winner.

Sam, Johnson and Sipho flew to Johannesburg for the finalization of the deal. At the factory they went straight to the board room to discuss the final points of the deal.

Five minutes before time they were told that Mr. Jones had arrived, and he was waiting at the reception. "Bring him through," said Sipho.

When Mr. Jones moved in, Sipho had stood up and went to the corner to attend to a call from his wife. Sam and Johnson greeted Mr. Jones and talked to him to put him at ease. They indicated that their boss was still on the phone. When Sipho was done he turned around to greet Mr. Jones. Unfortunately, Mr. Jones was still busy taking out some documents from his briefcase that was on the floor. He lifted his head with the documents in his hand and looked at Sipho. They were all still standing. Mr. Jones stretch out his hand to greet Sipho.

Sipho was shocked when he saw Eric. He stood there looking at him for a while without a word from his mouth.

"Are you Mr. Jones?"

"Yes, I am sir."

"Don't I know you?" he asked Eric.

"I don't know Sir, but my face is very common. You are not the first person to say so," said Eric.

He couldn't remember Sipho because Sipho had grown his mustache and looked more muscular.

Sipho felt some anger slowly creeping up. He requested to be excused for a minute. He went outside and took out his cell phone. He dialed his wife's number

"Baby he is here."

"Who my love," asked Thandi

"That Mr. Jones who won the bid, is Eric. Linda's boyfriend, the one I told you about."

Thandi could pick up some anger in her husband's voice for the very first time since they met.

"Baby, listen to me now my love. You don't have to be agitated about this. You didn't know that the Mr. Jones you have selected was Eric. Can you please allow this to be a business transaction without putting anger into it? Please my love."

"Sweetheart, are you aware that this is the man who pointed a gun in my face?"

"Yes baby, I am fully mindful of that. All that had to happen so that you and I could be together" said Thandi with a low soft voice try and ease her husband. "Baby do not allow anger to cloud your thinking. Let the past be the past. How do you know that it was God's plan for that to happen so that you leave Johannesburg and come to the Cape? Please deal with him as you would do the business with any other person. Don't allow what happened in the past to disadvantage him in whatever deal you will conclude with him. God used him to bring you down here to me."

"Ok, if you say so, I feel better now that I have talked to you."

"That's my man. Go back now baby and finish your meeting. I love you."

"I love you too, sweetheart."

When Sipho came back he asked Sam and Johnson to excuse them because he wanted to have a one on one word with Mr. Jones.

"Do you know a lady by the name of Linda Sibeko?"

"Yes, I know her very well. Linda is my wife," he replied. Sipho went on relaying the whole incident of that day. He went on telling Eric about him being the owner of the warehouse.

Eric was speechless. He didn't know whether to apologize or stand up and leave. He knew there and then that he was not going to get the business.

He stood up and said, "I am very sorry for what had happened to you Mr.?"

"Mokoena," responded Sipho.

"I wouldn't like to waste your time sir. If I knew you were the owner of this business I wouldn't have entered for the bid. I am very sorry Mr. Mokoena for everything I did to you. I was driven by the spur of that moment."

"Why are you on your feet? Where are you going?" "Sit down Mr. Jones, we are not done yet." Sipho stood up and called Sam and Johnson to join them.

"Sam is the press here already?"

"Yes sir, they are waiting outside."

"Mr. Jones let us allow bygones to be bygones. I am not a vindictive man by nature. I am not going to allow my bitterness to deprive you of what you want." He turned to Sam and said, "Sam, tell Mr. Jones what the whole deal is and out of it give him 15% discount." Eric was getting

60% of the company and 40% was shared between Daniel and Martha. The truck business was given to Seth and Thabo on loan by Community Steel. Seth and Thabo were working as drivers for the same company and have been friends and work colleagues with Sipho for long. Eric was happy with the deal. After the meeting there was press briefing.

In the evening Linda had visited Joyce and her family. She was busy in the kitchen and Joyce was watching the news from SABC.

"Linda! Linda! Quickly come and watch the news. Is that not Eric on the news. I wonder who is the man that is standing next him?"

Linda dropped what she was doing and rushed to the lounge. "Joyce you right that is Eric. When did he come out of jail? The man next to him looks like Sipho." Linda dropped on the floor with loud scream. She wept hysterically.

This took Joyce and her husband by surprise. "Linda what is it? What's wrong Linda?"

After some time, Linda stopped crying and looked at Joyce and said, "I owe you the truth Joyce, I owe you the truth."

"What are you talking about?" asked Joyce.

"Can you please switch off the television I want to tell you the truth about Sipho, Eric and myself. I lied to you Joyce, I lied about everything I told you from the beginning."

"What do you want to tell me, I'm all yours?" said Joyce knowing that the truth is going to come out at last.

"Do you remember the first time I told you about my parent's death?" she continued with the whole story. She ended up by saying to her, "Joyce in all what I have told you the bottom line is that I am now HIV positive, and my life is miserable," said Linda.

Joyce kept quiet for a while looking at her friend with eyes full of sorrow. Part of her wanted to say to her, "I tried to warn you, but you wouldn't listen to me," but her friendship to Linda was beyond that. She was holding tears from her eyes. In her, there was a deep sense of sympathy for her friend. She felt that was probably the first time in their friendship that Linda had been very level with her. It was then that she realized that her friend was in deep trouble.

"You know what Linda? In all what you have said it's not me that I am worried about, but Sipho. How I wish you could go back to Johannesburg and look for Sipho and tell him exactly what you have told me. It is very easy for me as your friend to forgive you and forget, but it is not me that you lied to and manipulated. You owe Sipho an apology for making a fool of him and taking his love for you for granted. If it was not the fact that you and I are friends, I would be saying something different to you."

"I know that Joyce. I don't deserve your forgiveness and your sympathy. I didn't treat you like a close friend. I am very sorry. What do I do now?"

"As I said to you earlier on that you owe Sipho all the explanation. The best thing is for you to go back to Johannesburg and talk to both Sipho and Eric. If you are correct that the man standing next to Eric is Sipho, from the look of things it looks like they have forgiven each other. The ball is left in your court right now. In whatever you do don't forget to tell Sipho that the pregnancy you had was not his. He was devastated when you miscarried."

"Sipho is not in Johannesburg, he is here in Cape Town," said Linda

"What are you talking about? How do you know that?" asked Joyce with an amazement

"You remember that rich lady, the one who gave birth to twin boys. What's her name again?"

"You mean Thandi?"

"Yes, Thandi, Thandi Mokoena."

"What about her?"

"She is Mrs. Sipho Mokoena. She is Sipho's wife"

"You are lying, how do you know that?"

"I have yet another confession to make, the day Thandi was discharged I was in the ward. Sipho walked in when I was busy writing something. I heard a voice like his behind me and I turned around. I was shocked out of my socks when I saw him. Strange enough he could not remember me clearly, he said I looked like somebody he knew, and I also tried not to reveal my identity. I quickly left the room so that he would not recall who I was. I went to my office, and I cried."

"Why didn't you tell me that you saw Sipho here?"

"I didn't want to because I knew how you were going to behave. Sipho is your favorite person Joyce so there was no way I was going to let you know. Now that I have come to my senses and need your help, I should think you deserve to know."

"Well, that's great then, you need to go to Sipho's house and talk to him. Let me accompany you to Thandi's place so that you can go and talk to Sipho and Thandi."

"What are we going to say to Thandi, where do we even begin?" asked Linda

"We will start by honoring her invitation that she extended to us."

"What if Sipho refuses to forgive me when I tell him the truth? How am I going to live the rest of my life with the guilty conscious?"

"The Sipho I know is not vindictive, he has a forgiving heart. I can assure you one thing that whatever you have done to him, he has forgotten about it. Look what he did for Eric. Do you think there is any man who can do that to his enemy? You saw yourself. Sipho shook Eric's hand on national television. Besides my friend, you have lived with this guilt all along. You were living a lie, telling the truth will definitely set you free no matter what the outcome will be."

"I know you are right there, Sipho won't say much and again being the gentleman he is, he will not ill treat me or say anything bad to me. I guess I just must face him and get this thing off my chest. After which I must then face Eric and deal with my issues with him too."

"Linda, do you think you still love Eric?"

"Yes, I do very much so. I have learned to love him and prepared to forgive him for all what he has done to me, provided he will also level with me."

"Do you love him as Eric or as the flamboyant rich guy?"

"I love him as an ordinary guy as Eric, I still regard him as my husband and besides who is going to take me with the virus from another man?"

"I think you need to go and tell him that. It looks like Sipho has moved on with his life and he has found his life partner, he has put the past behind him. I should think you need to do the same too, you deserve to be happy my friend. You will never be happy until you resolve all the outstanding issues in your life. Eric is one of them."

"What if Eric does not want me any longer?" asked Linda.

"Let him tell you that, rather than you sit here and be morose. Go to him and sort out everything including your status. Be level with him. I have a feeling that he is also hiding some things from you."

"Things like what Joyce?"

"The rape that you experienced Linda, if you are saying the child that you miscarried was not Sipho's child then Eric should know whose child it was. Eric was the last man to be with you that night, and now that we know about his drug dealings, I wouldn't be shocked to find out he drugged you and raped you that night. And that is why you could not remember anything."

"When do you think we should visit Sipho?" asked Linda trying to avoid the sensitive topic.

"Let me be the one who calls Thandi to make an appointment as early as tomorrow if Sipho will be back from Joburg," said Joyce as she took her cell phone and dialed Thandi's number.

"Thandi Mokoena, how can I help you?"

"Good evening Thandi. You are talking to Dr. Joyce Mayo here. How are you doing?"

"Good evening doc. I am well thanks and how are you doing?" ask Thandi with a smile.

"I am very well thanks for asking"

"How can I help you, my doc?"

"Can you please address me as Joyce? Most of my friends call me that and I regard you as a friend, so to call me Joyce would be most appropriate. Is that fine with you?"

"It is going to be very difficult because you were and still are my Gynae. I need to give you that respect."

"I understand that but the fact that you extended an invitation to me and Linda, this means that the relationship is now going beyond that of a patient and a doctor. We are now going to be friends outside work. Could you please feel free to call both Linda and I by our first names?"

"Ok Joyce I will. You called me. Is there something I can assist you with?" asked Thandi.

"Linda and I would like to pay you guys a visit when the whole family is available."

"Sure. When do you guys want to come through?"

"When will it be convenient for your family?"

"Is tomorrow too soon? I know that my husband will be around tomorrow evening. You guys you can then have dinner with us if that would be okay with you."

"Yes, Linda and I are available for tomorrow evening. We would love to join you guys for a dinner. Can we bring some red wine for the evening?"

"That's fine, you can bring some wine for you guys, Sipho and I don't drink."

"There is that name again, she started by saying Thandi Mokoena and now she is mentioning Sipho. Linda was right. The lady who has been my patient is my favorite guy's wife. She is extremely blessed to have a man like Sipho as a husband. Linda my friend was very stupid to dump a guy like Sipho. We will have to have a very diplomatic approach to this whole thing tomorrow. I wouldn't like to make Thandi upset; I just want to help my friend," she thought to herself.

"What time would you like us to be there?" asked Joyce

"Sipho is landing at 15h00 and it normally takes him 25mins to get at home if there is no traffic. You guys can be here any time after 18h00."

"Will do so, goodbye now Thandi. Will see you tomorrow."

Chapter 60

It was 18h10 when the intercom rang signifying that there was a person at the gate. Thandi and Sipho were busy in the kitchen cooking. "Are those our visitors already?" asked Sipho.

Looking at the monitor Thandi responded as she was opening the gate "Yes baby it's them."

"How many are they? Do you know honey?"

"It's only the two doctors my love."

The doorbell rang and Thandi quickly took off her apron and rushed to the door to receive her guest. She left Sipho in the kitchen. "Hi guys. Come in. Was it easy for you guys to find this place?"

"Hi Thandi" they both said that at the same time. "We didn't get lost. The directions you gave us were perfect. How are you doing?" asked Joyce. "And how are the boys"?

"I am doing well, and the boys are fine, they are growing well. Make yourself comfortable. Can I have the wine, Joyce? I want to put it on the table. Would you guys like something to drink?"

They both said at the same time, "A glass of wine please." They were starting to feel nervous. Linda was quiet and her hands were shaking like a leaf and the sweat was starting to go beyond the facial make-up. They both needed the glass of wine to calm their nervousness.

"Ok. Let me bring the glasses then and the bottle of wine," said Thandi as she was going to the kitchen. "Baby you need to come and meet my friends."

"Where are they?"

"In the lounge."

"Should I go and introduce myself or you will do it?"

"No honey I will do it, those are beautiful girls I want to do it myself," said Thandi jokingly.

"Ok love I will wait for you."

As Sipho and Thandi walked into the lounge, Thandi said with a loud vibrant voice "Girls this is my husband Sipho."

Joyce lifted her head and her eyes met Sipho's eyes and they recognized each other there and then.

"Wow!!! Joyce!!! Is this you? What do you want here?" asked Sipho with broad smile.

"I should ask you the same." responded Joyce with a smile.

"This is a small world," said Sipho as he moved toward Joyce and gave her a tight hug. They hugged each other for a while.

"He-e Sipho! Do you guys know each other? Joyce, I hope you not coming to take my man here," said Thandi jokingly.

"Sweetheart do you remember the lady I told you about who was Linda's friend in Johannesburg?" asked Sipho

The mentioning of her name made Linda more nervous. She was wondering what is it that Sipho had said about her to Thandi.

"Yes, I remember," responded Thandi

"This is the lady," said Sipho

"But baby, this is Dr. Mayo my gynecologist I also told you about," responded Thandi.

"Mayo is my married name. When Sipho and I were in Johannesburg I was not married then. I got married after he left," said Joyce. She turned to Sipho and said, "and you, what are you doing here in Cape Town with my patient?" asked Joyce.

"Shall we go to the dining room please guys," said Thandi. They all moved to the dining room with Sipho holding Joyce's hand to take up seats around the table.

"When did you come here? My wife has been talking about her Gynae Dr. Mayo and all along, I had never thought it was somebody I know," said Sipho.

At the table Sipho was sitting next to Thandi but opposite to Joyce and Linda sat next to Joyce but opposite to Thandi.

Linda was looking down all the time trying to avoid eye contact with Sipho as much as possible.

"Your patient is my wife" said Sipho as he turned around and faced Linda "Oh, I am sorry lady for being rude, it's just that I have not seen this lady for ages. The last time we talked was when we were still in Johannesburg. That cruel place."

Linda lifted her head and looked at Sipho. "I understand sir."

"Your face looks familiar. Are you not the lady I met at the hospital?" asked Sipho.

Linda was quiet and she looked down.

"Yes, Sipho this is Dr. Jones the pediatrician don't you remember her?" asked Joyce "My coming here it's a long story. It will need us sitting down not around the table like this. Seeing we are here now I should think I might as well talk," said Joyce trying to take Sipho's attention away from Linda.

"What happed to your friend Linda? Where did she disappear to?" asked Sipho not paying attention to the other lady. His interest was on Joyce and not paying much of attention on what Joyce was saying about the other lady.

Joyce was quiet for some few seconds. Then she said "In fact the main reason we are here with my friend was to come and talk to you and your wife. You remember the day you saw this lady at the hospital you told her that her face looked familiar."

"Yes, that is exactly what I said to her," responded Sipho.

"Sipho this is Dr. Linda Jones the former Linda Sibeko that you knew, your so-called ex-wife. You were right when you said to her, she looked familiar. Remember Eric Jones who bought the steel company in Wadeville? This is now his wife."

Sipho slightly jumped from his chair. He felt something moving from his shoulder to his neck. His forehead started sweating there and then. Thandi quickly noticed that, and she stood up and went to Sipho. She put her arms on his shoulders and pressed him down in saying cool down. Sipho looked down. Tears started flowing down his cheeks. He stood up and walked to his bedroom. Thandi followed him and indicated with her hand that the two must stay not go.

He started sobbing bitterly on top of the bed. Thandi sat down next to him and allowed him to cry for a while.

After some few minutes he said to Thandi, "what does she want here? After destroying my life, she has guts to come to my house. What does she want me to do? Thandi this is the woman that stripped me bare and left me with nothing. On top of that she ordered her husband to put a bullet through my brains. Does she want me to forgive her? My life with that woman sweetheart was a nightmare."

"Baby, I know how you are feeling right now, but she is here now coming to talk to you. Please my love, do not allow anger and bitterness to control you. I know you are very angry now, but it is the past that you are angry about. Your anger now will not bring back the past. Can you forget about it and start anew now? What has happened is gone and it will never come back, it should not determine your happiness and your future. This is not about Linda but about you. Can you learn to forgive her to be able to take away the heavy baggage from your shoulders? By forgiving her now you can then live a baggage free life. If you forgive Linda, it will liberate you from the burden of carrying bitterness in your heart. It will take away that pain you are feeling. You will feel free now and for the rest of your life every time you see her or think about her. Let the pain go my love and forgive her. Whatever she did to you was for our benefit. You are here with me now because of all that hurt you experience with her. Her intention was to hurt you, but God's intentions were to set you free for moments like these. Come let's go and talk to them," said Thandi persuasively.

Immediately Sipho stood up with tears, Linda started crying also. Joyce went to her and held her hand. She told Joyce that they should leave because the environment is not right. She said she does not want to cause more pain to Sipho by bringing the painful past.

"We can't go now. We came here to close the chapter of the past. If we leave both you and Sipho you will never heal. You need to forgive yourselves first and then forgive each other thereafter. It is good for Sipho to vent out his anger by crying. Don't hold yourself either."

Sipho and Thandi stood up and went back to the dining room. They found the two ladies waiting for them.

Thandi was surprised that the two doctors that she is trying to befriend are the same people that her husband had talked about. She could not imagine that her children's Pediatrician was the same Linda that Sipho was once married to. Linda had changed a bit. She had lost weight and a scar on her face. Not exactly the way Sipho described her. A sense of compassion toward Linda was aroused inside her.

"That is why Sipho could not recognize her at the hospital the first time they met," she thought to herself.

Joyce turned to her friend and said, "you need to talk now Linda." By now Linda's eyes were full of tears. Thandi could read between the lines about what was happening based on what her husband told her. She stood up and went to Linda and rubbed her shoulders to give her some encouragement to talk.

"Now that you took that first step of coming here to talk to Sipho, I should think you need to talk. Talking to him will help you to heal from the wounds of the past. Talking to him will set you free. Please Linda take out everything that is in your heart now. Don't leave a thing. You need to have a closure to your past both of you. Tell him everything don't sugar coat it, put it raw as it happened. When Sipho forgives you, it must be the forgiveness based on truth," said Thandi.

"I am so sorry Sipho for all that I have done to you," said Linda in a stammering voice. "I did not treat you right when you showed kindness to me. I lied to you all the time and cheated on you with Eric. I was mean to you when you did not have a job, yet you cushioned me when I lost my parents. You housed me and took care of me when I was in need, you even paid for me to finish my education. I know Sipho I don't deserve your forgiveness and sympathy. I was not the person you thought I was. You gave me love and I gave you hell. I am heavily indebted to you with my life. I am what I am today because of you. I am a doctor today because of you, for that I will always be grateful." Linda started crying louder and Thandi wrapped her hands around her shoulders and held her tight.

"It will be fine, you have to keep on talking, and it will make you feel better. You must off load now. Sipho is listening and this might be your last chance. This is therapeutic for you don't stop now please," said Thandi trying to encourage Linda to talk more.

"Sipho I never loved you and I lied to you with a lot of things……" Linda continued with the story and told Sipho everything about Eric, the rape, the child, her marriage to Eric, the plot to divorce him and the fact that she was positive.

Sipho was quiet all the time listening.

"Sipho, I owe you an apology and I am asking you to forgive me for all the wrongs I have done to you."

"As I am listening to you now Linda, I realized that you intended to harm me, but God turned it into a blessing. After Eric pointed a gun at me, I was completely devastated, and I intended to take my life…" he went on with his story until he met Thandi and married her. "With that Linda, I forgive you with all my heart. If I managed to forgive your husband Eric, I have no reason not to do the same to you. I respect your honesty and frankness. By the way if you would like Eric's numbers, I do have them, and I can give them to you. Tell me, why then the loss of weight? I really could not recognize you."

"Hey you silly. You don't ask a lady that," said Thandi to Sipho with a bit of a smile.

"Yes, I would like to have them please. I should think I owe him a lot and he owes me a lot too, thanks for your forgiveness it really means a lot to me. I feel like a heavy load has been lifted off my shoulders," said Linda with a relief.

They all settled down and enjoyed the meal. Thandi took her husband's hand and said to him, "I am very glad that God brought a man like you in my life. I am proud of what you have done for Linda and Eric. You are a very good man Mr. Mokoena with a good heart."

Joyce lifted her eyes and looked at Thandi after the words of encouragement and then looked at Linda. It was like she was saying to her friend this is what a woman does to keep a good man like Sipho. After the meals Joyce and Linda asked to be released and promised to visit again.

On the way back Joyce looked at Linda and said, "at some stage when we were at the university and you were playing around with Sipho I wanted to remind you of a song by the Whispers that says, 'If you don't know it now you will know it someday that you are throwing a good love away'"

"But I told you several times Joyce that Sipho was not my cup of tea. I have never loved him, but I just tolerated him. I love Eric no matter what or who he is. I will have to clear things with him. If he wants me back, I am prepared to accept him."

"It pleases me to hear you saying that. Growing up has a way of bringing sense to people. I never thought that I would ever hear you saying that you love a man no matter what or who he is. Congratulations. Welcome to the real world my friend," said Joyce

Chapter 61

Linda was sitting at the airport waiting for Eric. She was completely oblivious to the surroundings and in a pensive mood. Now and then, there were drops of tears from her eyes and would wipe them off. The past triggered the tears which she was not aware of. It was not what she had done to Sipho that occupied her mind but what Eric had done to her.

She gave him all her love and all she got was lies and deceit and to crown it all he gave her the virus. She knew how much she loved and still loves him. She was now at crossroads. She was not sure if Eric loves her or not. She was prepared to forgive him and move on with their lives together. "Is he prepared to spend his life with me?" she found herself whispering "Is he going to fulfill his promise of picking me from the airport? I can't take a cab and go to his place. I don't even know where he stays now." As she was talking to herself more tears came out.

"Good morning baby." Linda was brought back from the world of wonder by a familiar voice. She looked up and she saw Eric standing right in front of her. He stretched his hands to welcome her and help her to stand up. "Why are you crying my love?" asked Eric as he pulled Linda up from the chair to stand. He drew her closer to him and held her tight. Without a word Linda started to cry even more.

"I am here my love I am here for you. I will never leave you again," said Eric with a drop of tears out of his eyes.

"I love you Eric, I love you!!!"

"I love you too baby, I love you, my sweetheart. I am very sorry for all I have done to you. I will never leave you again, never." They spent some time holding on to each other and they were both crying. She turned her head and went for Eric's mouth to give him a kiss. For a while they were engaged in a deep passionate kiss. Eric wiped Linda' tears with both his thumbs and said, "I am sorry Linda I am very sorry for messing up your life. I hope you will find it in you to forgive me after I have opened my heart to you and tell you the truth. Can we go and sit down at the coffee shop so that I can talk to you?"

"Ok let's go. I also want to talk to you." They went up the escalator hand-in-hand.

Sitting at the corner of Mug & Bean, Eric was level and frank with Linda. He told her everything that she wanted to know and hear. After Eric's explanation Linda had no questions to ask and she felt that she was talking to a changed man.

Linda told Eric her side of the story and how she met Sipho and leveled with him.

"Eric there is also one thing I want to tell you and I don't know how you are going to respond to it."

"Yes, Linda I am listening, but I should think I know what you are going to talk about now. I also left it because I want to have your special attention for it. It is going to determine our future from now."

"If you know and you said you left it for my special attention then I am all yours," said Linda

"When I was in jail, I went for HIV testing, and I tested positive and my CD4 count was below 250 though clinically I was still strong. They started me on antiretroviral (ARV) drugs which I am still taking even now, that is why you see me looking strong. I contracted this before I went to jail, and I have been worried about you all the time. What is your status?"

"Eric, I appreciate your honesty and frankness. I am also positive, and I am on ARVs too."

"I am very sorry for putting you through this. I am still prepared to spend my life with you Linda. Are you still interested to our marriage?"

"Yes, Eric that is why I am here. I am still Mrs. Jones and I know we can work through this together as husband and wife," she said reassuringly

They stood up and went to the car walking hand-in-hand.

"Don't you think we need to call Sipho now and we both apologize to him. He is my partner in business now?" asked Eric.

"Dial his number now then and let us talk to him," said Linda as the car took off to town.

The same year Linda relocated back to Johannesburg to join Eric and she got a job at one of the hospitals.

Chapter 62

Later in Cape Town at the beach, Sipho, Eric and Joyce's husband were sitting on beach chairs basking in the sun with their swimming trunks on. They were watching their wives and children playing in the water and talking to each other.

Linda's son was two years five months old, and she was expecting a second child with Eric.

"Linda how did you get your son to be negative when both of, you are positive?" asked Thandi.

"Sipho and I were talking about it, and I told him that I will have to ask you as the doctor."

"Strange enough, that was also Eric's concern. That is why he did not want us to have children. I told him that there is a program for prevention of mother to child transmission of the virus, and if the mother is taking ARV's religiously and the viral load becomes undetectable, the chances of the child getting infected are very slim. The other thing both Eric and I we are on ARVs. His viral load is also undetectable.

"Oh! That's great. So, it helps to take your treatment as prescribed by the health worker," said Thandi.

"Definitely it does," responded Linda.

"Are you done now after the twins; don't you want another child?" asked Linda.

"Of course, yes. I am six weeks pregnant now. I am hoping that it is going to be a girl so that I can have somebody to talk too. The boys are always with their father. Sipho loves his children very much."

"It better be a beautiful girl like her mom my friend so that I can have makoti with the Mokoenas. You can see how handsome my son is." commented Linda.

Later the husbands joined their families, and they were all playing in the water joyfully.

Thandi got out of the water and brought a camera with her. She asked one of the stand-by people to take them a family photo. They all joined her and took a picture as one big family.

www.ingramcontent.com/pod-product-compliance
Lightning Source LLC
LaVergne TN
LVHW040135080526
838202LV00042B/2919